Deceitful Devotion

The Polaroid Reaper Trilogy - Book 1

Lyla Shepherd

3rd Edition

Contents

To everyone who feels lost.

Keep going, the storm will pass.

I promise.

Deceitful Devotion

Our official playlist

Everleigh Carlton & Tylan Blaese

Who's Afraid of Little Old Me?	Taylor Swift	5:33
Villains Aren't Born (They're Made)	PEGGY	3:14
Dangerous Hands	Austin Giorgio	3:10
I Don't Deserve It	Lisa Cimorelli	4:50
You Are Enough	Sleeping At Last	2:59
Burned	Grace VanderWaal	3:11
no body, no crime (feat. HAIM)	Taylor Swift, HAIM	3:35
human	Christina Perri	4:10
Built To Be Bad (with Alex Sampson)	Grace Gachot, Alex Sampson	3:07
If I Killed Someone For You	Alec Benjamin	3:05
Legends Are Made	Sam Tinnesz	2:49
Gasoline	Halsey	3:19
Figure You Out	VOILA	2:42
I See Red	Everybody Loves An Outlaw	3:50
I Think I'm In Love	Kat Dahlia	3:22
Dancing Without Music	BRDGS	4:08
Can't Help Falling In Love	Haley Reinhart	2:52

Content Warnings

Please note that whilst this is a work of fiction, the following topics are touched on. This book does include graphic explicit material intended for 18+ only. Reader discretion is advised.

- Anxiety/Panic Attacks
- Arson
- Blackmail (mentions of)
- Body Mutilation
- Child Abuse
- Choking
- Degradation
- Depression
- Edging

- Exhibitionism
- Explosions
- Firearms
- Grief
- Kidnapping
- Light bondage
- Loss of Family Members
- Murder
- Non-Consensual Drugging
- Praise
- Public Sex
- Sexual Assault
- Slight Torture
- Strangulation
- Suicide
- Suicidal Thoughts
- Stalking

- Trauma
- Use of sex toys

This book is written in British English.

Part I

Prologue

Everleigh

Murder is messy...I hate it.

What's worse? They never go quietly. Even when they're dying they still want to get the last word in. The headache after is the worst feeling, but still I drown it out with my female empowerment playlist that's currently blasting through my car's speakers. I hate driving in the dark, especially when it's a sixty road, but I'm all for being safe, hence me going twenty below it, the road too narrow to see clearly ahead.

I'm shimmying along to the beat, picking the dried blood off my hands, when bright lights illuminate around me. I gasp, swerving to the right, ending up in a ditch. I pant for breath, the panic calming, my eyes catching on the car pulled up behind me. I glare at the figure running towards my car, pushing open my door. "What the hell is your problem?" I shout, slamming my door closed behind me.

The man stills mere steps away from me. I glare up at him, and my heart skips a beat. Chocolate waves, sculpted jaw, lightly tanned skin, piercing blue eyes...*Shit.*

"Me? You were the one doing forty in a sixty." He glares at me.

I cross my arms, hiding my bloodied hands. The last person I want to see that is the man standing in front of me. "Because it's dark." I scoff.

His eyes appraise my body. "Are you drunk?"

My glare deepens. "No! Who gets behind a wheel drunk?" Should I be arguing with a member of the police force? Probably not. But it's not like I've committed a crime. He's the one who was driving recklessly.

He sighs. "Just be more careful. The world needs women like you in this world."

I don't miss how his eyes trail my body as he says that. "A woman like me?"

He holds his hands up, eyes widening as if he just realised what he implied. "I meant a woman who can stand up for herself."

I roll my eyes. "Whatever. Now if you don't mind, I need to work out how to get my car out of this ditch." I turn away from him, examining my car.

I freeze at the soft touch on my shoulder. "I'm sorry, I didn't mean to imply anything. I've never been good at flirting."

I blink slowly. *Flirting?* "No shit. It's no wonder you don't have a girlfriend."

"How do you know I don't have a girlfriend?" I can feel the heat of his body standing just behind me and I tense.

"You're Tylan Blaese. Millionaire turned detective, you were all over the news after you switched careers, and before that." He's also the man who could ruin my life but I keep that part to myself.

"I didn't realise I had an admirer."

I spin around, catching his smirk. "It's kinda hard to escape when the news is everywhere." I shrug it off.

He steps closer to me, brushing a lock of loose hair behind my ear. "What's your name, Pretty Girl?"

My breath catches, my heart pounding. Will he do a background check on me? Charge me if I tell him my name? Well my fake name. I know I should just walk away, somehow get my car out of this ditch and drive off, but then I get an idea. He's my way of getting inside information on what the police know. He's already, terribly, flirting with me, maybe I could get him to trust me, form some sort of relationship and make sure I'm not even on their radar. My mind made up I give him the name everyone knows me as. "Bea Featherstone."

The Polaroid Reaper

What's the problem with men...?

Their downfall is always going to be who they are. Take Theodore Black for example. On the outside he's a loving, caring, fifty-two year old husband and father who works long hours to help support his family. But on the inside? On the inside it's a completely different story – filled with filthy, disgusting, lust filled thoughts. The same thoughts that lured him right into my trap, yielding the same result as always – him lying here on the luxurious king-sized bed of an expensive hotel, with me straddling him in my lingerie, just as he dreamed about in his head.

Well, nearly.

In reality all you can see are the whites of his eyes, a portal directly to the inside of his soul – if he had one that is. Moving down, blood pours out of the smooth slit on his neck, the crimson trail leading down to pool and spill over from his belly button, staining the pristine sheets. To top it all off, his pride and joy, which I can safely say was definitely not something to brag about, is now all sliced up and piled into a hundred pieces next to him.

But none of that would be the reason for my notorious name, the Polaroid Reaper, generously provided by the vultures known as Little Bray journalists. That would be this old 1993 polaroid camera currently poised over this despicable excuse of a man.

One bright flash later and the little memento prints into my hand, a little wave of my hand and the beauty starts to come to life right in front of my eyes, just like a little movie. Of course I have to leave the cops a little present as well – they always get the second copy – the one that I throw on top of my victim's chest. Not that they're victims. What victim preys on young, vulnerable women just trying to have a good night?

After my work is finished, I climb off, standing to face the floor length mirror, the reflection is of someone that I don't recognise. A golden brown rat's nest sits on top of my head, rosy cheeks mixed with smudged blood red lipstick, or maybe it's real blood, who knows. Faint red fingerprints scatter the pale white skin on my neck, evidence of what the sick fuck liked to do – control a woman's breath to the point of passing out so that he could do whatever his sick heart desired. The white lace showcasing my most prized assets is now splotched with red. My sharp claws trace down my body, dried blood flaking off beneath them. My mind races at the memories of my parents racing through me, reminding me how much I look like them – the one thing that I have made sure to treasure every day for the past five, nearly six years.

My thoughts are interrupted by the faint buzzing sound coming from my discarded leather jacket. I reach down and pull out the little black phone from the pocket before answering the call. "Leigh? I was starting to get worried." I smile at my best friend's soft yet coarse voice filtering through the phone.

I wedge my phone between my shoulder and ear, sliding my black pencil skirt back on. "I should be offended that you doubt me, Cami."

"I never said I doubted you. I said I was getting worried. There's a difference."

I try to suppress my laugh at her defensiveness, failing miserably. "Why? You know I've mastered this by now, right?" I quickly put my phone down on the dresser, sliding my low-cut silk top back on.

"—getting reckless." Even though I only got the last of what I'm sure was one of her many rants, I still know exactly what she was saying. The same words I've been hearing since the night of my previous kill.

"You have to be more careful. You're getting reckless."

I'm sitting on the grey marble counter of my bathroom, facing the gold rimmed round mirror with nothing but my black silk bra covering my top half. Camilla stands behind me, reprimanding me whilst she stitches up the shallow stab wound at the top of my back. I haven't said a word since our phone call where I calmly asked her to pick me up. I've been too embarrassed. I've never had any close calls like this; I've never had any of these men openly stab me in the back before I've even pulled out my own knife. Although I guess technically it was my own knife he stabbed me with. Maybe that's what makes it even more humiliating?

Camilla's face softens from the scowl as she meets my haunted eyes in the mirror. She presses a soft kiss to my shoulder before speaking again. "I'm only saying all this because I love you, Everleigh."

I take a deep breath, counting to three, before replying. "I know. And I love you too, Camilla. I just—" I shake my head. "I don't even know what happened. One second I'm seducing him, the next I have a knife in my back."

"I'm not just talking about with the men. I'm talking about with the police," she sighs at my confused expression before continuing. "They're saying on the news that they found something at the latest scene."

"What did they find?"

"They won't say. We just have to hope it's nothing too incriminating." She wraps her arms around me from behind in a sisterly hug. "I don't want to see you go to jail for this, Leigh."

"I won't." My eyes darken in hatred. "There's too many men in this world who don't deserve to be here and I'm going to make sure they all suffer."

"Are you even listening to me?" Camilla's annoyed shout pulls me back to the present.

I roll my eyes, despite knowing she can't actually see me, ignoring her question. "I'm sending you the address. You know what to do." I don't hear what she mutters moments before she hangs up and I'm left in a silent hotel room with nothing but my own thoughts and a rotting corpse.

By the time I hear the signature knock at the apartment door I'm already clean and dressed once again. The rats nest now replaced by long golden curls cascading down my back. I swiftly open the door to two identical giants, both leaning either side of the door with one ankle crossed over the other. I swear they're literally the same person down to every detail, the only difference being the slight accents in their voices and their eye colour.

"Hey, Pixie." The silence is filled by the smooth posh London accent to the left of me, belonging to Freddie. I remain silent, stepping to the side to let them in.

They both saunter past me, his brother, Callum, letting out a low whistle. "You really did a number on this one, Cap." Callum's always been my favourite of the two. Maybe it's the quiet, gentle giant feel to him that has every woman he meets fawning over him, or it could be his subtle Irish accent. There's only three men I've ever let get close to me and that's the twins and my secret boyfriend, the only difference being that he doesn't know this side of me - he is a detective after all.

It feels like forever with the three of us standing there in the room silently looking at the body before I break it. "What are you waiting for? You know what to do." I pick my bag up from the floor, placing it onto my shoulder before opening the door again. "Message me when you're finished." And with that, I walk out, closing the door on man number four.

I climb into my navy blue Mini, locking the doors and connecting my phone to the radio via Bluetooth, selecting my 'post-justice' playlist full of songs that make me feel normal, despite knowing that I never will be, not anymore. I haven't been normal since the worst day of my life – December 24th, 2010 – the day an unknown man broke into my family home and brutally murdered my entire family.

Chapter Two

Black Bombay Cat

Tylan

1 week earlier

The Polaroid Reaper strikes again. I knew it wasn't going to be a good day when the minute I stepped into the station this morning I was called out to an alleyway. No further explanation is needed these days when the body of a successful businessman is found in an alleyway – naked. "There's no change to the previous two?" I'm currently towering over the rotting corpse.

"Other than one thing." My partner, Blake Sanders, squats down next to the body, lifting the cold limp hand to show me his fingernails. "He has blood under his fingernails."

I squat down next to him to get a closer look. "Is it his blood?"

"We've sent a sample to the lab to get it tested." He gently places the victim's arm down again. "But if it's not..."

"It's probably our killer's." I look around the scene before looking back at the body, examining the stab wounds closer. "These look shaky." Blake leans in to take a closer look.

"Could he have hurt her? Gained the upper hand before she took it back?"

"It's possible. He could've suspected something and attacked her to get away."

"But she was faster," I mutter to myself. "Is there a polaroid?" Blake wastes no time in handing me the picture inside of an evidence bag. I examine it closely. Just like the others. "We have a serial killer."

"And we might have her blood." His eyes sparkle in the low moonlight. "We might finally be getting somewhere with this case." I don't mirror his excitement. I have a strong feeling this case isn't going to be that straightforward.

Not if my theory is true.

Present Day

My team and I are sitting around the large oval table in the bright modern conference room, currently housing our case board. Photos from each murder, a map of Little Bray, news clippings, and other photos and notes all connected with red string linking our many theories for this case. I'm currently reading through my case notes when I receive an email from the lab. I click on the notification, pulling up the latest blood report. I scan it quickly, my theory being proved correct. "Fuck," I mutter to myself.

Blake perks up from his laptop. "Do they have a hit on the blood?"

I click off the report, pulling up the fake one I made a week ago. "It's our victim's." I print off the fake report, pinning it to the case board before passing a copy to the rest of my team.

"What about the cat hair found on Theodore Black?" Lyla, our newest and youngest addition to the team speaks up. "We know that he was allergic to cats, so why did he have cat hair on his clothes?"

"He was dumped in an alleyway, a stray could've found him and left it," Naomi speaks up from the other side of the table.

"That is an option, but she could own a..." Lyla glances down at the lab report on said hair. "Black Bombay cat."

I lean back in my chair, twirling the pen in my hands. "We need to look into black Bombay cat owners," I reply. "It's a long shot but it's better than where we are now."

"But if we look at her behavioural profile, she lacks the emotional empathy to look after an animal." Naomi voices her doubts turning to face the rest of us now crowded by the case board. "Look at how she kills. She does her research on each of her victims, respected men, all who take advantage of young vulnerable women, but they keep it hidden. You would have to do some serious research to find that out. Then she seeks them out and lures them in, offering intercourse, they think they're going to get what they want, at least until she gets them naked and takes them by surprise with exactly twenty stabs to their chest, followed by one smooth slit to their neck. At some point she mutilates their genitals and to finish it off, she finds the time to take at least one picture before moving them and dumping them in an alleyway."

"We already know she's getting justice." They all turn to look at me. "We got nowhere with the first victim's victims, but something had to have happened in her past for her to have this amount of hatred." I rub a hand down my face and sigh. "Lyla. Look into black cat owners within our kill zones. Blake. Look into hotels where the beds in the photos may be from, see if there's anything missing. Naomi. Look into sex offenders that may have died recently." They all give me a nod before heading back to the table and working on their own tasks. I turn back to the board and contemplate the evidence that we have so far, one question swimming around my mind.

Who is Everleigh Carlton?

The second the doors to the elevator open I'm hit with a strong delicious aroma drifting from the kitchen. I drop my black leather briefcase on the floor, shrugging my long coat off and hang it on the coat rail. I smile, untying my shoes, listening to the soft, but terrible, singing coming from the other room.

I place my shoes back in their spot on the shoe rack before closing the cloak room door and wandering into the kitchen. I lean against the marble counter closest to the door admiring the tight black jeans highlighting the drooling curves of my girlfriend. I admire her beauty for a few minutes, waiting for her to realise I'm here.

She turns around, jumping when her eyes land on me. "Don't mind me. I'm just admiring the view." I smirk at her.

She rolls her eyes. "Hello to you, too."

I walk closer to her wrapping my arms around her waist as she plates the food. "What have you made?"

"Chicken alfredo." She smiles, shrugging out my arms. "You're so touchy."

"Mmm. Your signature. And I can't help it when you look as good as you do." I try to reach for her again, but she holds the serving spoon out in defence. We jump around each other laughing in joy until I pin her arms to her side in a cuddle, placing her weapon on the side. "Gotcha," I whisper in her ear, placing a soft kiss on her cheek.

"Of course I got stuck with the needy boyfriend." She pouts at me, giving me the perfect opportunity to peck her lips. She pushes out of my arms picking up both bowls of pasta. "Let's eat before it goes cold." I take the seat opposite her as we both get stuck in. "How was work?"

"The same as always," I sigh, taking another bite.

She twirls the pasta on her fork repeatedly but doesn't eat. "They're saying there's a serial killer called the Polaroid Reaper?" She seems to zone out as she speaks.

"We don't know that for certain. We have leads."

She perks up. "Like what?"

I raise an eyebrow. "Bea, you know I can't tell you anything."

She leans back in her chair, her olive green eyes softening. "I know. Sorry I asked."

I reach over, squeezing her hand gently. "It's okay. You're a curious person." She smiles but it barely reaches her eyes. "What's wrong?"

"Are you sure you're okay with this? Keeping the relationship quiet?"

"We've known each other for four months, dating for one, and you're a private person. I'm more than happy to wait until you're ready."

"Thank you." She smiles at me, her breathtaking smile back on her face.

We spend the rest of the evening talking and watching movies until late into the night. I ride down with her to the lobby, offering her a kiss goodnight before watching her climb into her car. I wasn't lying when I said I'll wait for her, but I also can't fight the feeling that something feels off with her. Almost like she's hiding something from me.

Chapter Three

Coffee and Secrets

Everleigh

I didn't get back from Tylan's until gone midnight last night. I don't like lying to him about who I am but it's not like we're going to last. If I have the chance to talk to someone who makes me feel normal when I most need it, even if it's just for a few months, then I will make the most out of it. Yes, I started talking to him just to see if I could get an insight into the investigation but over the past few months I've come to like the normalcy of it all. I've even come to crave it.

I'm woken from my ultra rare peaceful sleep by my alarm clock, also known as Camilla. I blindly fumble on my bedside table searching for my phone, accidentally knocking my, thankfully empty, water glass over in the process. "You better have a good reason for waking me up at..." I barely open one of my eyes to check the time, "Five am."

"Good morning to you too." I can hear the eye roll in her voice even through the phone. I'm already starting to fall asleep again by the time she speaks up again. "I just thought you'd like to know that you're in the clear. The police just announced that the incriminating evidence they found was just a cat hair."

That wakes me up. "I'm sorry what? Are you telling me that the thing that's been keeping me up for two weeks, was a fucking cat hair?"

"I guess they thought it was human hair but after a simple test they discovered the truth."

"Let me guess. They're all men. The team working on this case?" I know it's not, but I have to keep up appearances.

"No. But why do you think that?"

"Because only an idiot can't tell the difference between a human hair and a cat hair."

Camilla lets out a soft laugh. "This coming from the girl who catnapped her neighbour's cat for two days before realising she had the wrong cat?"

"I was six and Mr tuff and Ollie looked as identical as Freddie and Callum." My defensive tone is obvious even to my own ears that I'm not surprised when Camilla lets out another laugh, especially when our chat is interrupted by the loud mewl from the only man I truly love, Muffin, also known as the black Bombay cat currently nestled in my lap.

"I better let you go so you can show Muffin some love. I'll call you if there's any updates. Love you, Leigh."

"Love you too, Cami." Camilla ends the call whilst I lean down, placing a soft kiss on top of Muffin's head which he affectionately returns by nudging his nose against mine before stretching out next to me on the bed. I join him in trying to fall back asleep.

Many restless minutes later I give up with the tossing and turning ultimately deciding to give up on sleep and instead go about my day. I quickly shower, brush my teeth, and wash my face before heading back to my bedroom, throwing my hair up into a ponytail, wrapping a black ribbon into a bow around the bobble, leaving my curtain bangs free to frame my face. The cool autumn breeze makes it the perfect weather to throw on my favourite outfit – my long sleeved cream turtleneck, black skater skirt, twenty dernier tights, paired with my fur lined ankle boots. I do a quick observation in my mirror before moving onto my makeup. I never go full out, just a simple natural look with a dark purple lip and extra blush to give my cheeks their signature rosy pink colour.

Once I'm ready to face the day I head out, opting to walk to my favourite café and bookshop – Forever & Ever – just a few streets from my house. The sun is only just starting to rise when I step out, taking a deep breath and closing my eyes, taking in the crisp fresh air. It takes me ten minutes to reach Forever & Ever – it's always been my dream to open my own just like it, but life clearly has different plans for me. I push open the white French door, the little bell above announcing my entrance.

"Bea!" The bright voice is supported with an equally bright smile from the owner of the store, Leah, currently stocking the pastry case full of delicious treats. "Let me guess. An iced caramel latte, with extra caramel, and a cinnamon roll?"

"You know me so well." I grin as I walk up to the counter to pay. I've barely even opened my bag when a small white bag is thrust in front of my face. I suppress a laugh taking the bag from her and handing over the cash. "Keep the change. Do you have any new books in? I need something new to read."

"I did just get in this hockey romance." She doesn't stop making my coffee as she reaches under the counter and hands me a book with two illustrated people on the cover. I open my mouth to voice my concerns, but she interrupts me, handing me my drink. "Don't be fooled by the cover. It gets spicy." I let out a little giggle, the one I always get when talking about books, they're my only escape from this cruel miserable world after all.

"I'll take it." I hand over more cash for the book before heading over to my favourite spot in the cafe. It's a hanging chair in the corner by the window with a little table next to it where I place my coffee and pastry, a pink fluffy rug sitting underneath. It truly feels like my own little reading corner, especially at times like this when the cafe's empty and the pink-orange hues of the sky are shining through the cottage style windows.

I'm staring out the window, sipping on my drink when the bell above the door rings, announcing the unexpected visitor. I come here often enough that I know no one else ever comes in before eight and it's only seven-thirty.

My breath catches in my throat as I'm greeted with the 6'2 god of a man I've gotten to know over the past few months. My eyes drift over the soft chocolate brown waves down to the broad shoulders and strong back covered with a long black coat. I don't think I'm imagining things. I'm pretty certain Tylan is standing at the counter of my favourite hangout spot.

I quickly avert my eyes when he spins around...I meant to look out the window but instead my eyes land on his ocean blues set into his perfectly sculpted, clean shaven face. I audibly swallow as we continue to stare at each other for an eternity before I break it, taking another sip of my coffee. "Mind if I sit here?" I look up at the sound of his sexy London accent.

"I-I—" *He's acting normal, Everleigh, why aren't you?* I clear my throat. "Sure, but there's plenty of other seats here."

"Yes. But none of them have a view quite as beautiful as this one." He takes a seat on the couch opposite me as I look back out the window at the low sunlight shining through the trees.

"It always looks beautiful in the low sunlight." Looks like instead of coffee and books, my morning's going to be full of coffee and secrets.

"It definitely does." When I turn back to look at him he's already staring at me intently, a light blush rising on my cheeks as I realise he wasn't talking about the outside view, his lips tip up into a small smirk. *Are we really going to act like we don't already know each other?* "Are you new here?"

Looks like we are. "Nope. I was born and raised here."

"Hmm."

"What?"

"I'm surprised I've never met you before. I never forget a pretty face." His eyes flick down my body causing the blush on my cheeks to increase so much that I have to cover my cheek, disguising the action by tucking my hair behind my ear. His eyes watching every movement.

"I don't tend to get out much during the day," I lie. He sits back, resting one ankle on top of his knee, stretching an arm across the back of the sofa. He looks so dominating right now. I subtly rub my thighs together to try to ease the small ache between them.

"Why's that?" His lips twitch up, my tongue running over mine subconsciously as my mind wanders back to the feel of them on mine.

"I...–Um. I'm more of a night owl I guess."

He raises his eyebrows at me. "A night owl?"

"Yep. I'm barely awake during the day."

He nods. "So you're like a vampire?

I giggle. "I guess you could say that." My eyes flick back to his lips. I wish I could kiss him right now but I can't break my cover.

He saves my urge when he stands up. "I'll see you around. Unfortunately, I have to get to work."

"Have fun." I smile at him, watching him walk out the door. Part of me wishes we didn't have to act like strangers, but another part of me likes the forbidden nature of it.

Chapter Four

Not Working Alone

Tylan

I was not expecting to see my little firecracker when I walked into the coffee shop this morning, but it's enough to put a smile on my face before my, what I already know will be stressful, day. My smile is quickly wiped away when I turn the radio on in my car

"We still do not have any more details about who the Polaroid Reaper could be. Theodore Black is now the fourth victim of the infamous serial killer living amongst us. Her previous victims include local social worker Matthew Anderson, local politician Daniel Williams, and local philanthropist Jake Peters. Many locals are speculating that she could be the modern day Jack the Ripper. Police are urging every man in the Little Bray area to be cautious around any young attractive women they may come across."

The fourth man. This psychopath is taunting me and now everyone knows it. I have to admit, this Polaroid Reaper is impressive. Her ability to lure these men and kill them leaving no trace behind must've taken a long time to perfect. Or maybe not. Men like Theodore Black are the most likely to end up as victims of a female seeking revenge. As impressive as she is, she is still a massive pain in my ass.

I arrive at the latest discovery site – a dumpster in an alleyway in one of the quieter areas of the city – just like all the others. The scene is chaos with multiple police vehicles and news outlets, as well as curious bystanders watching the busy work of the investigators. Parking my car, I climb out walking up to the police tape that an officer generously lifts up to allow me to walk under. "Tylan! Over here!" I walk up to the dumpster where Blake is observing the scene.

"Is it the same as the others?"

"Yes. Except for this." He hands me an evidence bag, inside of which there is a silver cuff link.

"Is this the victim's?"

"No."

"But the killer's a woman? Why would she have a cuff link?" He gives me a sideways glance and I answer my own question. "She's not working alone."

He takes the evidence bag back from me before any of the public or more importantly, the reporters, can see anything. "We need to keep this out of the public eye for now. If she still thinks that we think she's working alone she or her partner might slip up."

He turns to face me. "This is beginning to feel like it's about something bigger and I can't see what it is."

The sun is only just starting to set as I look up from my mahogany desk to look out the floor length windows overlooking the Little Bray skyline. Today has been the most unsuccessful day I've had in years. I've been doing extensive research on the victims and trying to find connections between them and Everleigh Carlton, as well as trying to find who her partner could be. Why would she be working with a man if she clearly hates men?

I rub my eyes, catching a glance at the time – six-fifteen – I let out a heavy sigh, turning off my computer. There's no way I'm going to be getting any more work done today so instead I leave the office, heading back to my penthouse a few blocks away. The minute I enter, I head straight for the drinks cabinet, pouring myself a glass of scotch, shrugging my coat, blazer, and tie off, hanging them up neatly before undoing a couple of my shirt buttons, rolling my sleeves up. I sink into my usual seat, taking slow sips of my drink.

I sit in silence for a few minutes until it's interrupted by the quiet patter of little feet that appear to be running. Before I have the chance to blink the little golden ball of fur is on my lap, licking all over my face. "Hey, buddy." I scratch behind the fluffy ears of my little golden retriever puppy, Bailey. After he calms down from his initial excitement, he curls up in my lap. I stare out the window petting him subconsciously, my thoughts running wild.

After ten minutes I sigh and stand up, Bailey now peacefully sleeping in his bed in the corner of the room, looking at my now empty glass. I'm going to need something stronger. With that thought, my mind is made up. I don't bother changing, instead I fill up Bailey's food and water bowls before heading out to the local upscale bar down the road.

Chapter Five

Bubbles

Everleigh

I spent all day perfecting my plan for tonight. I normally wait six months in between my kills, it gives me more time to do thorough research and plan every last second, but lately I haven't been able to fight the urge. Jack Harrow will be my third kill in two weeks. I always wondered why serial killers go on sprees but now I get it. Most of them don't have the same morals as me though, I do it because I need to rid the world of predators and the faster I do it, the better. But we all share the same addiction that courses through our bones like a drug. We have a burst of adrenaline that drives us, and we don't want to fight it. Is that really so bad?

It took me all of two seconds to find out my target's plan for tonight. He's spending the night at his upscale nightclub, Harrow Bar. I rolled my eyes at the creative name. I spent the rest of the day researching the bar and studying the blueprints, they were surprisingly easy to get my hands on.

Tonight is going to be my hardest yet, the previous four men were all alone in random bars and clubs, but this is Jack Harrow's bar, everyone who works there knows who he is. I need to be careful how I go about this. I finish the final touches on my makeup, taking a quick glance in the mirror. My tight black mini dress is complete with black fishnets – Jack's weakness. My hair is tied up in a simple half up-half down hairstyle with my bangs framing my face and the ribbon securely tightened. I always ensure I dress up in whatever my target for the night loves – it makes it easier to seduce them. I order my Uber, feeding Muffin before making my way to the nightclub.

I arrive at the bar twenty minutes later. The dark interior with purple fluorescent lighting is striking but it still looks classy. I will admit Jack knows how to decorate. It even smells subtly of lavender compared to the pungent cologne riddled scent most clubs have. I take a seat at the bar where I have a clear view of the upstairs VIP area, which is roped off to the public, with a bouncer standing guard.

"What can I get for you?" I turn my attention to the young bartender.

"I'll have a glass of champagne please." I tap my card on the card reader, scanning the room as I wait for my drink. The layout has changed slightly from the blueprints I found but the majority of it is still the same. The ground floor consisting of a dance floor and stage that take up the majority of space, the bar I'm at sitting on the opposite side. To the right there's a hallway that leads towards the bathrooms as well as the back exit and to the left is the main entrance and smoking area. Overlooking the floor is the balcony with a glass barrier that houses the VIP area. I need to get up there.

The bartender places my drink in front of me. I cross one leg over the other, taking a sip. The hairs on the back of my neck tingle. I glance over my shoulder, my eyes catching on the brown eyes staring down at me from above, heat in his eyes. I sip on my champagne, refusing to break eye contact. He doesn't break it either as he speaks to one of his bodyguards, pointing directly at me. I hide my smile behind my glass, taking another sip. So predictable.

I've barely turned back to the bar when his bodyguard taps on my shoulder, leading me towards the VIP area. My jaw literally drops at the sleek black booths overlooking the main area, complete with a smaller bar near the back of the room. The man leads me over to one of the empty booths just as a server comes over with an ice bucket, a bottle of Dom Perignon, and two glasses. "I didn't order this."

"It's on the house," the sever says before quickly walking away. I'm left alone watching the sea of people mingling below. I feel like a queen watching over her kingdom. I'm already three-quarters of the way through the bottle of champagne when I finally get some company...but not from the man I was expecting.

"Mind if I sit?" I look up into the ocean blues I'm all too familiar with. *Shit. What is he doing here?*

I nod. "Are you stalking me?"

He chuckles, sitting next to me, so close that our thighs are touching. “Maybe.”

My mouth drops open but I cover it by taking a larger sip. “What are you doing here?” He doesn’t answer, instead he picks up the bottle of champagne starting to pour himself a glass before I slap his hands away. “That’s mine.” I’m full on pouting now. “Get your own.” He chuckles once again and, fuck, it’s the sexiest thing I’ve ever heard.

“You’re very protective of your drinks, Bubbles.”

“No one touches my champagne.” I finish my current glass, glaring at him picking up the bottle again, but my gaze softens when he pours the rest of it into my glass for me.

“How many glasses have you had?”

“One bottle’s worth.” My head is definitely starting to feel its effect but I’m still very much sober. I found out years ago that I am not a lightweight.

His eyes widen. “And you’re still sober?”

I roll my eyes. “I know how to handle my alcohol.” He raises his hand and a server rushes over taking his drink order of some sort of whiskey, I wasn’t really listening. I was more focused on how his shirt stretches across his chest, highlighting his muscles– *Snap out of it, Everleigh!*

“Look, I...” My voice trails off at the sight of his arms sprawled across the back of the booth behind me. In return, I turn to face him, my nose instantly hit with the intoxicating manly cinnamon scent of him that I wish I could bottle up, so much so that my body instinctively leans closer to him just to try and get more of it.

"Careful there, Bubbles." I realise that I'm basically sitting on his lap, stopped by his hand stretched along my hip. My skin heats under his touch. Maybe I could have some fun with this.

"What's your name?" Who says a little role play isn't fun? Instead of moving, I twist until I'm straddling his lap, his arms wrapping around my waist.

I see confusion flutter over his features quickly replaced by mischief. "Tylan. Tylan Blaese." His thumb gently strokes my lower back. "What about you, Pretty Girl? Or should I just stick with Bubbles?"

"Bubbles is good for now. You'll have to prove yourself worthy of knowing my name." I swear I hear a small growl as his arms wrap around me tighter, pulling me closer until our chests are touching. I can feel the hard bulge sitting between my thighs, unconsciously moving my hips ever so slightly just to feel it more.

He grabs my hips, stopping the movements, leaning in so close I can feel his hot breath against my ear. "Stop."

I playfully pout at him, my body automatically stopping. "You're no fun."

He doesn't reply. Instead he reaches around me, passing me my drink before picking up his own, his other hand never loosening its hold on me. We sit there, silently staring at each other, our eyes full of heat. I block out the outside world savouring the moment of the two of us alone. We've never done anything more than making out but, fuck, I really want that to change tonight. There's only so much a girl can control herself around a man like Tylan Blaese.

I place my hand on his chest, slowly trailing it up until I'm cupping his face, the stubble gentle against my hands. We both slowly lean forward until our lips meet. The kiss starts off slow and gentle, but it quickly turns into rough passion. We fight for dominance, at least until his hand grips my hair, not too tight, but tight enough to keep me in place – not that I want to go anywhere else. We pull away an eternity later, our breathes heavy, foreheads resting against each other.

"Take me home," I whisper breathlessly, kissing along his cheek all the way to his ear. "Take me to your bed." I tug on his ear lobe. "Please."

Next thing I know, he's gently pushing me off his lap, fixing my dress for me. "Let's go." He leads me out the bar by my hand and I happily follow, completely forgetting the reason I came to the nightclub in the first place. Jack Harrow can wait.

Good Girl

Tylan

My day is definitely taking a turn for the better. I only went to Harrow Bar tonight to have a drink or two, but the moment I stepped into the VIP area I spotted my little firecracker sitting alone drinking from a bottle of champagne. I have no idea what she was doing there alone all dressed up but she looked like she could use some company...so I made myself her company for the night. Out of all the possibilities for tonight, bringing my feisty girlfriend back to my place was not one of them.

The second the lift doors close my lips are back on her addictive ones. I'm practically dragging her out the lift when we reach my penthouse to an echo of her giggles. I know I should wait and take her to my bedroom, or at least offer her a drink, but I don't want to waste any more time. I push her against the wall, smothering her cute gasp with another passionate kiss. It takes her a second until she's returning the kiss, pushing up onto her tiptoes, her arms reaching up to pull me down to her 5'4 frame.

I wrap my arms around her thighs, pulling up until she locks her perfect legs around my waist. Once I'm certain she's secure, I trail my hands up the back of her thighs and onto her round ass with a firm squeeze, her response nothing but an adorable gasp. I take the opportunity to slip my tongue between her partially open lips, both of us fighting for dominance but I quickly gain the upper hand, her hands gripping my hair, her hips grinding against my hardening cock.

We break the kiss, both of us panting for breath. I take the time to admire her swollen lips, her dark red lipstick smudged. Unable to hold back, my lips trail down to her soft neck, kissing all over as her head lulls back giving me the perfect room to explore and bite, leaving my mark on her. I pull back smirking at the reddening mark, before continuing my way down to her beautiful breasts. Her hands tug on my curls, forcing me to look at her.

"Take me to bed." I can hear the desperation in her whispers, latching onto me tighter when I pull her off the wall, carrying her down the hallway and into my bedroom, placing her back on her feet.

I take a couple of steps back trailing my eyes down her body. "Strip." Her eyes widen ever so slightly before she reaches behind her unzipping her dress. I lean against my desk my eyes tracking her every movement. She moves the straps slowly, teasingly pulling both of them down one at a time, it takes all of my control not to push her onto the bed and have my way with her.

Her eyes drop to my hand that is palming my cock through my trousers, trying to ease the ache forming from the tightness as she continues to push her dress down over her hips and, fuck me, I have the literal girl of my dreams right in front of me.

She steps out her dress kicking it off to the side, standing in the middle of my usually cold bedroom now warmed by her presence, in nothing but her black lace lingerie set and fishnet tights. I push off the desk stalking towards her, taking all of her in as she stands there shuffling from foot to foot, avoiding my gaze.

I reach her, placing a gentle kiss on the spot just below her ear, the sexiest little moan escaping her. "You're beautiful." Her skin flushes pink. "How much do you like these?" I ask, running my finger along the waistband of her tights, her skin pebbling along my path.

"Why?" Her voice is nothing but a breathy whisper. I don't answer. I rip them right where her panties are covering her noticeably wet pussy. "You could've just taken them off." My fiery goddess glares at me but she still has that playful smile on her face.

"Where's the fun in that?" I give her another quick kiss, whispering in her ear. "Besides," I gently tease one finger over the front of her panties, her breath hitching, "you liked it."

Catching her off guard, I pick her up, throwing her onto the middle of my black bedsheets. She lays there like the goddess she is, waiting to be worshipped, her swollen bottom lip captured in between her pearly whites, watching as I undo my belt, her thighs rubbing together. I pull the belt off tossing it to the side smirking at the whimper she lets out. My girl might not be as innocent as she looks. She begins to sit up but I glare at her, stopping her. “Stay.”

She stays leaning back on her elbows for a few seconds before laying back flat on the bed again. Once she’s back in position, I throw my shirt and trousers off, her eyes widening at the scars on my chest left from my loving bastard of a father. I don’t give her long to look before I’m crawling over her, her hands wasting no time in tracing along one of my scars before I grab her hands pinning them over her head, her eyes narrowing. “Who did that to you?”

“I don’t want to talk about him right now.” I gently kiss her, moving down to her neck, marking her some more, my fingers following the trail left behind, a small shiver running through her. My kisses trail down to her chest, my hands reaching behind her as she arches her back giving me the space to unclip her bra and pull it off her body.

I have no restraint at this point.

Grasping her breasts in my hands, I kiss around them alternating between kisses and nips, my tongue flicking over her hard nipples. Her low moans urge me on, her hands reaching down to my hair but I pull away pinning them above her head again. "Do you want to come tonight?"

She nods her head vigorously. "Yes."

"Your hands stay here or I stop. Understand?"

"Yes," she whines.

"Good girl." She squeezes her legs together again, my path continuing down her body starting at her round stomach, moving down to her hips, kissing along her panty line battling against her squirms, using her skin as a cover for my small chuckle. Note to self: Bea does not like to stay still.

"Take them off," she breathes out, forcing my eyes up to meet hers, my eyebrow raising. "Please? Please take them off."

I smile at her, using both hands to silently tug her panties off. I sit back on my knees admiring her naked form. It's official: My dreams did not live up to reality.

"Spread your legs." I admire her soaking pink pussy, the desperation in her eyes telling me exactly what she wants. "Tell me what you want, Bubbles." Starting at her ankle, I trail gentle kisses up her leg waiting for a reply.

"Please make me come."

I place teasing kisses over the inside of her thigh and up, placing a singular kiss on her beautiful pussy before pulling back, a little whimper falling from her lips. She's so responsive. I repeat my kisses on her other leg forgoing the little kiss on her pussy as I pull away.

"You'll have to be more specific."

She pouts at me, letting out a small growl. "You'll have to show me how good you are first. Or are you just one of those guys who thinks he knows what to do but doesn't actually?" She raises an eyebrow at me and this time it's me who lets out a low growl.

"Just remember you asked for this when you're screaming my name later." I don't make either of us wait any longer, using one hand to spread her pussy open exposing her little clit, my tongue gently swirling around it, purposefully avoiding the little button.

Spurred on by her little moans and whimpers, I finally give her what she wants, sucking gently on her clit, slowly increasing the pressure until she cries out, her muscles tensing. I continue at the pace she likes, holding her hips down against her squirms, her moans are the sweetest sounds to my ears.

I run a finger down her slit gathering her wetness, gently pushing one finger inside her tight hole. Her back arches, giving up the fight and placing a hand in my hair, grinding against my face as I slowly add a second finger using both of them to stroke the spot inside her that will make her scream. She doesn't last much longer, her cries pouring out of her as her body tenses before relaxing, little shudders taking over her.

I lick her release as she comes down, her grip on my hair loosening as she gasps in breaths. I crawl up her body dragging my fingers out from her warm centre, bringing them up to trace them along her lips until she opens up allowing me to slide my fingers inside her mouth, she wastes no time in sucking and licking them clean. I pull my fingers out and kiss her, still tasting her on my lips and her tongue.

"You're delicious." The blush that rises on her cheeks is nearly obscured by how flushed the rest of her body already is. "You're so fucking beautiful," I whisper, looking down at her, her olive green eyes trying to refocus on me.

"That was...intense," she pants, grinning. "But good."

"Just good?" I raise an eyebrow at her, pushing my boxers down revealing my hard length. "Why don't I show you amazing?"

She looks down and gasps, her eyes widening. "I don't think that's gonna fit."

I peck her lips. "You're made for me, it'll fit. Now be a good girl and take it." I reach over grabbing a condom from the draw, wasting no time in rolling it over my hard length. Crawling over her again I soften my features at the wary look shining in her eyes. "Are you sure you want this?"

"Yes." Her silky legs wrap around my waist pulling me closer until my cock is nudging at her entrance. "Please fuck me."

How can I say no when she asks so nicely?

I guide my cock into her waiting entrance. "Fuck." I let out a low groan, pushing further until my cock is fully seated inside her, watching how she stretches around me. "You're so tight, baby." Her only response is a moan, her head tilting back.

I give her a minute to adjust, kissing her hard before I start moving inside her. It doesn't take long to find a rhythm we both like, her back arching, her sharp nails clawing at my back, our moans pouring into our kisses. Her face burrows into my neck, smothering her loud scream as pleasure takes over her. I follow soon after, taking a moment to bask in our closeness before I pull out of her, kissing her lips softly. "You're amazing."

"So are you." She smiles at me placing a peck on my lips before she collapses back on my bed. I leave her lying there, going to the bathroom to discard the condom and grab a warm wet cloth for her. When I return she's still lying in the same spot staring at the ceiling with a dazed smile, her skin glowing. *Why did we wait so long to do that?* I can't stop my smile as I climb back onto the bed next to her feet. She jumps at the warm cloth running between her legs. "I-I can do it myself." She blushes again.

I peck her lips. "Let me take care of you." She blinks, swallowing, tears forming behind her eyes. "Hey. Hey." I lie down next to her pulling her into my chest. "What's wrong?"

"Nothing." She pushes off my chest, heading to the bathroom without a second glance at me, her body tenses once again. She returns after ten minutes, her hair brushed, makeup removed, and fully dressed, minus her tights. "My friend's here to pick me up. Thanks for tonight."

“Bea,” I call after her, but she’s gone. I sigh lying back on my bed, her intoxicating scent consuming me.

Chapter Seven

Messed Up

Everleigh

I step out the lift into the fancy lobby only to be greeted by a furious Camilla glaring daggers at me. I roll my eyes, walking straight past her out into the street. I hear her walking behind me but neither of us speak until we're both safely in her car.

"What the hell, Everleigh?!" I wince at Camilla's furious shout.

"It was just a one night stand," I lie.

"What about Jack Harrow?"

I roll my eyes. "I'll deal with him tomorrow."

"Tomorrow's too late, Everleigh."

"Don't give me that." I glare at her. "In case you're forgetting. I'm the one running this operation. Not you." We sit there glaring at each other until she turns her attention back to the road, driving to my house.

"Do you know he assaulted another girl tonight? She only just turned eighteen two days ago." I look at her too stunned to speak, tears brimming my eyes. She scoffs. "Of course you didn't. You were too busy sucking a random guy's cock." She shakes her head in disbelief. "How did that even happen? You hate men. You never let any touch you without killing them. Not since—"

"Don't! I don't need that memory right now." I think about what she said. I was supposed to kill Jack Harrow tonight to stop him from hurting any other girls, but instead I ran off with my secret boyfriend and now there's another girl who's going to be haunted by what that despicable man did to her. Just like my foster parents did to me. Just like my therapist tried to do. I'm slipping into the memory of sixteen year old me sleeping, being woken up by the man and woman who took me in, pinning me to the bed, ripping my clothes off—

"I'm sorry." Camilla's voice pulls me back to the present. Almost as if she could sense me going back to that dark place. "I shouldn't have said that."

"No. You're right. I should've stayed focused tonight. It won't happen again." And I will make sure of that.

I reach over switching to a radio station running the news.

"Breaking news. It has been revealed that police now have a new lead on the Polaroid Reaper case. At the last crime scene investigators discovered a cuff link that didn't belong to the victim, Theodore Black. They now believe that the Polaroid Reaper is not working alone and that she is working with a male partner. Police are urging for anyone with any information to call this number—"

Camilla and I stare at each other with wide eyes.

"Take me to the twins. Now." She makes a sharp U-turn towards the twins' apartment as I stare out the window, biting at my fingernails, letting my mind wander.

Twenty minutes later we're pulling up to the twins' apartment complex. Before the car is even shut off, I'm jumping out, opting for the stairs as I run up to their door, frantically knocking. "Hey, Cap. Now's not really a good time." Callum opens the door with just a towel haphazardly wrapped around his waist.

"Then make it a good time. Now." I push my way in, immediately covering my eyes at the sight of a naked woman and a naked Freddie on the couch. "Freddie!"

"Pixie?" Freddie's voice is as surprised as I am.

"Oh my God! Thanks for the warning, Leigh." I turn around to face Camilla shielding her eyes.

"I didn't know either." I cross my arms.

"Who are you?" The mystery girl is now dressed in an inside out dress.

"None of your business. Get out of here."

The girl huffs, closing the door behind her as she leaves. Freddie leaves the room at the same time Callum walks back in thankfully properly dressed now. I go to sit on the couch but swiftly change my mind and sit on the coffee table instead as we wait for Freddie.

Two minutes later he returns fully dressed. “What’s so important you had to ruin my happy ending, Pixie?” If looks could kill Freddie would be dead. His playfulness drops when he sees my face. Camilla turns the TV on and sure enough the same news story is running. The twins watch it as I sit there, glaring at them, anger boiling inside me. No one speaks until it ends.

“Whose is it?” I ask calmly. After waiting too long for an answer my glare deepens. “Answer me!”

“It’s mine,” Callum replies, we all turn towards him. I hate getting mad at Callum, but I can’t fight the fury bubbling inside me. The need to kill coming in full force. Killing is like an addiction for me and without it, I’m struggling with withdrawal. “I didn’t even know I lost it. I’m sorry Everleigh.”

“Do you know how careless that is?” I storm over to him, clenching my fists at my sides. “I could go to jail for this, we all could, and these horrible, disgusting men will get to keep walking around like they own the world, assaulting every woman they come across. Do you know the trauma that that leaves?” When he doesn’t answer I end up screaming in his face. “Do you?!”

“Okay, you need to calm down.” Camilla pulls me away from Callum, but she struggles, my feet refusing to move. “Everleigh Bea Carlton look at me.” Her voice turns stern forcing me to look at her.

I break.

She catches me before I collapse on the floor, tears running down my face, struggling to catch my breath. She sits next to me, holding me close to her.

“I messed up. I messed up. I messed up.” I keep mumbling the same three words over and over again, sobbing hysterically. Both of the twins join us on the floor, all three of them holding me. I already knew it, but in this moment I’m reminded that these three people are the only ones who know the real me and still love me. That thought just makes me cry harder.

“You didn’t, Cap. I’m so sorry for what our parents did to you. You didn’t deserve it. No one does.” Despite his best try to keep it hidden, I can hear the hurt in his voice.

I look at Callum. “It’s not your fault,” I manage to say between sniffles. “Your parents are the ones who decided to...do that to me.” I’m squeezed tighter in our four-way hug, my sobs eventually quieting down to whimpers.

I glance around at the three people surrounding me. My chosen family. Callum and Freddie. The twins who are my brothers, the brothers from my foster family. When they found out what their parents were doing to me, they killed them for me without an ounce of remorse, it turned out that their parents did the same thing to Callum before I showed up. They were horrible people and I wish I could’ve killed them myself but at least they’re not around anymore.

I turn my attention to Camilla. My best friend from nursery. She’s always been my ride and die, she’s never left my side for anything. She's like a sister to me, but she'll never be a replacement for my twin sister. I pull away from the group hug, wiping my tears away whilst taking a deep breath. "What are we going to do about this?"

"Don't worry. I've got a plan." Camilla smiles.

"What is it?"

"It's best if you don't know before I do it." Camilla winks at me, helping me to stand up again. I dust my dress down, Camilla and I both turning towards the twins, matching smirks on our faces.

Freddie looks up from his phone, noting our expressions. "What?"

Camilla and I share a look before she answers. "So, that girl—"

"Don't say another word." We both burst out laughing.

I hold my hands up in mock surrender. "Hey, we don't judge. Any girl would love to be taken by two guys at once."

"Or more," Camilla adds.

Freddie rolls his eyes whereas Callum blushes to his roots. "Didn't you have a kill planned for tonight, Pixie?"

"Yeah, about that," I drag out. "That's been moved to tomorrow night."

"Why?"

"Because she got distracted by her own man," Camilla replies for me.

"He's not my man. He was a one night stand," I lie.

"Are you sure about that?"

If the ache between my legs could speak it would definitely disagree with my statement. Thankfully it can't.

"I never thought I'd see the day the great Everleigh Carlton willingly touched a guy." This time it was Callum picking on me.

I roll my eyes at all of them. "I hate you all. I'm going home." I turn to walk out.

"Do you want a ride?" Camilla shouts.

"No. It's only a ten minute walk. What could happen?"

Famous last words.

I'm about halfway home when the hairs on the back of my neck prickle, my senses heightening. I keep walking, listening out for anything strange, the sense of being watched growing stronger with every step. I stop at a pedestrian crossing when I hear a twig snap behind me, willing the car coming to go faster so I can cross. The second it does I rush across, taking the opportunity to look over my shoulder but I walk straight into a wall of muscle. I look back at the man holding me tight, struggling against him. "Let me go." I lift my foot to stomp on his but he's faster than me, moving it before I can.

"You're not going anywhere." His eyes scan down my body, lingering on my chest. "Not when you're dressed like this." He's dragging me to an alleyway out of sight from any prying eyes, but I don't stop struggling. "Stop struggling.

I'll only make it hurt more." He throws me against the wall, my head bouncing off it, knocking the breath from me. He crushes me between him and the wall as I fumble in my bag his grimy hands yanking the top of my dress down.

Where is it?

He knocks my bag out of my hands but thankfully I manage to get my knife out as he does. In a heartbeat I stab him right through his heart, he stumbles back.

I pull my dress back up as he looks at the knife in disbelief, the blood pouring down like a trickle of water from a tap. "You shouldn't have underestimated me." I pull the knife out causing him to fall back and collapse onto the ground. "You should really be more careful." I stab him again. "You should know there's monsters running the streets at night." I stab him a total of twenty times, finishing with one slit across his neck, and one clean swipe against his cock, cutting it clean off.

I reach into my bag, pulling my polaroid camera out. This might not have been a planned kill but this man was a vulture just like the rest of them. I snap two photos, placing one of them on top of the body and the other one in my bag along with the camera. Unlike my usual crime scenes, I don't have to move the body. Instead, I leave him to rot against the piles of rubbish he fell on top of, continuing my walk home.

Chapter Eight
Vengeance

Dear Miss Reaper.
Beware, beware, the ghost of past.
Prepare, prepare, to say goodbye.
Despair, despair, you're too late.

Do you know what I hate most in this world? The psychopaths who never get caught – who never get what they deserve. The psychopaths like you, our dear Polaroid Reaper. I'd forgive you if you weren't killing innocent men, men like my brother-in-law. You broke my little sister, yet you have no remorse. Do I know who you really are? Yes. Could I get you locked up in jail? Yes. But you deserve worse.

I pull the final photo out of the developing fluid, swinging around to pin it up next to my latest line of photos. There's very little I find more relaxing in life than watching as the photos slowly develop – the little unsuspecting people coming to life right in front of my eyes. You don't know I have these, of course. You never know I'm there watching you in the shadows, capturing your every movement. This one's my favourite – you, Miss Reaper, sitting on the very lap of the detective in charge of your case. It was obvious in person, but it's clear as day in these photos that he's fallen under your enchantment, completely clueless to your secret activities. It's pathetic really.

I stand back from my latest addition to view the entire wall full of photos of you and your little crew, taking up the entire back wall. My hand clenches tight, anger and remorse for my sister at the forefront of my mind. You won't get away with this but as my father always says, "patience is key".

Count your days, Miss Reaper.

Deja Vu

Everleigh

The purple fluorescent lighting and sleek black booth surrounding me combined with the pounding music are giving me a major sense of deja vu – minus the attractive distraction from last night. My phone buzzes from my purse. I'm debating whether or not to look at it when it buzzes again. I sigh pulling my phone out. *Speak of the devil.*

Are you still coming over tonight?

I'd like to talk to you about last night

Just let me know you're ok, Bea

I sigh. I haven't spoken to Tylan ever since I ran out on him last night. The truth is I don't know what to tell him. It's not like I can tell him I'm the person who he's spent the past year tirelessly working to catch.

I'm ok

I can't come over tonight

His reply comes a second later.

Promise me you're ok?

I promise

I take a deep breath, pocketing my phone, I can't afford to be distracted tonight. I bring my glass of champagne to my lips, keeping my eyes trained on the colourful dots merging together on the dance floor below. The hairs on the back of my neck raise, spotting my target out the corner of my eye, watching me intently as he talks to some random guy I've never seen before. *Time to turn on the flirt.*

I flick my lightly waved hair over my shoulder, crossing one leg over the other forcing my dress to rise up, showing off the majority of my thighs. I don't turn to look but I can feel his eyes tracing a burning trail over my body. My instincts are shouting at me to curl up and hide, but hatred wins out calling at me to continue the seduction.

It works. I'm finishing my champagne when my nose is assaulted with the overwhelming, sickening scent of cigarettes. I force the bile in my throat down at the feel of his rough calloused hand on my bare shoulder. His pungent breath whispers over my cheek when he speaks, "What's a beautiful thing like you doing alone?"

I fight the need to stiffen and brush him off, instead I relax into the hand on my shoulder, turning my face towards Jack Harrow. "I'm waiting for a man to impress me."

Without my permission, he sits directly next to me, as close as Tylan was the night before. I wish more than anything that I was with Tylan right now instead of this predator.

"What about the man from last night?" My look of surprise causes him to chuckle, brushing a lock of my hair behind my ear. "I had my eye on you last night."

I can't stop the small gasp that leaves my mouth when his hand grasps my hair tightly, I cover it quickly, placing a small smile on my lips. "He doesn't know how to pleasure a woman," I lie. Tylan Blaese definitely knows what he's doing.

"Do you want to know what I think?" His hand tightens in my hair, a sickening smirk crossing his face. "You're just a whore who will take any guy who looks her way." *Shit.* This is not how tonight was supposed to go. It's a miracle but I press on, hiding the panic currently stirring inside me, his hand tight enough that I couldn't escape even if I tried. I'm still trying to think of a way out of this when he releases his death grip on my hair, circling his arm around my waist yanking me closer to him.

I can feel the small pocketknife pressed against my waist. He doesn't give me a chance to panic, instead he presses my now full glass of champagne against my lips, whispering in my ear, "Here's what you're going to do. You're going to finish this champagne and then walk out with me so I can take you to my special room and give you what you so desperately want." My heart thumps hard against my chest. Much against my better judgement, I swallow the champagne currently being forced down my throat. "Good girl." I can't fight it anymore. I stiffen up causing him to press the knife closer to my waist.

I try to drag it out, but I finish the champagne way too quickly. Jack grabs my hand, dragging me out the booth with him causing me to stumble into him at the force of his tug, he catches me by my waist. I take a couple of deep breaths, cloudiness starting to take over my brain. *This son of a bitch drugged me.* I try, and fail, not to stumble as he drags me down a back staircase.

It feels like forever until we reach what I can only assume is a basement level – a level I didn't even know existed. By the time we stop outside a door I can barely see straight but I force myself to hold on. If I lose consciousness, it's game over. I force my eyes open at the sound of Jack's voice to see him talking to a bouncer guarding the door. I meet his eyes silently begging him to help but he doesn't. I hate to admit it, but I'm scared.

The bouncer leaves, leaving me alone with Jack. He wastes no time in opening the door, shoving me inside. I lose my footing, falling hard on my knees, the sound of Jack's chuckle a mile away. My eyes close again just before a firm hand is in my hair again, dragging me up until I'm standing. "They'll be plenty of time for that later my little whore." I swallow the lump in my throat, refusing to open my eyes against the spinning in my head. I should be able to fight him off just like

I did last night to that random man, but I can barely keep my eyes open right now.

One second I'm standing, held up by the strong grip in my hair, the next I'm being thrown onto a soft bed, barely able to stop the need to vomit. "Stop throwing me around," I hiss. *You idiot.* I reprimand myself too late, if the murderous look in Jack's eyes is anything to go by.

I don't even get the chance to blink as he climbs on top of me, pinning me by my throat so tightly I can barely breathe. He snarls at me, his wretched breath assaulting my senses. "I'll do whatever I want to you, and you'll take it like the good little whore you are." I'm clawing desperately at his arms, blood dripping onto my skin from the wounds forming from my desperate attempts to try to get him to let me breathe again. One more tight squeeze completely blocking my airways is quickly followed by my gasping breaths, my lungs trying to refill with much needed air.

I'm still gasping for breaths, my breath fogged from whatever drugs he used, when my dress is ripped from my body into tiny scraps of black satin. *Think!* My panicked brain is screaming at me to do something, but what can I do? I subtly move my hands over the plush bedding searching for anything I can use to defend myself.

The next thing to go is my fishnets, leaving me in my black lace lingerie set. His weight shifts off the bed giving me a chance to open – well squint – my eyes, catching on the piece of metal hiding in my purse laying just a small distance away from me.

I peek a glance at Jack to see his back turned to me facing a table full of what could only be described as torture devices. I take the opportunity whilst he's distracted to reach into my bag, pulling out my trusted knife. I realise I got too confident when my bag drops onto the floor with an echoing thud. My attacker's body whips around, staring angrily at the knife held in my hand before he lets out a low chuckle.

"Now what are you going to do with that?" His condescending voice is emphasised by his slow but menacing prowl towards me, his hand outstretched. "Give it to me before you hurt yourself." I can feel myself slipping out of consciousness as I pretend to go along with what he wants, reaching my shaky hand holding the knife out towards his outstretched one. "That's it. Good girl."

I snap.

I push up onto my knees forcing the knife directly through his heart, his hands coming up to try to stop the bleeding. "You bitch." I block him out, stabbing him repeatedly until we both black out.

My eyes slowly blink open at the warm light flooding through the room. *Where am I?* "Come on Pixie. Wake up."

I glance towards the direction I think the voice is coming from. "You can't leave me alone in death either?" My voice is scratchy from the dryness in my throat.

"Stop being dramatic." I can just about make out his eye roll.

My eyes open fully as he gently flicks my forehead – an annoying habit he's always had to wake me up. "I suggest you stop before I cut your hand off." I glare at him sitting next to me on what I'm now realising is my bed.

"Stop winding her up." I turn my head towards the door just in time to see Callum's eye roll. My eyes wandering down to the plate of cinnamon rolls in his hands, licking my lips subconsciously. "How are you feeling, Cap?"

My eyes never stray from the plate of deliciousness even as he sits down on the other side of me. "Like I could devour that whole plate." I reach my hands out to him with grabby hands. "Gimme."

"Say please."

He moves the plate just out of reach as I glare at him. "I don't beg."

This time I'm the victim of his eye roll. "I'm not telling you to beg. I'm telling you to ask nicely."

Realising my glare's not working, I switch tactics. Sticking my bottom lip out in a pout, widening my eyes giving him my signature puppy dog eyes that he can never resist. It's not long before the plate of goodies is placed in my lap. I snap out of it immediately, my face lighting up as I dig into the first one, moaning at the warming sweetness coating my tongue. "Where's Camilla?" I speak around a mouthful.

"She had to meet with someone." I swat Freddie's hand away as he reaches towards the plate on my lap. "You need to learn to share."

"Make me." I stick my tongue out at him. I love this side of our friendship, Freddie and Callum have always treated me like their little sister ever since their villainous parents took me in, always protecting me but also always teasing me.

"We saved your life, I think you can spare one cinnamon roll."

"I may not remember last night, but I know that I saved my own life."

"You may have literally, but we got you out before the cops showed up."

I shrug taking another bite. "It would've been self-defence."

"Everleigh." The sound of my name coming from Callum has me pausing towards my next bite, slowly turning my head to face him. "You could've been caught and thrown in prison for life."

"They wouldn't have been able to prove anything." I shrug. "I met the detective in charge." *I'm dating him.* "Trust me, they have no clue about anything to do with me. I'm pretty sure they could catch me in the middle of the aftermath and still have no clue."

"Let's not test that theory." He passes me a bottle of water, distracting me as Freddie steals one of the treats from my plate.

I glare at him but he just shrugs. "You snooze you lose."

"That makes no sense in this situation." I've nearly finished the whole bottle, listening to the twins talk about random things when a burning realisation comes to me. "I didn't get a picture!"

Callum turns to me, his eyebrows pinched. "What are you talking about?"

"Last night. I need the pictures." I cross my arms.

"We took one for you." He reaches into his pocket pulling out a small polaroid picture and handing it to me. I observe it. *This isn't right.*

I shake my head. "I didn't kill him."

I hold the picture out to Callum for him to take back. "Yes, you did."

"No. Look, there's only ten stab wounds. I always do twenty. And look at his neck, there's no slit."

He takes my hands in his, looking into my widened eyes. "Everleigh. You were drugged. You probably blacked out before you could."

I shake my head, tears forming behind my eyes. "No. It's not right. Everything has to be perfect, or it doesn't count. This..." I point at the picture. "Wasn't the Polaroid Reaper."

"He's dead. Isn't that what matters?"

"But—" I'm interrupted by a soft knock at my door. "Who's that?" I whisper. The only person who would be here that I can think of is Camilla, but she wouldn't knock. All I get in response is shrugs from the twins. "Come in," I speak louder so the intruder can hear.

The door opens to a stunning petite red haired girl dressed in a light yellow sundress. "Good. You're awake." I pinch my brows, frowning at her, trying to work out who she is when she lets out a giggle. "Boys, did you forget to tell her about me?" I break my stare from her turning towards the "boys" in question. Both of their eyes are zoned in on the bubble of sunshine. She reaches Freddie who's sitting closest to the door, flopping onto his lap completely oblivious to the way they're both staring at her. I roll my eyes as she takes a bite of the half-eaten cinnamon roll from Freddie's hand.

She swallows her bite before turning her attention back to me. "I'm Summer Harrington." She holds her hand out to me with a blinding smile, making my head ache even more.

"What are you doing in my house?" I refuse her hand.

"The twins asked me to check you over, seeing as you were drugged." I blink at her. "I'm their private doctor. They're my best clients, seeing how much trouble they seem to get themselves into." I notice her directing pointed stares at both of them before looking back at me. "You ingested Flunitrazepam, or as it's more commonly known as, Rohypnol—"

"The date-rape drug," I cut her off, my heart racing. I'm no stranger to the horrid drug or its effects. I close my eyes, my head spinning, barely able to make out the sound of her voice.

"Listen to me." I look towards the direction of her voice through the fogginess. "I need you to breathe with me. In. One. Two. Three. Out. One. Two. Three. And again. In..." I follow her directions as she counts my breaths for me until my head starts to clear again, my heart returning to its normal rhythm. "That's it. How are you feeling now?"

"I can breathe again."

She's no longer sitting on Freddie's lap as she gets to work checking me over. "You just need to rest for today, but you should be fine." She giggles as Freddie pulls her back onto his lap. "I have to get going I have an audition to get ready for. But you—" She turns back to me, pointing a stern finger in my face with a look that could kill. "Are on complete bed rest." She leans in closer to me pretending to whisper but it's loud enough for the twins to hear. "I have these two wrapped around my little finger and they will call me if you so much as stick a toe out of this bed." She may be intimidating to some but to me she just looks like an adorable golden retriever puppy standing up to the much bigger Doberman. I fight to keep my smile hidden, instead offering her a nod, which she accepts stepping back, her bright smile back on her face. "Bye boys." We all watch her practically skip out the room.

Once I hear her car engine move off in the distance, I swing my legs off the bed, standing up shakily. "Where are you going?" Callum asks.

"To shower. I feel...ugh." I walk towards my ensuite bathroom.

"You're on bed rest." Instead of answering I simply offer him my beautiful middle finger before closing my bathroom door on their chuckles.

Chapter Ten

A Lead

Tylan

I've been going crazy all night. Bea is barely talking to me, even her messages are short. I can tell something's on her mind but I don't know what and it's killing me. My frustration, from her refusing to talk to me, is tampered down when I decide I need to face the music and reveal to my team my lead on the Polaroid Reaper...just so I can shoot the idea down in a couple of days. At least it will get Everleigh Carlton out of the picture. I would rather let this case go cold than risk the truth about her family coming out.

I'm just finishing up my notes to present my findings when I'm interrupted by my phone ringing. "Detective Tylan—"

"Get to Harrow Bar, now." I'm interrupted by the agitated voice of Lyla, a feeling of dread settling inside me.

"Who is it?"

"There's three victims."

"I'm on my way." I end the call with a sigh, leaning back in my chair. Three victims?

It doesn't take me long to get to our latest crime scene, the bustling crowd already forming outside the popular night club. Reporters hound me searching for answers as I push my way through the crowd.

The stark contrast once I make it inside to the main room is almost calming, the silence a welcome feeling. I savour it until I make it to a door at the back of the building, usually covered with a thick black curtain, where just inside lays the first victim, his neck covered with a singular angry red line wrapped around it.

Manoeuvring my way around the first body I walk down the steep stairway, at the bottom of which lays the second victim, a pool of now dried blood leading from the back of his head. I continue my journey down the dark narrow hallway to where a secondary door lays open to the final victim, a picture of what I've come to expect when we find a man as powerful as Jack Harrow.

I step closer to the body, crouching down to take a closer look, Lyla stepping over to me voicing her thoughts. "I don't think this was her." I tilt my head up to look at her over my shoulder, silently encouraging her to continue. "All three victims were killed in a different way. Mr Harrow was stabbed ten times, no slit on his neck. Mr Richards was hit hard on the back of his head, and Mr Stephens was strangled. And then there's the fact that they were all found here where they were killed instead of in a random alleyway..." I walk around the room, listening to Lyla continuing her explanation. “We don’t have her signature polaroid picture. His genitalia is still intact. If this was her, why are there so many differences from her previous victims?” I’m about to agree with her when I notice a loose floorboard in the corner of the room.

Lyla peers over my shoulder as I pull it up, pulling out a wooden box and passing it to Lyla. I reach further inside touching a small plastic bag filled with pills. “Maybe she couldn’t.”

Lyla looks at me, her brows furrowed beneath her round glasses. “What do you mean?”

I pull the bag out, examining the pills. “Rohypnol.”

“You think he drugged her but she killed him before they took over?”

“It’s a theory. We’ll have to look into his past—”

“Maybe not. Look.” Lyla turns the now opened box towards me. Why does a man like Jack Harrow have a box full of women’s accessories? She closes the box, placing it into an evidence bag as I do the same with the bag of drugs. “If you’re theory’s correct, what about the other two men? There’s no way she had the time to kill them as well.”

I stand up from the floor. “Let’s get back to the station. I may have a lead.”

“What lead?”

“I may know who she is.”

“You know who she is?” Her eyes widen.

"I might. But I wouldn't get too excited, it's not as good as it sounds."

One hour later, my team and I are seated around the oval table staring at our case board, our individual case files scattered around in front of us. Lyla leans over my shoulder as I pull out my lead. "Everleigh Carlton." She drags the name out reading the name scattered amongst the files. "Why do I recognise that name?"

"The Carlton family were a young family of five. At three am on Monday 25th December 2010, Amy Carlton, thirty nine, Kayden Carlton, forty one, Maya Carlton, sixteen, and Ethan Carlton, five, were found brutally murdered by their other daughter Everleigh Carlton, also sixteen." Both of us turn our heads to the right where Naomi is currently looking through her files rambling off details of our newest lead without me needing to say a word. "Everleigh was put into foster care and the last anyone's heard from her was when her foster parents were found strangled in their family living room. She's been off the grid ever since." She finally looks up at our shocked faces and shrugs. "My Dad worked both cases."

"So what happened to her?" Lyla moves back to sit on her chair.

"It's speculated she killed herself shortly after." Blake pipes up from his spot in front of the case board. "I wouldn't be surprised. Her family and foster parents were all killed within a couple of couple of years and she was left to deal with the pain all alone at eighteen—"

"I don't think she's dead." *Shit I said that out loud. Think, Tylan, think.* "She knew the first victim. He was her social worker." Not entirely a lie. It's not like I was going to reveal her fingerprints that were found at her latest successful victim's site.

"That doesn't prove she's alive now though," Lyla voices her doubt.

"I never said it was a solid lead. I just think we should look into her, she could be seeking revenge."

"Vengeance is a dangerous thing," Lyla mutters from beside me as we go on discussing other updates on the case. I half listen to their discussions but I can't stop my mind from wandering back to Everleigh Carlton and the picture of her now staring back at me from my file. I can't fight the feeling that I know her. It may be twisted but I can use her for my own personal gain. I just need to find her.

Chapter Eleven

Dead Ends and Broke Memories

CRIME SCENE DO NOT CROSS

Everleigh

The dark clouds outside intensify the warm lights of Forever & Ever, creating an ominous atmosphere. I've had this uncomfortable feeling all day, my stomach constantly doing somersaults, my heart racing at random times. Everyone tells me it's the aftermath of the drugs but my gut is telling me it's something else, something bigger that I can't quite put my finger on just yet.

I'm sitting at my usual spot by the window, my laptop resting on my legs and my half-finished iced caramel latte on the table next to me. Once she finally came to visit me, Camilla made me promise to wait a week before my next kill, claiming I need a rest so I stop making mistakes. At the time I didn't have the energy to argue with her about it, but now I can't stop the need from bubbling up inside me.

I'm distracted by the warming scent coming from the plate being placed on the table next to me. "I didn't order—"

"Someone brought it for you." Leah's smile lights up her entire face as I look around frantically.

"Who—"

"They called up. I think you may have a secret admirer, he even brought you your next coffee." She winks at me but one second later her smile drops. "That was such a tragedy."

My brows draw together before I realise she's looking at the news articles currently pulled up on my laptop. "Yeah it was. It's a shame the killer was never found."

"Why are you looking into it now?"

I shrug. "Just for fun. Imagine if I found out who the killer was." I do imagine it. I've imagined it too many times to count. My knife mutilating his body one agonising second after another. I wouldn't make it quick. I'll make sure he feels every inch of my pain and more, to the point where he's begging me to kill him. I wouldn't. Not until I'm satisfied, or until he bleeds out, whichever comes first.

"You're a strange girl." Leah's smile is back on her face as she teases me before she heads back to the counter to serve another customer. Once I'm certain I'm alone, I pull up my password protected word document, multiple pages filled with notes and theories from the past six years. Six years and I'm still stuck with multiple dead ends and broken memories from the most important day of my life.

I pick up the plate, devouring the cinnamon sweetness quickly whilst I scour through my notes, trying to find something I may have missed.

"Bea...Bea...Bea!" I didn't realise I had fallen asleep until my eyes blink open to Camilla calling out my fake name, and an otherwise empty café, minus Leah cleaning behind the counter. "Here, this will wake you up."

I uncurl from my cramped position, taking the coffee she thrusts in front of my face. "How long was I asleep?" I take a sip of the sweet hot drink, cradling it to warm up my freezing hands.

"No idea. I only just got here." I don't fail to miss the bags under her eyes, despite her efforts to cover them. Nor do I miss the droopiness in her eyes.

"When was the last time you slept?" We've known each other long enough that it's not hard to miss whenever Camilla's overworking herself.

"I haven't had the chance to."

"Cam! You have to stop doing this to yourself." I sigh softly watching her take the seat on the sofa opposite, the same one I've tried, and failed, to avoid looking at in order to limit the visions of the man I can't seem to get out my head even if I have been distant the past few days.

"I promise I'm not doing this on purpose. I'll be fine once I sleep tonight." She appears completely oblivious to the images currently swirling around in my head of a naked Tylan sprawled across the sofa his naturally dominant nature drawing me in— "You found anything new?"

I blink myself out of the visions. "Other than a crippling headache...no." I shut my laptop, unable to miss the worry in Camilla's eyes as she observes me, silently sipping on her hot chocolate.

We chat about anything and everything until the sun goes down and Leah finally kicks us out half an hour after closing. I bask in the moments like these whenever I can – the ultra-rare times where I feel like a normal person just hanging out with her best friend. I can pretend to be someone I'm not, at least for a couple of hours. I savour them, praying that one day I can be that normal girl, that I can have that family I've always wanted and that carefree life without any resentment...a girl can only dream, right?

We reach Camilla's doorstep, the porch light turning on as we approach. "Promise me you'll get some sleep. I need my feisty Cami back."

"I promise." I don't miss the eye roll she gives me in response to the puppy dog eyes I'm giving her. "You get some as well. I can tell you're still feeling the effects of the drugs." Her head drops slightly, taking a deep breath.

"I will." I reach out and squeeze her hand. I know no matter how many times I tell her differently she feels guilty about that night. "I'm just going to head to the basement first." She gives me a single nod, guilt written all over her face as she rushes to open the door, closing it on me just as fast once she's inside. I sigh at the closed door before heading back to my car and driving to the one place I know will help me feel in control again.

I step out of the lift into what we like to call "the basement", aptly named as it is the basement of Freddie and Callum's apartment building, comprised of multiple different rooms for many different situations. I walk down the short hallway until I get to the "lobby", really it's just a red carpeted room with sofas dotted around, similar to a green room. Freddie walks out from one of the rooms to the left that we like to use for casino nights, dressed in one of his pristine suits. "Aren't you meant to be resting, Pixie?"

I shrug in response. "Yes. But I'm tired of feeling out of control." I walk over to the door housing the small changing area, turning around and leaning against it. "Is Cal here?"

"He's in the gym." He looks up from his phone looking at me with scepticism. "Where do you want him?"

"Boxing room in five."

He chuckles. "Perfect timing. He's getting too cocky for his own good."

I roll my eyes. "Go." He gives me a mock salute as I enter the changing room. There's nothing here but a row of lockers, a small bench, and a full length mirror on the wall. This room was a storage room at some point but it's a useful place on the rare days we aren't already dressed in workout gear.

I open my locker pulling out my emergency workout clothes, a simple black sports bra with matching shorts just long enough to cover my ass. I finish by throwing my hair into a messy but practical ponytail, and of course my little ribbon.

When I leave the changing room Freddie's nowhere in sight. I head down the hallway leading towards the boxing gym, it's a small room with a couple of mats on the floor and punching bags dotted around the perimeter but it's just large enough for practising. I push open the door to the sight of a shirtless Callum stretching, his skin glistening in sweat from his prior workout.

His head twists towards me at the sound of the door. "Hey Cap."

I step onto the mat, making my way to the centre where he's currently standing. "Ready to get your ass beat?"

His eyebrows raise with a smirk. "You want me to take it easy on you?"

"No!" The one word comes out so sharply that he jumps back a little causing me to close my eyes and take a deep breath before putting on my best fake smile. "Give me a challenge for once." I try to avoid his sceptical eyes by stretching but no matter how hard I try to avoid them I can feel his eyes burning into me. "Take a picture, it'll last longer." I glance over my shoulder at him, the fake smile still plastered on my face, my arm stretched across my chest.

He doesn't say anything as he comes up behind me, placing his hand on my arm to help me stretch further. It's not until I switch arms that he finally speaks up. "I'm worried about you Everleigh." My breath catches in my throat at the sound of my name, something I rarely hear from Callum.

"I'm fine." My answer is short as I move away, sitting on the floor a step away from where we were, stretching my legs out either side of me. I'm not even surprised when he lets me continue my stretches in silence, he knows what I'm like. He knows that I bottle up my feeling and emotions, never wanting to be a burden on someone else, a contrast to the girl I used to be when my family was with me.

I used to be that girl who wore her heart on her sleeve, but now I keep the million tiny shards locked away out of sight from everyone. I want to tell him why I've been so on edge lately but I can't because I know the moment I do will be the moment I finally lose it. I'm losing control of myself and it's a terrifying thought. I need to be in control of my life otherwise it will all unravel into a knotted mess.

The silence as we start practising is usually a welcome friend, but today it just plunges my mind into darkness. Bloody faces of the four men bombarding my thoughts. My mother lying dead on the kitchen floor, my father with blood running down his chest, my twin sister and little brother huddled together in a pool of crimson. I'm so caught up in the horror that I don't even realise I'm straddling Callum, my hands tight around his throat as he claws at my hands, not until Freddie bursts into the room tugging me off his brother, my arms now thrashing and clawing at him—

"Everleigh!"

Everything stops. My mind clearing as I look into Freddie's hazel eyes filled with a mix of confusion and horror. My head turns to where Callum's now sitting up coughing on the mats. My mind remains numb as everything comes back into focus. I'm frozen still, trying to work out what just happened. "I think you've had enough practice for today." Freddie's hands slowly leave my arms before he rushes over to his brother, red fingerprint marks forming on his neck – my fingerprints. I'm frozen in place, watching the twins talking, unable to hear anything other than the ringing in my ears. I finally snap out of it when they both look towards me a mix of horror and concern written all over their faces.

"I-I'm going to go to the shooting range." The truth is I had no intention of going there but I know that it's the only room in this place I can let all my emotions go without the potential of harming someone I love. The short walk to the shooting room is filled with my racing thoughts but only one stands out.

I'm quickly losing control and I'm terrified.

She's Dead

Tylan

I'm used to bad days but this may be my first agonisingly long day consisting of nothing but endless research leading nowhere. I'm about five minutes away from losing it when a knock sounds on my door. I glance at the time on my laptop and it's just gone six. "Come in," I speak up. The door opens to my biggest headache, Michael Knotts. He stands there in his custom tailored suit oozing cockiness. Without an invite he waltzes in taking a seat on the other side of my desk barely giving me time to shut my open file before he has a chance to see any of it.

"What do you want, Blaese?"

I resist the urge to roll my eyes, opting to rest my arms on top of my desk before my fists end up on his face where they really want to be. "How did you know Everleigh Carlton?"

He tenses for a mere second before relaxing again. "Who?"

"Everleigh Carlton. You were her therapist after her family was killed six years ago."

"You answered your own question, Blaese. I knew her professionally. Why do you care? She's dead." He crosses his arms.

"You stopped being in contact with her when she still needed help. Why?" I narrow my eyes at him.

"Are you accusing me of something?" He narrows his eyes back at me.

"Should I?" I lean back in my chair.

"Are you forgetting, Blaese? About those images I have?" He smirks, fury growing inside me.

"That has nothing to do with this case."

"You'll keep me out of whatever investigation you have or I hit send. Understood?"

I clench my fists harder, my nails digging into my palms, holding back the need to punch the man in front of me. "Get out of my office," I hiss.

He stands with that smug smirk plastered on his face. "Good chat."

I wait for him to leave before smacking my hand hard on my desk in frustration. *Deep breaths Tylan.* I take a couple of breaths but they barely do anything. I log out of my laptop heading back to my car. I need to get out of here.

It takes ten minutes for me to arrive at my destination. On the outside, and the majority of the inside, it looks a little bit like one of those old fashioned hotels converted into apartments. The basement is a different story – filled with multiple rooms varying from a boxing gym to poker rooms, to rage rooms, and to my destination, the shooting range. The access to the basement is limited to only a handful of people – the owners, me, and a couple of their friends. I step into the lift, using my personal pin code and fingerprint to select the basement level, taking a deep breath I swear my mind is going crazy as I'm hit with the addicting mango scent I can't seem to escape.

I push the thought aside, stepping out of the elevator and making my way to the shooting range only to be stopped by one of the owners, Freddie Archer. "Tylan? You're here early."

I shrug. "I have a few issues I need to iron out."

He crosses his arms, raising an eyebrow at me. "Boxing or shooting?"

"Shooting." I walk over to the small changing room needing to change out of my work clothes, muttering under my breath. "Before I actually kill someone again."

He smirks at me. "You won't be alone in there."

I spin around to face him, my hand on the door handle. "Who's in there?"

"Everleigh Carlton." He glances at his phone as though he was just talking about a normal person, not someone who's meant to be dead.

"Everleigh Carlton? As in the one who's family was murdered Christmas Eve six years ago?"

"Yeah." He doesn't look up from his phone.

"She's dead."

He glances up at me for a second. "I think I'd know if my sister was dead." I don't get another word in, watching him walk off in the direction of the elevator I just came from. *His sister?* Then it hits me. The Archer's, Everleigh Carlton's foster parents, had twin sons.

I waste no time in throwing my coat and bag into my locker, changing into grey jogging bottoms and a simple white t-shirt, rushing towards the shooting range. I close the door behind me noting the empty space, except for the familiar figure standing with her back to me in nothing but a black sports bra and matching shorts, tension riddling her body, gun aimed at the target in front of her, although her aim is slightly off.

I walk closer to her, her mango scent drawing me in to her until I can fully recognise the pale skin, and golden brown hair thrown up in a messy ponytail, with that ribbon wrapped around it, portraying an image of fake innocence.

I stop dead in my tracks. Bea, my secret girlfriend, the woman who's been pushing me away the past couple of days, is Everleigh Carlton. The person I've been protecting for my own selfish gain. It all makes sense now, it's why Everleigh's picture looked so familiar to me. I'm dating her. But why did she lie to me?

Without thinking, I step up to her, gently placing my hand on her shoulder just as she fires the gun, missing the target. She jumps spinning around hitting me hard on the face with the gun in the process. "What the hell are you doing?!"

She pulls her noise cancelling headphones off giving me her signature scowl. I turn my face to look at her, the colour draining from her face. "Tylan?"

"Hey, Bubbles."

She crosses her arms. "What are you doing here? And why the fuck did you think sneaking up on me was a good idea?" She leads me over to the bench at the side of us pushing me to sit down. She dabs at the little cut above my eyebrow with a tissue.

"I have some steam I need to blow off." I shrug, reaching out to grab her waist pulling her towards me until she's straddling my lap.

"Answer my other question." She glares at me continuing to clean the cut.

"Because you had these on." I point at the headphones now around her neck.

"You could've just left me to it."

"I couldn't. Not now that I know who you really are, Bea."

Her eyebrows pinch together. "What are you talking—"

I grip her waist to keep her on my lap. "Or should I say Everleigh Carlton?"

Chapter Thirteen

Normal's Easy

Everleigh

My hand pauses mid-air, my heart racing. "H-How—?"

"You really need to talk to your brothers about not giving your name to strangers. Especially considering you're supposed to be dead."

"I'm going to kill them," I mutter.

"Why did you lie to me, Everleigh?"

I look away from his hurt-filled ocean blues. "Because everyone knows me as Bea."

"Why is it so bad to be known as Everleigh? The real you."

I try to pull away but he holds me close to him. I sigh, wrapping my arms around his neck. "I'm guessing you know my story?" He nods. "Between the time my family and my foster parents were killed, every time I introduced myself I got an "I'm sorry" and a damn fake sympathetic look. I hated it. So, when the Archer's were killed it was my one chance, fake my death and become someone else, Bea." I look up into his eyes, the ones already staring down at me. "Bea's just a normal twenty-three year old girl creating her own life, no family trauma to deal with. Everleigh's not. Everleigh will never be normal. *I* will never be normal, not until I find who killed my family."

"Why would you want to be normal? Normal's boring."

"Normal's easy." I shrug. We sit in silence whilst I clean up his small cut.

"Were you ever going to tell me?" He runs his hand up and down my side.

"I don't know." I look down, unable to look him in his eyes. "I want to be Bea. It's easy being her." I huff a laugh.

"But she's not real." He tucks two fingers under my chin forcing me to look at him. "I want to get to know the real you, Everleigh. I want to know all your perfections and all your flaws."

"You do?" I blink back the tears forming. No one's ever wanted to know the real me.

"I do. I have one question though."

"Just one?" I raise an eyebrow.

"Why'd you run out on me the other night? Normally I'm the one running out."

"I guess you've found your match then." I close my eyes in embarrassment at what I just said.

"My match, huh?" I can hear his smirk.

"Shut up." I push him back, climbing off his lap. "I ran out because I'm not used to nice." Not entirely a lie. I walk back to my position in front of the shooting target, picking up my gun and firing it, missing the target entirely. I huff in frustration.

“You’re holding it wrong.” Tylan steps up behind me, tentatively placing his hands on top of mine. “Just place your fingers here.” His rough hands are a direct contrast to my soft ones as he moves mine to a more comfortable and stable hold. “Straighten this arm a little more.” He moves my left arm until it’s not as bent. I’ve missed his touch. “And pull the trigger.” I do. The bullet hits the target directly in the middle.

I spin around hugging him tight a bright grin on my face. “I did it!”

“You did.” I pull away, his arms tightening around me. His eyes fall to the scar on my collarbone. “What happened to you?”

I step away from him. “It doesn’t matter.” No one knows the real truth about how I got this scar and I don’t fancy changing that today.

His eyes darken in...anger? “I know your story, Everleigh.”

“No one knows my story. Not fully.” I turn my back to him, aiming the gun at the new target.

“I know your family was killed when you were sixteen, your foster parents when you were eighteen. You went to a therapist called Michael Knotts in between.” I pull the trigger, trying to keep the tears currently lining my eyes from falling. His arms wrap around my waist. “I know you only have three people you trust. I hope I can make that four one day though. Freddie Archer. Callum Archer. Camilla Rivera—"

"Stop!" I try to keep the strength in my voice but I can hear it wavering. "I don't need you to drag up my past."

"Let me help you, Everleigh."

I spin to face him, our bodies pressed up against each other. "No one can help me." I shrug in defeat.

"You don't want revenge?" His hand caresses my side. "You don't want to find the man who killed your parents? The man who killed your little brother? Your twin sister?"

"Of course I do!" I throw my hands up, snapping at him. "But I don't need help. I never have and I never will so just drop it!" I pull out of his arms, storming towards the exit.

"I can help you make this case go away."

I pause in my stride, going stiff as a board. "I don't know what you're talking about."

"Come with me." He holds his hand out to me and I reluctantly take it, letting him lead me back to the locker room. I stand by the mirror watching as he opens one of the lockers, rifling through a black satchel bag.

"These don't look familiar to you?" He places a brown case file in front of my face. I take it tentatively, my hands shaking as I open it. Inside is filled with pictures of all the men I've killed, each with their own notes and copies of the polaroids I left for the cops.

I shut it, turning to face him. "What do you want?"

"We have a common enemy." His voice is monotone, no emotions present.

"Who?" I'm tentative to ask.

"Michael Knotts."

My eyes widen. I run towards the open door but he's too quick. Before I know it I'm pinned to the now closed door. "You can trust me," he whispers in my ear, pressing addictive kisses to my neck.

"Tell me something," I whisper softly.

"What?" He doesn't stop the kisses peppering my throat.

"Tell me a secret. Something to prove that I can trust you."

He pretends to think before answering me, looking me in my eyes. "Michael Knotts is blackmailing me."

I try to suppress my shock but fail. "Why?"

My eyes track his lips as they lift up into a smirk. "Let's just say that I have a few skeletons of my own, Bubbles." His lips brush against mine. "What do you say we get him out of our way together? Don't worry. I'll help you tidy up after."

"How do I know you won't frame me for his death?"

"Everleigh, you're my girlfriend. In case you've forgotten."

"Your girlfriend who lied to you."

"Doesn't mean my feelings have changed," he whispers in my ear, placing a soft kiss.

My heart races. "I have my own clean-up crew. I don't need your help."

He presses a kiss to my cheek. "Keep telling yourself that. Call me when you change your mind." I watch him walk away from me, back to the shooting range.

I'm practically sprinting to the lift, my bag and clothes barely contained in my arms, my mind racing with everything that's happened over the past couple of hours. It's not until I'm standing alone in the lift that I finally take a much needed breath. I didn't need to run; I already made my mind up about Tylan. There's this unexplainable energy between us that pulls me towards him whenever he's nearby. I want to take him up on his offer but I need to make sure I can trust what he says first...I'll just have a little fun along the way.

Chapter Fourteen

Duty Calls

Tylan

It's been a week since I found my mysterious Everleigh Carlton, she may not have accepted my offer of helping her but that doesn't mean I'm not going to. The day after, I set out on my mission to rule her out of the official investigation, nothing that a fake death certificate couldn't fix. As far as the rest of my team is concerned, Everleigh Carlton drowned herself after the death of her foster parents, and with their wrongly placed trust in me and my fake evidence, none of them doubted it. Not even in moments like these where we're all sat around the table once again discussing the case.

"It makes no sense. She was on a spree so why has it been a week since her last victim?" Lyla sighs out her observation from the far end of the table.

"Maybe she's done? Jack Harrow was her last target?" Blake speaks up from next to her. I nailed my poker face years ago when my parents were still around, at the time I had no idea how much that skill would help me in the future. I have no idea why she hasn't done anything in a week but I do know that she's not finished. I've spent the last week waiting for my phone to ring just so I could hear her sultry voice again but so far I've had nothing but silence.

"That doesn't help us out. If we're not careful she'll become another Jack the Ripper." Lyla shrugs. "We'll look like idiots."

"We can't solve every case," I speak up. "I hope we find her and soon though," I lie. "She's out there somewhere."

"We're just going round in circles. We need a new lead that's actually going to lead us somewhere."

"We're not going to get that unless she kills again. We've scoured each crime scene hundreds of times now and there's nothing."

"There might be something." We all turn to face Naomi standing by the map of Little Bray, placing string around each of the pins representing where each of the victims were found, minus Jack Harrow and the victim before him, forming the beginning of a strange looking star—*Shit!* "She's trying to tell us something."

"What do you mean?" Lyla observes the deformed shape. "It's just random lines."

Naomi rolls her eyes. "It's making some sort of shape, almost like a star."

"How does that help us?" The scepticism is clear in Blake's voice.

"It looks familiar. We should look into it."

My heart races. I know exactly what it means, even in death he can't leave me alone. My mind scrambles trying to come up with anything to steer her away from this theory. "They were all dumped close to places they liked to hunt; it just so happens to be forming something reminiscent of a star. There's nothing to it." Blake and Lyla voice their agreement. I breathe out a silent sigh of relief. I need to speak to Everleigh.

I'm sitting in my leather armchair, staring out at the Little Bray skyline, twinkling in the darkness of the night, combined with the soft snores coming from Bailey curled up on my lap create the calming atmosphere filling my apartment, a contrast to the chaos of the day. He perks up as my phone rings, interrupting my controlled pets. I don't look at the number as I answer it. "Hello?"

"You said I could trust you and I swear to God you better not be lying to me or I will—"

I chuckle at her fierceness. "What do you need, Bubbles?"

I can't work out what she mumbles before she lets out a sigh. "I'm sending you a location, meet me there. Alone, or you will end up like the others." The call ends abruptly, cutting off the voice I've missed hearing.

Bailey looks up at me, tilting his head at me his collar jingling at the movement. "Sorry, Bailey. Duty calls." I tap him gently. He takes the cue, jumping off my lap and into his bed, a text coming through with my destination for tonight. I already changed into black jeans and a t-shirt when I got home so I simply pick up a black hoodie before heading towards the abandoned hotel.

At first glance you wouldn't think this hotel was abandoned, the only indication would be the cobwebs in the corners and the lack of people, but the lack of dust and working electricity tells a different story. I opt for the stairs, deciding that it's probably a safer bet, making my way up to the third floor. I walk down the carpeted hallway stopping once I reach 315. I take a second to listen in. I listen for so long that I'm convinced I'm in the wrong place until I hear the voice of my angel. "I know you're there."

I smile to myself, pushing the door open to a literal crime scene. I take note of the blood splotches on the carpeted floor leading all the way to the bed. The body of a man slaughtered to death, lies on top, with a small polaroid photo placed neatly on his chest.

My eyes travel past the bed to the woman standing next to it, she looks so different to how I've seen her before. Her golden hair darkened and tangled; her face covered in nothing but her natural beauty. Even her clothes are different, instead of the tight dresses I normally see her in, she looks like a literal goddess dressed in a red fit and flare dress hugging her waist. She rolls her beautiful olive green eyes at my appraisal of her body, cleaning a bloody knife in her hands. "Is this going to be your regular greeting? Checking me out?"

I don't hesitate in my reply. "You already know it is."

She rolls her eyes at me again, placing the knife in her bag resting on her shoulder before she walks over to me. "I'm giving you a chance to prove yourself. Do you know the alleyway between Primrose House and Primrose Bar?"

I try to look her in the eyes. I swear I do. But I can't help my gaze from drifting to her heart shaped lips. *I just want one taste.* "Yeah. What about it?"

She stops walking when she's close enough that our toes are touching, but that's not close enough for my liking. "Dump his body there, you know how I like it." She winks at me. "And then come back here and clean up for me."

"Why can't you do that?" I reach out to her but she steps back.

"It's not my thing. Do this and I'll let you in." She pushes up on her tiptoes to whisper in my ear, "I'll let you touch me again." Without another word she pushes me back playfully, spinning on her heel and strutting out the door. "You know where I live." Is the last thing I hear her say over her shoulder before I'm left alone with a rotting corpse. *This woman is going to kill me.*

It's gone two when I finally finish scrubbing as much blood off the carpet as I can. Standing up I take one last look around the room, searching for anything I may have missed.

Confident I've erased all existence of what happened tonight I head off towards my next destination.

I pull up to a small cottagesque house that is a complete contrast to my little firecracker. The only light on in the house is the upstairs one which I assume is her bedroom – this is my first time coming to her house after all. I imagine her lying on her bed in all her beauty reading one of her little romance books that she loves, waiting for me to show up. I park my car on the street, stepping out and walking up to her door. I knock.

I wait patiently, listening intently to the creak of a door followed by soft footsteps down the stairs. I hear the turn of the lock but before it opens there's the sound of glass breaking followed by an adorable shout of "Muffin!" My panic quickly turns to confusion, my brows furrowing. I stare at the door as it slowly opens revealing a real life angel dressed in a black silk baby-doll nightgown, stroking a midnight black cat, just like a villain in one of those cheesy movies.

"Did you do it?" Her face is expressionless when I finally drag my eyes away from the little creature burrowed in her arms snarling at me.

"All done. There's not a single trace of you anywhere near him."

"Good." She opens the door further, stepping to the side giving me space to step inside. I take the few seconds she's distracted by locking the door to observe the small cosy living room, it's very minimalistic with a small three-seater leather couch covered in fluffy blankets, a small wooden coffee table set out in front of it facing the brick fireplace, on top of the mantelpiece are photos of her family. When she notices me looking, she rushes over turning them away but I don't miss the way she holds the cat in her arms closer to her.

She turns around to me with a fake smile that could easily be mistaken for real if it wasn't for the sparkle missing from her eyes. She lets the cat, Muffin, out of her arms. We both watch him saunter towards me with a small hiss, sniffing me before he stretches and rubs against my legs with a purr. I hear a small sigh from the fireplace. "Muffin..." His only response is a high pitched meow as he keeps rubbing against me. I take the opportunity to crouch down, petting him as the two have a little conversation, I'm distracted by how adorable it is to see this fierce woman talking to an animal like it's a small child. "We'll talk about this later."

I look up to see her eyebrows raised, arms crossed, in a staring contest with the cat who's now lying on his back happily accepting all the belly rubs I offer. It only lasts for thirty more seconds before he gets bored, wandering off to his water bowl. I straighten up to see Everleigh's eyes trained on me, full of lust.

I stalk towards her, every step I take echoed by one back from her. "I want my prize now." My eyes remained trained on her widened olive ones, portraying an image of fake innocence.

"What prize? I don't remember playing any game." She blinks sweetly at me, our little stalking game never stopping.

"Reward then." She takes another step back, her back hitting the wall behind her. I take my time eating up the rest of the space between us. "I believe I was told I could touch you." I close the distance until our chests are touching, peering down at her. I hook my finger under her chin forcing her to look up at me, taking the time to truly observe her, my thumb running softly over her cheek and the small acne scars dotting her chin that are normally covered by her makeup. Her cheeks however are as rosy as ever, highlighting the small scatter of freckles.

"How did you like your reward?" she breathes out, pressing her body impossibly closer to mine.

"I haven't taken it yet." I don't give her a chance to respond, tracing my fingers over her soft pink lips, tugging the bottom one down softly, pulling away to a chorus of soft whimpers. "Is there something you want, Bubbles?"

"Just kiss me." She pouts at me. I return to tracing her lips again, leaning down to brush mine gently against hers, barely touching. I smirk at the small frustrated moan she lets out but I still don't give her what we both want. I need to know she's as desperate as I am, as into this – us – as I am.

I place a soft kiss at the corner of her lips, peppering kisses down to her neck and across to the spot just behind her ear that drives her crazy. Her soft whimpers and moans are music to my ears. I place a soft kiss on that spot again only to be met with a strong grip on my hair, pulling my lips to hers.

"I thought you would last longer." I smirk as she pulls my lips back to hers. There's nothing soft or calm about the kiss. Instead it's filled with desperation and hunger from the past week of longing. We reluctantly pull away, pants escaping from both of us, her cheeks flushed. I place my lips back on her neck, her hands moving to the hem of my hoodie, pulling it off in desperation. I revel in the small gasp she lets out as I softly suck and nibble on her neck, leaving my mark, despite her hands trying to push me away.

I pull back to meet the angry daggers she's shooting me, despite her warm hands drifting underneath my t-shirt pulling it up, her fingers tracing my torso underneath it. I trace the red marks on her neck, accompanied by her shivers. "My marks suit you."

"I'm going to kill you." Her voice holds no conviction, pulling me impossibly closer, simultaneously tugging my t-shirt off. Our hands run over each other, me savouring her softness through her nightdress.

I run my fingers over her thighs at the hem of her night-dress. "You look so sexy in this." I move my hand slowly up the outside of her thigh, watching the gown moving up with it, exposing more of her luscious skin. I continue until I reach her hips tracing along them, searching. "Where are your panties?"

She blinks up at me, batting her eyelashes innocently. "I don't wear them when I'm sleeping."

"Fuck," I breathe out, locking that piece of information away for the future. I place my hands on her ass, hinting at her to jump up but her feet stay firmly planted to the ground.

"I'm too heavy." A blush rises to her cheeks, avoiding my eyes.

I tilt her chin, forcing her to look up at me. "No you're not. I've carried you before. Now..." I pat her ass softly. "Up." I don't miss the hesitation before she reluctantly jumps up, locking her legs around my waist.

"You're poking me," she whispers, the blush deepening on her cheeks.

"What did you expect? I have a literal goddess in my arms." She shifts slightly, grinding against me, burrowing her face in my neck. "Why are you so shy tonight?" I ask, genuinely curious.

"I'm not used to going slow. Normally we'd be done by now." She buries her face further into my neck.

"That changes tonight. I want to take my time with you, the way I should've last time." I hold her in my arms, walking upstairs to her bedroom, trying not to trip over Muffin weaving between my feet.

"How do you know where my bedroom is?" she mumbles against my neck in between the kisses she's placing there.

"I saw the light when I got here."

"Hmm, and here I was thinking you were a stalker."

"How do you know I'm not?" I whisper in her ear. Everything about her is adorable and sexy all at once, including the little gasp she lets out when I throw her onto her luxurious queen bed. For the first time tonight I can feel how hard my heart races whenever I'm around her. I just know that Everleigh Carlton is going to be trouble.

Aftercare

Everleigh

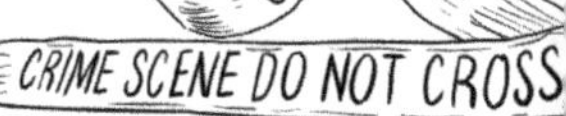

"Take it off." Tylan's standing at the foot of my bed, watching me with a predatory gaze. When I woke up this morning I considered this a possibility, all week I've been waiting, wanting, needing to see him again but I had to stay strong. I needed to make sure I can trust him before I let him in completely. I still don't fully trust him, especially not now that he knows who I really am. I won't until he's fully proven to me that he won't turn against me, but it doesn't mean I'm not going to give him a chance, and if that includes a way for me to release my stress then that's just an added bonus.

I sit up, staring at Tylan, biting my lip as I slowly trace the neckline of my gown. He's been teasing me all night, now it's my turn. His glare intensifies, following the path of my hand pushing one strap down my arm and then the other until the top half falls down to my waist, leaving my breasts on display. His gaze drops to them, goosebumps forming on my skin from the hunger in his eyes.

"I said take it off," he growls, moving his eyes back to mine. I stop teasing him, grabbing the hem and pulling it off over my head. "Good girl." A shiver runs through me. "Lie down." I don't hesitate, lying back resting my head on my silk pillows. He taps my ankles, not moving any closer. "Spread them." I suck in a breath, slowly spreading my legs, blushing as his eyes drop to in between them. "More." I do what he says, his gaze trained on my pussy, a smirk forming on his lips. "So wet for me already." My breath speeds up feeling the wetness dripping down my thighs. "Touch yourself. Show me what you like."

My breath catches in my throat. "W-What?"

"You heard me." I suck in another breath, hesitantly reaching my hand down towards my dripping centre. My fingers gently graze my clit, a small moan escaping. It takes a few minutes but the more I touch myself, the more I relax. I touch and rub all the spots I know drive me crazy, using my other hand to slide two fingers inside, my eyes drifting closed as the pleasure takes over.

A sharp slap lands on the inside of my thigh, my eyes flying open to glare at the man observing me. "What was that for?"

"Eyes on me or you stop." His eyes drift up to mine, narrowing in response. "And lose the attitude or we stop completely." I huff but soften my eyes not wanting tonight to end just yet. I pleasure myself, keeping my eyes locked on the man I've been craving for weeks, but his eyes aren't on mine, they're wandering all over my body, like he's trying to sear my body into his memory. I'm so close to the edge, my body tightening, my back arching. *Just one more—*

"Stop." I let out a sharp gasp, staring at the cheeky smirk that I just want to slap off Tylan's face as he pushes my hands away from my aching centre.

"But I was right there," I stutter out in between my panting breaths.

"I know." He climbs on top of me, looking down at me.

"Why did you stop me?" I glare at his devilishly handsome face.

"Because, Bubbles..." He leans down kissing that one spot behind me ear that drives me crazy. "When you're in my bed." Kiss. "Your orgasms." Kiss. "Your body." Kiss. "All of you." Kiss. "Is mine," he growls, biting and tugging on my ear.

"This isn't your bed though." My glare is plastered on my face despite my racing heartbeat.

His eyebrow raises, his smirk stuck on his face. "I should've known you'd be a brat." I didn't think it was humanly possible for my glare to deepen. "I like it," he whispers against my lips before pressing a deep kiss against them. "Why don't you put that bratty mouth of yours to use?" I don't get the chance to respond before he's climbing off the bed, pulling me up with him. "On your knees." He grabs a cushion placing it on the floor before gently guiding me down until I'm eye level with the impressive bulge of his boxers. I lean into his hand stroking my cheek softly, looking up at him as he stares down at me, softness written on his features. "Have you ever done this before?"

I close my eyes, the memories flooding back to me in full force. I can see my foster dad pinning me down, forcing himself all the way down my throat, cutting my air supply off. In this memory it's the time where he almost killed me, holding himself so deep despite my struggles telling me to just take it—

"Hey, hey, hey. Look at me." Tylan's soothing voice brings me back to the present, my eyes opening at the feel of his thumb pushing away a stray tear, his eyes full of concern as he crouches down to my level.

"Sorry. I just...I...I—" I stammer, trying to calm my racing heart.

"We're not doing this," he announces sternly, his thumb continuing to rub soothing circles on my cheek.

"No." I take a deep breath to make my voice stronger, placing my hand gently on his forearm when he tries to pull me up. I look into his eyes. "I want to do this." *I need to do this.* I don't tell him the truth as he studies my eyes, like he's trying to find a lie within them. He must be confident enough as he stands back up keeping his hand resting gently on my cheek.

"I'll be gentle. Tap my thigh if you need me to stop." We keep staring into each other's eyes, no matter how hard I want to, I can't bring myself to look away. Before I let myself get into my head to examine any deeper meaning behind it, I reach up hooking my hands in his waistband but he tightens his grip on my cheek making me look back up. "Do you understand?" I nod. "I need words, Everleigh."

I nod again as I answer, "I understand. Tap your thigh if I need to stop."

A small genuine smile appears on his face. "Good girl." I move my eyes back down to his crotch, my hands tugging his boxers down his strong defined legs. I can't help but place a gentle kiss on the side of his knee, kneeling back up to eye level with his impressive length. Throughout it all, his thumb never stops rubbing soothing circles on my cheek. I lean forward until the tip touches my lips, tentatively giving it a small lick causing Tylan to suck in a breath.

His hand tenses but never stops the soothing circles as I take a couple of long licks down his cock before taking just the tip into my mouth, swirling my tongue teasingly. He lets out a low groan, his hand clenching gently on my cheek like he's trying to control himself. I move my eyes to his other hand at his side, noting how it's also clenched. I reach out taking it in mine my eyes focusing on the crescent shaped marks present when it unclenches at my touch. I don't let go, looking up into his eyes, taking more of him into my mouth, stopping just before it hits the back of my throat.

His groans are music to my ears every time I find a spot he likes. I bring his hand to the back of my head before letting go, resting both my hands in my lap once again. I suck harder giving him my best small nod at the desperation in his eyes. He takes the hint, grabbing a fistful of my hair, not tight and never taking control, just holding it letting me know that he could if he wanted to. I can't go deeper but I continue pleasuring him, reaching my hand up to stroke what I can't fit, his moans and groans echoing around the room. It's not long until he's pulling my head back and off his cock. I pout up at him trying to take him back in my mouth but his grip remains strong, keeping me in place. He chuckles in between panting breaths, shaking his head at me. "Your mouth is too good, Bubbles. I need to be inside you."

I half expect him to just grab me and throw me on the bed, he wouldn't hear any complaints from me if he did, instead he holds his hand out to me which I happily take, allowing him to guide me to standing. "Bend over the bed." I blush, turning around to face the bed, bending over the edge, my toes barely touching the ground whilst my chest lies flat on the bed. Goosebumps raise all over my body at the feel of his hands running down my back with feather light touches all the way down until he reaches my ass. "I missed your body." I barely hear his whispered words. His knee pushes my legs further apart, his hard cock brushing against my wet centre.

I don't know how I manage it but the sensible part of my brain speaks up. "Wait. Condom."

"Fuck." I hear his quiet mutter as he steps back. "Do you have any?"

I turn my head nodding towards my bedside table. "Bottom draw." He leans down pressing a soft kiss to my ass before walking over and grabbing one.

He turns back to me, smirking at me watching him roll it on. "I should have you bent over more often." He walks back to me, my blush deepening to the point that I have to bury my face into the bed. His mocking chuckle taunts me. "Don't get all shy on me now, Bubbles." His hand in my hair pulls my head up, his mouth next to my ear as he stands in between my legs again. "I want to hear you." And he does. I can't stop the loud moan that escapes me when he slides inside me, feeling his smirk against my cheek. "That's it." He places a soft kiss on my cheek before standing up straight. I prepare myself with a deep breath before he pounds into me, making it impossible to control my moans and whimpers as his hand snakes underneath me until he reaches my swollen clit. He holds his fingers hovering just above it, taunting me. I buck my hips towards his hand. "So impatient." I hear the chuckle in his voice but in this moment I don't care. All I want is the orgasm he denied me earlier.

"Please," I whimper.

"Please what?" I don't reply, instead I continue trying to move my hips as he continues to pound into me. At least until he stops completely, holding my hips tight, stopping my movements as well. "Use your words."

I let out a frustrated whimper this time. "Please. I need to come. Please."

"That's good enough this time." His hand finally touches my swollen clit, his thrusts relentless. It's not long before my climax hits me like a tidal wave. He continues pounding me through it until he finishes not long after.

He collapses over me, using his hand to hold himself up so that he doesn't squash me, placing soft kisses on the top of my back. I struggle to catch my breath. "How are you feeling?" He kisses up my back, up my neck, across my jaw, until he reaches my lips, placing a soft kiss on them.

I push myself up until I'm standing, forcing him to do the same, my back touching his bare, sweaty chest. I step out of his embrace grabbing my silk robe and sliding it on. "You can leave now."

"What?" The look on his face is nothing but shock and confusion, as I try to keep my eyes from drifting lower, and lower, and lower—

Snap out of it! I lift my eyes back to his. "Don't worry, I know how it goes." I sit down on my bed, Tylan's eyes still boring into mine like he's struggling to understand what I'm saying. "You got what you came for so now we go our separate ways. It's not my first time doing this."

"Everleigh..." He sits down next to me, taking hold of my hand that's playing with the tie on my robe. "I'm not leaving without giving you proper aftercare."

I tilt my head to the side looking at him like he's just grown two heads. "Aftercare?"

"Everleigh." His voice has an edge to it. "Please tell me you've had aftercare after sex before."

"I'm confused." I shake my head. "What's aftercare?"

He curses under his breath, closing his eyes for a few seconds to take a couple of deep breaths. Eventually he looks back at me keeping hold of my hands. "Aftercare's one of the most important things after sex. I need to make sure you're in a good mindset before I leave you alone. It looks different for everyone; it just depends on your needs. The more common ones are food, water, washing each other, dressing each other, and cuddles—"

I stand up abruptly, dropping his hands like they've burnt me. "I don't need any of that. You can leave now."

He rolls his eyes in response. "I'm not leaving. You ran out on me last time and I'm not letting it slide this time. Or any time in the future."

I fold my arms across my chest, glaring at him. "What makes you think there will be a next time?"

His eyes run up and down my body slowly before he looks back at me with that stupid fucking smirk. "I have no doubt that there will be. Now, come here and let me look after you."

I continue glaring at him, refusing to move from where I'm standing, battling with my own mind. I have one side telling me to let him in, that I need to let someone in at some point and I'd be stupid to let this opportunity pass. It's the same side that has the shattered pieces of my heart fluttering every time I so much as look at him – the fluttering that grew stronger when he was gentle with me tonight after bringing me back from my nightmare. My heart wants to be fixed by this man and if I'm not careful I very well may let him.

On the other side, I have my head screaming at me to keep my walls up, to protect myself like I always have, but it's getting exhausting. Every single day I can feel myself getting closer and closer to the edge of the cliff, getting closer and closer to falling off, and I'm terrified that when I do I'll have no one to catch me. My own mind will be the death of me.

I sneak a glance at Tylan sitting on my bed, naked except for the boxers he must've slipped on when I wasn't looking. He's watching me so intently that I can feel his ocean blue eyes searing into me, almost like he's trying to reach inside my mind. *You don't want to do that, Tylan.*

I stand there looking at him, yes he has a body that must've been sculpted by the gods themselves, but he also has a heart of gold. I think back to the very first time we met at the coffee shop after nearly running me off the road the night before, how I couldn't look away from him and for the first time in a long time, I actually wanted to talk to a man.

My mind moves onto that night at Harrow Bar and how it just felt right to leave with him, that night he let me forget the rest of the world. It was a break I didn't know I needed. Or that day at the basement where I was so close to losing control but the minute he touched me I felt grounded again. I know men don't heal broken hearts, but maybe Tylan Blaese could glue mine back together one piece at a time.

I finally make my decision. I'm tired of closing people out, I need someone to catch me when I inevitably fall and I have no problem with that person being Tylan. I finally quit thinking, walking over to the bed and straddling his lap, tentatively wrapping my arms around his neck. "What were you thinking about?" He tucks a stray piece of hair behind my ear as we stare into each other's eyes.

"It doesn't matter. Just hold me?"

"That I can do." He wraps his arms around my waist, pulling my body closer to his, allowing me to bury my face into his neck. All of this feels so natural that it scares me, but not as much as being alone does. I close my eyes and for the first time in a long time it's not a nightmare that appears, instead it's a glimpse into a future I hope I get.

The late evening summer sun glistens against the calming water of the lake, the trees swaying slightly in the breeze guarding our lakeside cabin. The rocking chair I'm sitting on rests upon the wraparound porch, empty minus the pile of toys by the back door. I split my attention between the breathtaking view and my beautiful twins playing together by the steps. I close my eyes taking in the clean air and the sounds of nature calling my name, when I feel a pair of strong hands resting on my shoulders. Looking up I catch the ocean blue eyes of my husband as he smiles down at me. "Hey, Bubbles. How's our little one doing?" I look down at our mini-me swaddled against my chest smiling to the point that my cheeks hurt. "She's perfect. Everything's perfect."

My mind races. Could I really have that life? What will it take for my dream to become a reality? Am I ready for the consequences that come with it? I take comfort in knowing that I don't need to make that decision right now. After all, I barely know the man taking over my dreams, but I hope that one day I will.

Chapter Sixteen

Cinnamon Rolls

Tylan

If I could reach into the beautifully crazy mind of the woman in front of me I would. I can tell she's in her own little world, battling with her own mind – I hope one day she will be comfortable enough to open up to me but I'm no fool, I know that day won't be anytime soon.

I watch her whilst she's zoned out, my heart beating like crazy. Yes, she may not be society's fucked up idea of beauty, but she has the body of a goddess. Her curves are beautiful, her stomach so soft, and her rolls that I know she hates are my favourite. I wish I could kiss them and kiss all her insecurities away. But it's not just her flawless body that I love about her. I know underneath everything that she has a heart of gold shielded with armour from all her pain. I hope she'll let me past the armour one day.

Ever since the first day we met there's been this invisible string pulling us together, no matter how far apart we are she consumes my entire world. As much as I know she will very much be my downfall, I can't find it within me to care in this moment. The realisation hits me so fast that it nearly takes my breath away. I'm falling for Everleigh Carlton and I don't ever want to stop.

She glances towards me and for a moment I think she's going to yell at me to leave again but she forever surprises me, climbing onto my lap and wrapping her arms around my neck. I stare into her eyes, brighter than I've ever seen them before, tucking a stray piece of hair behind her ear. "What were you thinking about?" I selfishly wish she would tell me even though I know she won't.

"It doesn't matter. Just hold me?" She sounds so vulnerable when she asks me to hold her that it physically pains me to imagine how she's been treated in the past.

"That I can do." I wrap my arms around her waist, pulling her as close to me as possible, she takes the opportunity to nestle into my neck. I rest my head on top of hers breathing in her scent, sweet mango with a hint of sex, it's addictive. I run my hand up and down her back soothingly, holding onto her, not wanting to let her go just yet. "Do you need anything? Water or a snack?" I speak quietly not wanting to disturb her peace.

"Both sound good please." She pulls back with a sleepy smile.

"You lie down and relax. I'll be right back." I give her a quick peck before laying her down and tucking her in, leaving her to get what she needs.

I switch on the kitchen light looking around at the wooden counter tops and forest green cupboards. In the middle sits an island with the same colours as the rest of the kitchen that looks like it belongs in a countryside cabin, not in a semi-detached house in a town on the outskirts of London.

I walk over to the stand-alone fridge-freezer noting just how organised and tidy it is, just like the rest of the house. Closing the fridge, I pull out two bottles of water, looking around at the cupboards trying to guess which one would have the snacks in when I notice a glass topped cake stand in the middle of the island.

I smile when I see four cinnamon rolls, thinking back to the first time we met and the half-eaten cinnamon roll she was nibbling on. I think it's safe to say I know what her favourite food is. I open each cupboard one at a time until I find where she keeps her plates. I take one out before going to the island and placing one of the treats on the plate. I'm placing the glass top back when I feel something soft brush against my legs glancing down to see Muffin rubbing against me, looking up at me with his green eyes. "*Meow.*"

I crouch down, scratching behind his ears, which he enjoys just as much as Bailey. "You don't look much like a 'Muffin' to me."

"*Meow?*" He tilts his head at me.

"Your mum is a beautiful strange woman." I smile at the cat giving him one last scratch before standing up and taking the water and snack back up to said woman, Muffin not far behind me. I open the door, smiling at my sleeping girlfriend curled up under the covers.

We've only been together for a couple of months but this is the first time I've ever seen her sleep, as she's never stayed the night, she looks so peaceful, a contrast to the tension she's always holding onto. I quietly make my way to the bed placing the items on the bedside table before carefully sitting down next to her on the bed, trying not to wake her.

"Tylan?" She sits up, rubbing her eyes.

"We have a little friend." As if on cue, Muffin jumps up onto the bed and onto her lap.

She smiles. "Hi, Handsome." He rolls onto his back, happily accepting the belly rubs she gives him. "What did you find?" She nods towards the bedside table.

I turn around picking up the plate and one of the bottles. "Your favourite."

She raises her eyebrow at me. "How do you know they're my favourite?" She gratefully accepts the plate, holding it at chest level to not disturb the ball of fluff cleaning himself on her lap.

"You had one the day we met, and again last month." I move closer to her so that our bodies are touching.

"So just because I happened to have one both of the times you've ran into me at Forever & Ever, and I also happened to make some this morning, it means they're my favourite?" She takes a bite letting out a small moan at the taste.

"Am I wrong?" She doesn't reply, opting to roll her eyes as she finishes the rest in a couple of bites. I take the empty plate from her placing it back on the bed side cabinet, exchanging it for the bottle of water. She takes it from me with a shy smile – her smile is perfect. She finishes her water at the same time Muffin jumps off her lap, wandering over to the cat bed in the corner of her room. "He's a smart cat."

She tilts her head at me. "What do you mean?"

"He jumped off just in time for us to cuddle." She blushes again as I stroke her cheek gently.

I climb under the covers with her, lying down on my back and pulling her towards me. She follows suit, resting her head on my chest. I stroke her hair as she idly traces the scars on my chest and, for the first time ever, I don't back away from the touch. "How did you get these?"

"Do you know about the private jet that crashed in the Amazon rainforest two years ago?"

She leans up onto her arms, her eyes widened. "Were you on it?"

"It was my parents' plane, one of the perks of owning the airline. I was the only one who survived." My voice is monotone, void of emotion, the way it always is when I talk about that day.

I don't like to talk about my childhood, too many bad memories plaguing it, but everyone in Little Bray knows about it. I was always known as the heir to Blaese Airlines, set up to take it over from the day I was born. I never really wanted to take over the company but my father trained me in his own way that it felt like I had no other choice. My escape was university where I studied criminology, graduating top of my class, but that didn't stop my father from forcing his company on me and I was stuck as his shadow.

Then my parents died on one of their own aircrafts, making national headlines, and it gave me the escape I needed. I was now the new owner, with enough money to set me up for life. A few months after I'd taken over, investigations started to ramp up, talks of foul play beginning to arise and that's when I realised I needed to put my degree to good use to keep my name out of it. I shut the airline down, paying the staff enough to keep them going until they found another job, and I applied to join the police academy, working my way up to Detective by the time I turned twenty-six, but even that's not working out, given that the Polaroid Reaper is my first case as the lead detective. I might have to start looking for a third career.

I can sense her wanting to ask more about it, but I'm guessing she can see something on my face that says I don't want to talk about my family right now. Instead she asks a different question. "Why did you close down the airline?"

I stroke her hair absentmindedly, staring at the wall, my voice emotionless. "Technical difficulties caused the crash, we couldn't guarantee that passengers would be safe. I couldn't risk the lives of millions of people." It's a lie I've told enough times that sometimes I even convince myself it's the truth. It's better than what really happened, the truth that Michael Knotts holds over my head every time he needs to get away with something. I don't want to lie to Everleigh but she lied about who she was, I can lie about this. I have to. I can't bear the thought of her looking at me differently, like I'm some sort of monster.

A soft hand under my chin turns my attention to the bright olive green eyes I love to get lost in. "It's admirable, what you did. You could've covered it up, but you gave it all up to protect the lives of strangers."

"Covering it up was never an option. I have morals. I don't believe in killing or hurting innocent people—" *Not anymore.* "But I'm more than happy to rid the world of monsters."

I feel her stiffen beside me, despite her face showing no change in her emotions. "Let's get some sleep." She turns over onto her side curling up into a ball. A wave of uneasiness floods through me. Did I say something wrong? My mind races through every possibility trying to figure out what ran through her mind. Unable to find one, I turn onto my side pulling her into me, drifting off into a dreamless sleep.

My eyes blink open at the sound of purring in my ear and a heaviness on my chest. I look down to see a sleeping Muffin on my chest. At some point in the night I must've turned onto my back as my arms are no longer wrapped around a sleeping Everleigh. Instead she's star-fished across the bed, half of her body on top of mine.

I didn't think it was possible for her to look even more beautiful but seeing her in the early morning light, drooling on her pillow, her hair a tangled mess from tossing and turning all night, and our late night activities, her eyelids fluttering as she dreams – *Slow down!* I force myself to look away. I'm falling too hard too fast, just like I always do, except normally I deny it as much as I can but I can't this time, no matter how hard I try to push the feelings away they're there in full force making me confront them.

"What are you still doing here?" She shifts beside me, her voice raspy with sleep.

"And miss out on the opportunity of seeing you in the early morning?" I tease her.

"It's not an attractive sight, and don't even try lying to me." Even after just waking up she's still as sassy as ever.

"It's an adorable sight."

She rolls her eyes at me, pushing the sleeping cat off my chest who hisses at her in response. "Don't hiss at me." I hide my smile at her reprimanding her cat. God she's adorable. She wastes no time in resting her head on my chest right where he just was. "Don't you have work? There's a serial killer out there you know."

"I know and she's a massive pain in my ass."

"Hmm. Is she now?" I feel her smile against my chest.

"I think she's going to get away with it, and that's going to create a lot of paperwork for me and damage my reputation." I idly play with her hair.

"If she's such a pain why not throw her in jail?"

I tilt her head up to me. “Because she means too much to me.” *Shit.* I did not mean to admit that.

She smiles brightly. “So you’re a detective who lets killers out on the loose?”

I lift her chin up to look at me. “I’m not a detective because I want to be. I’m a detective because I need to be.” I watch her eyebrows burrow. “Despite what everyone thinks, I’m not a good person, Everleigh.”

“That’s good. Because neither am I.” I don’t get the chance to reply before she’s off the bed and walking into the bathroom. I let out a sigh talking myself out of following her, that would definitely be too much too soon. Instead I sit up, taking the opportunity to observe her room, the three forest green walls complimenting the printed leaves on the wall behind me. The only furniture in the room is the dressing table near the bay window, the bed, and the bedside tables.

I don’t know what comes over me but an image flashes in my mind of what I found in her drawer last night, besides the box of condoms. I look towards the bathroom door, listening closely for the sound of running water. I should’ve just got off the bed and joined her in the shower but instead I end up opening the draw and taking out the small polaroid picture. I examine it taking note of the young family, my heart racing in recognition. I flip it over not expecting the date on the back – July 28th, 2006 – maybe it’s not the family I’m thinking of. I don’t even think before I’m reaching into the pocket of my discarded jeans, pulling my wallet out and placing it in front of the other picture I keep hidden in there.

I hear the shower shutting off and rush to put my jeans back on, sliding my wallet into the back pocket. I turn around at the sound of the bathroom door opening. She looks like an angel, the steam from the bathroom surrounding her, making it look like she has a glow, with nothing but a flimsy towel wrapped around her body. However, I can't focus on the beauty of her, my heart won't stop racing, my wallet burning against me through my pocket of my jeans. "I have to go."

I don't give her the chance to respond before I'm practically running down the stairs only stopping to throw my t-shirt back on and pick up my hoodie, rushing out the door. I race away from her house, only slowing down a few streets away, not prepared for my eyes to connect with the ghost of my past driving past me. Our eyes connect and I see the shock followed by panic, feeling like time slows down as she drives past me in the direction I just came from. This can't be good.

Chapter Seventeen

Invisible Force

Everleigh

I'm still standing in the doorway of my bathroom when I hear my front door slam closed. I blink. *What just happened?* Before I can overthink it, I walk over to my wardrobe pulling out my favourite pair of black jeans and white crop top, placing them on my bed along with my comfy cotton underwear. I quickly go through my post shower routine and get dressed before Camilla gets here.

I take a seat next to Muffin on my cushioned bay window looking outside at the dark ominous clouds, also known as typical Little Bray weather, brushing the knots out of my tangled hair. I don't plan on going out today so I don't bother with makeup.

I've only just finished when I notice Camilla's silver car pulling up in my driveway, made even more clearer by Muffin jumping up, hissing at her through the window when she steps out her car. I can't help but notice how uneasy she seems, clearly not noticing that I'm watching her. I've known her nearly my entire life and she's even better at hiding her true emotions than I am.

I don't get up until I hear my front door being opened followed quickly by Camilla's worried voice ringing through the house. "Leigh?"

I saunter down the stairs, Muffin rushing past me to his food bowl meowing loudly. "Hey, Cami."

"Why was your door unlocked?" She crosses her arms, hitting me with that angry-mum look. When I lost my family Camilla took me under her wing, treating and protecting me like I'm her sister. If I didn't already have a sister, I would happily call her my older sister but no one could ever replace Maya. I try to avoid it but my mind wanders back to my last birthday before I lost her...

Our family home is decorated with multiple pink and gold decorations; balloons, banners, table decor, whatever you could think of for a sweet sixteen is here. My pink fit and flare dress matches the exact shade of all the decorations – baby pink – a testament to just how well my parents know me. "Oh. My. God!" I turn around to my sister, dressed in a tight fitting gold gown, her chestnut eyes wide – the only physical difference between the two of us – she always has been the over the top twin. "It's perfect!"

I smile at her. "They really went all out for our sweet sixteen." Maya rushes over to me, pulling me into a tight hug. You'd think having your birthday five days before Christmas wouldn't be very fun, that your parents would combine the two together, but our parents have always made sure that our birthdays are extra special. Maya and I gossip until our mum interrupts us.

"Happy birthday, Pumpkins."

We both groan at her in unison. "Mummm." She always calls us her pumpkins, don't ask me why because she refuses to tell us, although I have a strong feeling that the baby photo I found of us surrounded by pumpkins whilst also dressed as pumpkins has every reason to do with it.

"You winding them up again, Ames?" Our dad walks into the room wrapping his arms around her waist. Maya and I share a look. Our parents have never been shy about showing their love for each other. My attention turns to the door at the sound of small running footsteps coming from the hallway.

I gasp with a smile, crouching down and holding my arms out to my five year old brother, Ethan. "Well aren't you looking dashing in your suit today." He rushes into my arms clinging to me in our usual greeting. I stand up, holding him on my hip. Our parents struggled for years after Maya and I were born to have another child. It took them ten years at which point they'd already given up. Ethan was quite literally a miracle baby.

"Let's get this party started." Maya smiles, pressing play on the speaker.

Four days later, they were all gone.

I push the memories aside before they can overwhelm me like they have in the past. I don't fancy breaking down today. "I must've forgot to lock it."

She crosses her arms, staring me down. "Why are you lying to me?"

I roll my eyes at her. "I'm not."

"Does this have something to do with why the twins were told they didn't have to tidy up for you last night?" Of course they told her.

"Fine. I had someone else do it. Someone who could help us all out."

"I feel like I'm not going to like this answer—"

"Then don't ask the question. Do you have anything—"

"Who is it Leigh?"

I stall trying to make up a lie she'll believe but I come up short. I sigh realising I'm just going to have to face the music. "The lead detective on the Polaroid Reaper case..."

She blinks at me slowly as I stand there waiting for her to explode. "Please tell me you're joking." Her voice is surprisingly calm...this isn't good. "You're sleeping with Tylan Blaese?"

"How do you know his name?" I raise my eyebrows at her.

"Because in case you haven't noticed, one of us has to keep track of what the media knows. His name is all over the case." She closes her eyes taking a deep breath. "Why are you being so stupid?"

"Excuse me?" I huff out a surprised laugh.

"Come on, Leigh. I know you're smarter than this."

I sink down into the couch. "I know but I can't help it. It's like there's this invisible force pushing me towards him."

"Everleigh. No." She sits next to me on the couch holding my hand tight.

"I think I'm falling for him." I hold off from telling her the relationship part. It always has to be one step at a time with Camilla.

"No, you're not. He's just the first guy to give you attention."

"Is that such a bad thing?" I shrug. "To have a guy who pays attention to me and actually cares for me?"

"Yes. You barely know him. How do you know you can trust him?"

"I don't. But maybe I don't care." I sigh. "I'm tired, Cami. I'm tired of being this emotionless robot who thinks she can't be loved."

"Leigh. I know that somewhere out there, there is that guy who will give you that dream family you've always wanted. But I know it's not Tylan."

"You've never even met him." I glare at her.

"Then let me meet him. So I can show you how right I am."

I think it over for a second. "I can ask him."

She nods at me seemingly happy with my answer. "Good. Now onto what I actually came here for." She reaches into her bag pulling out her laptop and a couple of binders. "I still think we should wait a little longer until we make a move on Michael Knotts. He has a holiday booked soon which I found out actually means he plans on holding a girl for a few days." She turns to look at me with a smug smile. "We just have to make sure that girl is you."

"I'm sorry?" My eyes widen.

"Nothing will actually happen to you. You just have to let him kidnap you and then you kill him."

"You're forgetting he knows me."

"We make him come to you."

"How do we do that?" I stand from the couch walking over to the kitchen as Camilla lays all her stuff out in a neat organised mess. I pull a glass out the cupboard taking it over to the fridge and pulling out my water filter jug, filling it.

I sneak a glance at Camilla still awaiting her answer when she suddenly perks up, flicking her head towards me. "Let him see you with Tylan. Everyone know he's a detective, make it sound like you're telling him about Michael."

"That," I put the jug back in the fridge before turning back to her, "might actually work. But Tylan wants to help with Michael's death."

I don't miss how her shoulders tense. "And he will be, just unknowingly."

"No." I shake my head. "I'll let him in on the plan. Plus it might be helpful to have him watching over me just in case something goes wrong."

"Fine. But not until I've met him. Freddie and Callum are meeting him as well." She turns back to her laptop powering it on as I walk back to the couch with my drink in my hand.

"They already know him."

Her head snaps to me. "What?"

I shrug. "He was at the basement the other week. He's not who you think he is, Cami." I watch the cogs turning in her brain, leaning over to place my drink on the coffee table when her hand reaches out and snags it out of my hand.

"Hey!"

She just shrugs. "It's rude not to offer your guests a drink."

I roll my eyes at her going back to the kitchen to grab another drink for myself. "So who's my next kill?"

"Michael Knotts."

My eyebrows scrunch together. "But you just said—"

"He's a dangerous one. We need you at the top of your game, otherwise it could be a disaster. Don't you remember what happened with Jack Harrow?"

I cross my arms. "Of course I do. I beat him." I'll never admit it out loud but I was terrified about the Jack Harrow situation. I'd lost control of the situation, worrying about everything. I can't let that happen ever again. Camilla gives me a pointed look. "Okay. Fine. I'll try to suppress the urge."

"That includes no killing random men."

"To be fair, he tried to assault me. He deserved to die just as much as the others."

She rolls her eyes at me, muttering under her breath. "You're crazy but I love you."

"Love you too. Now, what do I need to know about Michael Knotts?" I nudge her playfully.

It's dark by the time Camilla leaves, we've spent all afternoon coming up with a foolproof plan to get rid of Michael

Knotts for good, and a couple of backup plans just in case the impossible comes true. We also both agreed that she should meet Tylan before that night, just so that I can prove she's wrong about him. I pick up my phone contemplating whether I should call or text him, or neither. I eventually opt for texting. I sit staring at our string of messages contemplating what to message him. Eventually I land on the basic greeting.

Hey

I wait. Staring at the screen like an idiot. It takes exactly eight minutes before I get a reply. *You timed it?* I scold myself.

Who's death am I covering up tonight?

No one's

Do you have any plans for tonight?

I watch the three dots on the screen. What am I doing? Am I really staring at my screen waiting for a guy to message me? The dots disappear replaced by a photo of a bunch of paperwork strewn across a mahogany desk overlooking the Little Bray skyline. With it there's another message.

A date in the office with paperwork

Fancy a nicer date?

Delete. Delete. Delete.

How do you feel about Chinese?

Too late.

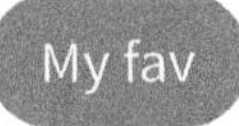

It'll be here when you are

Looks like I'm having Chinese in an office with my secret boyfriend tonight.

Chapter Eighteen

All Your Dreams

Tylan

The deadline for our monthly case updates is coming up and as usual that means long days and nights stuck in the office. Normally I'd be stuck trying to juggle the updates with trying to solve a case but this month I don't have any cases, seeing as I know who we're looking for and I don't plan on turning her in any time soon. I'm making notes when my phone buzzes on my desk.

Hey

Speak of the angel. Our text exchange is brief but it's enough to bring a small smile to my face. I never asked what she wanted so instead I order one of all the most popular items. I put my phone down planning to finish my current case file before she gets here but instead my mind keeps wandering to the woman on her way here. I don't even know how long I've been staring out the window when I spot her navy blue Mini pulling into a parking spot outside the building. Shortly after she steps out the car my phone buzzes again.

Should I come through the main entrance?

I can see the anxiety coursing through her.

Go round the side

There's an entrance directly to the offices

She sends one single thumbs up emoji making her way across the street. I unknowingly rush down the stairs towards the side entrance, taking a deep breath composing myself before opening the door where she stands shuffling her feet. "This was an unexpected surprise." I smile at her.

"I hope it's a good one." She tucks her hair behind her ear glancing behind her. I take the opportunity to check her out, her body perfectly framed by the flowy black dress that reaches just above her knees.

"You look beautiful. Come in." Her cheeks turn red as she steps inside. I'm about to close the door when I notice a delivery person walking up to the door, I take the food from him closing the door behind me. I turn around noticing how uncomfortable Everleigh looks, offering her my hand but she just stares at it. "Are you okay?"

With that one question her head snaps towards me. "Yeah. I've just never really done this before?"

She takes my hand and I lead her up to my office. "Done what?"

"Oh, you know. Been inside a police station."

Shit. I forgot that in most people's eyes she's a criminal trying everything to stay out of the police station and a prison cell. What was I thinking? "Do you want to go somewhere else?" I rub my thumb over her knuckles.

She shakes her head offering me a tiny smile. "No. We're already here."

I squeeze her hand gently, opening my office door and ushering her inside. She stands in the middle of the room looking around before making her way to the couch and sitting down. I join her, not quite touching, placing the bag of food on the coffee table in front of her. "I hope I got something you like."

She hums ripping open the bag and looking through the selection, her eyes lighting up when she reaches the chicken chow mein. "How did you know my favourite?"

"Lucky guess." I smile at her and she repays me with her stunning smile.

Her soft heart lips form a small pout. "There's no forks."

"It's a good thing I have some in case of emergencies." I walk over to my desk pulling out two plastic forks from the draw.

"Do you often eat at the office?" Her giggle is infectious.

"More than I'd like. Although if I had someone as beautiful as you joining me I'd do it a lot more often."

She rolls her eyes at me taking one of the forks and digging into the food. Her little moans going straight to my cock, making my trousers feel tighter.

"Can I ask you something?" she asks me in between mouthfuls.

"What do you want to know?" I dig into my own food.

"You don't have to answer if you don't want to. I-I just want to get to know you better." I look at her letting her take her time to ask. She takes a deep breath. "What were you like before your parents died?"

I pause with my fork halfway to my mouth. Out of all the questions she could ask I was not expecting that. I take a couple more bites before answering her. "My relationship with them was always strained so I didn't really change." I shrug. "I guess after I felt free."

"W-What..." She coughs a little, looking away from me. "What were they like?"

"Let's just say they weren't good parents." We both sit in silence eating our food.

"I'm sorry. I can't imagine what you must've been through." She tentatively places her hand on my knee and I give it a little squeeze.

I shrug. "That's just life. I was a mistake. They never wanted children so they treated me like the only thing important in life was money. They threw money at me instead of parenting." I squeeze her hand tighter. "And my father expected me to pay him back in the form of beatings."

She gasps looking at me in horror. “He hit you?”

I turn to look her in the eyes, needing to change the subject. “What was your family like?”

Her hand tightens on mine and I take the chance to pull her closer to me until our bodies are touching. “They were perfect. My parents were the most caring and attentive people.” She takes a deep breath, blinking back the tears forming in her eyes. “When we were growing up they always made sure to give Maya and I each the same amount of love and attention.” Her eyes focus on a random spot on the floor, a sad smile gracing her lips. “Even when they were devastated about every negative pregnancy test they tried to keep it hidden from us wanting to keep us happy. They never pulled away from us not even when they were hurting.” She huffs out a sad laugh. “They even made sure our birthdays were a separate event from Christmas, and they always made sure our parties were equal parts of both of us.”

“Wait, when’s your birthday?”

Her eyes snap to mine, taking her out of her trance. I watch her take a deep breath, her smile dropping. “December twentieth.”

My eyes widen. “When you lost your family...”

Her eyes fill with tears. “The last day we all spent together was our sixteenth birthday.” She lets out a sad laugh that turns into a sob. “My birthday and Christmas are forever tainted.” I’m at a loss for words, my heart breaking for her and all the pain she’s been through. She wipes her eyes taking another deep breath before turning to me, a fake smile plastered on her face. “Enough of the sad stuff.” She lets out another half laugh. “What’s the one thing in life you want more than anything?”

To be loved. “I want to fix my parents’ mistakes and make everything right again.”

Her soft hand touches my arm gently. “You don’t have to fix your parents’ mistakes.” I look into her eyes, pulling her onto my lap. She’s hesitant at first but relaxes into the hold.

I press a kiss to her forehead. “What’s yours? What’s your greatest dream in life?”

“It’s kinda boring.”

I grip her chin turning her face back to me when she looks away. “I want to know everything about you. The real you. All the good, and all the bad.”

“It’s more messy than bad.” She blushes.

“I still want to know it all. Starting with your dreams.”

“Okay. Well I’d love to move out of the city to a small countryside village, open my own bookstore with my husband and create my own little family. I want to stop having to hide but I won’t do any of it until the men who ruined my life are dead.”

I stroke her cheek gently. “Then I’ll help you get there until all your dreams come true.”

“That’s such a cheesy line.” Her smile this time is genuine. We stay like this until late in the evening, talking about anything and everything and at the end of it I feel like I know the real Everleigh better. I feel myself falling for her even more. At some point in the past few hours we moved around on the couch to where she is now, lying with her head on my lap, rambling about anything and everything. This girl switches topics so fast it's almost impossible to keep track. I'm pretty sure this conversation started with talking about travelling the world, and now she's talking about pixies. "And that's why Freddie calls me Pixie." Her mesmerising eyes turn back to mine.

"Because you were obsessed with Tinker Bell? Isn't she a fairy?"

"Technically yes but also because I got a pixie cut one day. Biggest regret. Of. My. Life." She physically cringes at the memory.

I chuckle. "Do you reckon he has a picture?"

"Oh I know he does. But you are never seeing it." Her face scrunches in the most adorable way, pointing a perfectly manicured finger at me.

"I'll just ask him when you're not around." I can't help my chuckle as she slaps me playfully.

"That would put you off me for life!" It doesn't take long until her infectious laugh fills the room.

"I have one more question." I stroke her hair, her laughs quieting.

"What is it?"

"How do you choose the men you kill?"

She shrugs. The conversation is so leisurely that you'd think we were just talking about movies or something equally as casual. "I don't. Camilla picks them for me. She's scarily good at digging up people's pasts."

"Why doesn't she kill them herself?"

"Because she doesn't have the same urge as me." She sits up, her back now facing me. "I've always said that killing is like an addiction for me, I tried it once and now I can't stop. I lasted two kills before I couldn't last the entire six month wait any longer. I just go crazy with the need."

"You? Crazy? I don't see it." I tease her but her body remains stock still. "Hey." I press my chest against her back, wrapping my arms around her waist and placing a soft kiss to her shoulder. "You're not crazy."

She takes a deep breath before turning her face to mine. "We have a plan for Michael Knotts but Camilla wants to meet you first."

"Should I be worried?"

Her face breaks into a grin. "Of course not. Just don't piss her off."

I roll my eyes with a smile. "Very helpful advice."

"I'm sure you'll be fine." We share a brief kiss. "I should get going." She pushes herself up off the couch. "I've got a cat to feed who's known to get hangry."

"Just like his owner." I chuckle placing a soft kiss on her cheek, releasing her from my embrace.

"I do not get hangry." I raise my eyebrow at her adorable glare as she stares me down. "At least not all the time."

"Don't worry," I pull her by her waist to stand in between my legs, "it's an adorable trait." I lean in to give her another kiss but she pushes me back gently.

"Not now, Romeo." She winks blowing me a kiss before walking out my office. The more time we spend together the more I realise that I'm playing a very dangerous game with fire, and I refuse to lose.

Chapter Nineteen
Vengeance

Dear Miss Reaper.

Beware, beware, the ghost of past.

Prepare, prepare, to say goodbye.

Despair, despair, you're too late.

You don't know I can see or hear you. You don't know about the bug I placed in Tylan's office. You don't know you've just added Tylan to my list. I thought he was just naïve like he normally is but he knows who you are and he's helping you. I have my camera perfectly poised at his window, the two of you perfectly in frame of the camera lens, but I let my fingers do their work, snapping the multitude of photos but I'm not focused on that. I feel cheated. I confided in him about what he did to my sister and he's just cosying up to you. Betrayal hits hard but I'll get my justice soon.

Count your days, Miss Reaper.

Chapter Twenty

Risky

Everleigh

Tylan and I have been messaging every day for the past week and with every message I can feel the butterflies flurrying in my stomach, my smile growing wider every time. *Quit whilst you're ahead, girl.* I wish I could, but all sense of self control flies out the window wherever Tylan is concerned. He makes me nervous, but for once it's a good kind of nervous.

I'm standing in nothing but my towel, staring at my wardrobe trying to decide what to wear. *Why does it matter?* It doesn't. It's just a normal dinner with friends so why am I overthinking it? I sigh pulling on a simple wine red summer dress just in time as a knock rings through the house. Muffin runs to the door scratching relentlessly as I make my way downstairs. I pick him up, holding him in my arms as I open the door, gasping in surprise. "This is a first."

"What's that meant to mean, Pixie?" Freddie grins at me.

"You two are normally the last to arrive." I raise my eyebrow at them, stepping aside to let them in, Muffin hissing in my arms.

"We couldn't miss out on seeing how that one," he points at said cat, "reacts to your new man."

"He's not my man." Lie. I roll my eyes, shutting the door behind the twins turning around to catch them sharing a look. "What's that look for?"

"Nothing." Callum fails at hiding his knowing smirk.

"He's just my hookup buddy. Nothing more."

"Is that what they call crushes these days?" He chuckles.

"You're one to talk. I see the way you look at Summer." For just one moment his body tenses.

"It doesn't matter. She's engaged."

Before I can speak Freddie calls out from the kitchen "Did you make all this, Pixie?" Callum and I join him in the kitchen, the island filled with multiple dishes.

"Make. Reheat...it's all the same thing right?" I smile innocently.

"We already know you can't cook, Cap." I elbow Callum in his side when he wraps his arms around me in a brotherly hug. I open my mouth to retaliate but I'm interrupted by another knock at the door. I was definitely not expecting to see Camilla and Tylan in a heated stare down when I open the door. They don't seem to notice I'm there until Muffin meows loudly in my arms, their heads snapping towards me in unison.

"I see you two have met..." The awkward tension is broken by Muffin leaping out my arms to rub against Tylan's legs. As he crouches down stroking him I catch Camilla rolling her eyes, hissing at her when she walks past me. "Be nice." I don't get a reply as she walks to the kitchen.

"I don't think she likes me." Tylan looks up at me from where he's crouched.

"She just has a lot of trust issues." I shrug holding my hand out to help him up which he graciously accepts. "Let's get this awkward phase over with."

"You planning on keeping me around, Bubbles?" I may have my back to him but I can hear the smirk in his voice.

"You could be useful." I shrug, leading him to the kitchen. Camilla is standing by the fridge glaring at the food on the island whilst the twins talk amongst themselves sitting at the stools at the end of the island. Camilla's glare turns to our hands when she spots us. I let out a silent sigh, squeezing Tylan's hand before dropping it and walking over to Camilla. "Give him a chance, Cami."

"I don't trust him." Our voices are hushed but I can feel Tylan's eyes on us.

"You don't even know him yet."

Camilla hesitates for just one second, uncertainty flashing through her eyes. "You know I have good instincts about this stuff though."

She does. "You can't always be right." I shrug.

"I don't want you to lose yourself." Camilla squeezes my hand currently resting on the countertop.

"Maybe he's the one who's keeping me from doing just that." I give her hand one more squeeze before joining the boys at the end of the island, the twins on one end, Tylan on one side, their plates piled high with food.

"Did you miscount, Pixie? There's only four chairs," Freddie asks between mouthfuls.

"That's because I only have four chairs. It's okay though I'll just stand—" My words change into a squeak as Tylan pulls me onto his lap.

I try to stand up but he holds me tight, whispering in my ear, "Stay." Camilla rolls her eyes taking the final seat opposite us but the twins both have their stupid grins plastered on their face.

"How did you two meet then?" Callum asks before eating a mouthful of lasagna.

"At Forever & Ever. I was just getting my daily coffee but I could feel a set of eyes ogling me—"

"I do not ogle," I protest, glaring at him.

He chuckles before continuing, "I would've been stupid to pass up the opportunity of talking to a beautiful woman like her." I turn to him, smiling at the adoration in his eyes.

"Sounds like a fairy tale meeting," Camilla mumbles quietly. I turn to see her pushing her food around on the plate, her eyes narrowed at Tylan. *Am I missing something?*

"It wasn't quite. He kinda put his foot in it." I giggle softly at the memory. The twins eyes open wide, forks paused halfway to their mouths. It doesn't take a genius to work out their shocked, I've never giggled around them before.

"What did he do?" Camilla perks up.

"He implied I was a slut trying to get attention, which I'm not." I lower my voice to whisper directly in Tylan's ear, "Apart from in the bedroom." His cheeks flush the slightest hint of red, his hand tightening on my waist. I'm pretty sure if I moved just a little bit I would be able to feel him pressing against my body.

"That was never what I meant, I've just never been the best at compliments." He clears his throat taking a sip of water.

"Turns out he nearly ran me off the road the night before," I continue.

Freddie chokes on his drink at the confession. "Why would you do that?" he asks between coughs.

"She was doing forty in a sixty whilst dancing around to music." Tylan shrugs.

"She does that a lot." Callum laughs.

"Well excuse me if I want to be safe when I'm driving."

"That's not being safe, Bubbles. We both know that night could've been disastrous." I sigh leaning into Tylan, wiggling into a comfortable position, only stopping when his hands tighten on my waist and he growls in my ear, "Behave." And then I feel it. His hard cock pressed against my hip. I suppress my giggle with a cough, Tylan shooting me a pointed look.

"I don't get it." All playfulness is sucked out the room as Camilla looks at the two of us. "You're a detective. This case could ruin your career if you don't catch the killer but here you are..." She points at us. "She's sitting on your lap, why are you not arresting her?"

"My career means nothing to me. What Everleigh's doing is admirable. Everyone thinks the law is everything but really all it takes is a good lawyer and money and you're free, your reputation squeaky clean. If the legal system's not going to punish these men for what they're doing then I am more than happy to join Everleigh to make sure justice is served." I smile contentedly at his confession, resting my head on his shoulder, anxiously waiting to see what Camilla will say next.

It takes a whole five minutes of Camilla locking Tylan in a staring contest, tension filling the room, until she finally answers, "Okay. You still need to prove to me why we can trust you but you could be useful." I sag in relief mouthing a silent "thank you" to Camilla. "But mark my words. If you betray or hurt her in any way at all..." She glares at Tylan, holding his gaze. "I will make sure you die a long and agonising death until you are begging me to end it all...and then I'll feed you to the rats. Got it?"

I let out a sigh, dropping my head into my hands. "Got it," Tylan replies, squeezing my waist in reassurance. For the next hour Camilla explains our plan, and backup plans, for Sunday night. By the time she's finished the only thing left on the island is empty plates and dishes which I am not looking forward to cleaning up later. We eventually move on to talking about random stuff and I can't help but smile at how normal this all feels. It takes me back to when I was a teenager and we'd have sleepovers every month. There was no need to worry about anything, just a group of friends hanging out and having fun.

I'm so caught up in the normalcy of it all that I can't help my next suggestion. "We should have a sleepover tonight. We could watch movies or play some board games."

The twins look at each other, shrugging at the exact same time that it's almost creepy. "We're down for that," Freddie replies.

"So am I." Camilla smiles at me. I turn my attention to Tylan.

"Sounds fun." He kisses me softly and for a moment I forget we're not alone as I deepen the kiss only to be interrupted by someone coughing. We pull apart smiling at each other. This is the life I want.

It took a long argument to decide on a film to watch. Camilla and I wanted to watch a horror movie, but Freddie and Callum wanted to watch a Disney film, of course that meant it was down to Tylan to choose and he obviously chose the horror film. The twins grumbled at not getting their choice, sinking down on the couch. It's kinda amusing. You wouldn't expect two grown men who could kill you in a single second to sulk over not getting to watch a Disney movie. Camilla took the final spot on the couch which left the armchair at the side of the room where I'm currently curled up on Tylan's lap, a blanket draped over both of us.

My head is resting on Tylan's shoulder, his hand resting on my thigh just below the hem of my dress. I shuffle slightly to get more comfortable his hand sliding further up at the movement. I can feel the heat rising between my legs, silently urging his hand to continue higher but instead he grips my thigh, forcing me to look up only to be met with his ocean blue eyes. He raises an eyebrow at me, silently questioning me, when I place my hand on top of his slowly guiding it up my thigh. I know it's risky. My friends are mere steps away but their attention is on the movie where a girl is being chased by the killer. I don't care. I let go of Tylan's hand when it reaches the edge of my panties, burrowing my face in his neck to whisper in his ear, "Please."

His fingers trace the edge of my panties refusing to move any closer, he whispers in my ear disguising it as a cheek kiss, "Why are you so wet?" I blush hard, burying my face even deeper into his neck, his chest shakes in silent laughter. "Does this turn you on? Do you like being scared?" I suck in a breath when his finger traces my slit over my panties. "Or do you like that we might be caught? Your friends are right there." He presses his thumb against my aching clit. "One little sound and they could turn their heads. See you acting like a little slut." *Fuck!* I've always loved his dirty talk but this? This is a whole new level.

I subtly spread my legs a little further to give him more room. He takes the hint, hooking my panties to the side. I bite his neck to stop from moaning out loud when his fingers trace my bare slit. "Acting like *my* little slut." He doesn't stop whispering in my ear as his fingers play with my soaking pussy, I can feel it dripping down my thighs. "Do you want my fingers inside?" I nod against his shoulder, too afraid of opening my mouth to speak. His comforting kiss to my forehead is a contrast to the feeling of his two fingers stretching me open. I bite my lip hard enough that I can taste blood. Why is it so hard to stay quiet?

Tylan strokes my hair and back as his fingers bring me to the edge, I can feel the tension growing, the need wanting to escape. Just one more touch...He stops. I can't stop the quiet whimper that escapes, glaring at him. "Shh. You're okay." He strokes my hair, calming me down as I wiggle desperately on his lap. "Stop moving." He hisses in my ear. I reluctantly stop which he rewards by thrusting his fingers back inside, his thumb pressed against my clit. My climax builds again, running throughout my entire body. I'm right there muffling my moans against his shoulder. My body tenses ready to release. He stops.

I glare at him again. "Do I need to do it myself?" I whisper in his ear, taunting him.

"I dare you to try," he whispers in my ear, challenging me. Not one to back down from a dare, I stare directly into his eyes, moving my hand down to my desperate pussy. I let out a silent gasp as my fingers touch my clit, Tylan's eyes darkening. His grip on my wrist is strong as he stops my hand, pulling it away. I pout, a small whine escaping, making me blush hard. "Shh. Unless you don't want to come?" I bury my head back into his neck, finding comfort in his masculine scent. He brings me to the edge again...only to stop.

"Make me come," I whisper, glaring at him. He raises his eyebrow at me, causing me to soften my eyes. "Please?" He smirks, not saying a word as he moves his fingers again. I can feel the pleasure building throughout my entire body, clutching at Tylan as I explode around his fingers not stopping as I ride out my climax. The second he moves his hand I collapse against his chest panting for breath. He looks into my eyes, licking the evidence off his fingers, my blush growing deeper.

Our moment is interrupted by Freddie pausing the movie, rushing over to my vintage style radio sitting on the side table in the hallway. Tylan and I share a confused look as Freddie turns it on. The reporter's voice filling the room.

"If you are just joining us I am live from Westmoor Park where just twenty minutes ago the body of a twenty-three year old male has been pulled from the river. We do not have much information as of this moment but with London's newest serial killer, the Polaroid Reaper, seemingly lying dormant for the past couple of weeks there is speculation that she may have changed her choice of weapon."

I huff a laugh. "No way. Throwing someone in a river is far too risky."

"We do, however, have a name. Jason Richards—"

Freddie shuts the radio off, sharing an alarmed look with his brother.

"Shit," Callum mumbles.

"Do you know him?" I ask. Neither of them reply as they grab their jackets and phones, running out the house. The three of us watch after them, unsure of what to say.

"What was that about?" Tylan asks, looking at me for answers.

"I have no idea." I shrug, looking over at Camilla who bears an equally confused look.

"I guess that's the sleepover over." She stands up from the couch. "I'll leave you two to finish your um...activities." Can you die from embarrassment? I can feel the heat from my blush as Tylan chuckles.

"You knew?" I cover my cheeks, trying to hide the blush.

Camilla raises her eyebrow at me. "Girl, you are not subtle at all. But do me a favour," she places a hand on my shoulder, "never have sex in front of me again."

"We didn't—"

"Bye, Leigh." She waves over her shoulder walking out the door and closing it behind her. Tylan bursts out into a fit of laughs as I turn back to him, mortified.

"It's not funny!" I cross my arms pouting at him.

"You should see your face right now. You're as red as a tomato." His laughs don't stop as he tucks a lock of hair behind my ear, his laughs are so infectious that I can't stop my own from escaping. He pulls me in closer to him, his arms wrapping around my waist, mine wrapping around his neck. How have I missed out on this my entire life? For the first time in six years I feel normal. It doesn't feel like we're a detective and a serial killer, traumatised by our pasts. It feels like we're just two normal people finding comfort within each other. I want this so bad it hurts. I want this future. I want to put in the work to make this happen. Life's dealt me a shit hand in life but now it's my turn to be happy.

Chapter Twenty-One
She's Gone

Tylan

The air around us is overwhelming, pungent with a mix of sweat and a variety of colognes, but the sweet smell of mango grounds me, a reminder of who I'm here with. I hold on tight to Everleigh's hand as we weave through the sweaty mass of bodies on the dance floor, not stopping until we reach the end of the bar where there are thankfully two seats free.

I help her onto one of the stools, her baby blue dress swaying at the movement. I was surprised when she picked this dress out, it doesn't hug her figure like her usual club dresses do, instead it flares out at the waist, giving her an air of innocence. Don't get me wrong though, she still looks as sexy as always and I can't wait to see it on my bedroom floor later, it's just different.

I even asked her about it and three simple words "He likes it" was the only explanation I needed. She might never admit it but I can see how he affects her. She may have known the first victim, but she's different with Michael Knotts –

vulnerable. A part of me is nervous that she might not be ready but this is her call to make.

I catch the attention of the bartender, ordering a glass of their most expensive champagne for her and a water for myself. I need a clear head to watch over her tonight. "I can't afford that."

I grab her hand when she tries to raise it to get the bartender's attention again. "It's on me tonight."

"Are you sure?"

I lean over, kissing her temple. "Don't worry about it." The bartender places our drinks in front of us before moving onto another customer.

Everleigh sips from her drink, eyes scanning the crowded room. "Do you see him?"

I join her in searching the room, my eyes landing on our target sitting in a booth surrounded by two blonde women but his attention is squarely on us. "He's watching us."

"Do you think he'll hear us?" She speaks quietly so that only I can hear.

"If he doesn't we'll move closer," I reply, her response a small nod.

"Is there anything I could do to put him away for good or is it too late?" she asks our prepared questions loud enough for our target to hear. I answer her questions honestly, taking note of Michael sending the girls off before talking to one of his friends, pointing directly at Everleigh.

"He can hear us," I lower my voice and she takes a deep breath.

"I guess it's now or never then. Right?" I can see the anxiety in her eyes.

I reach out, subtly squeezing her free hand as she downs her drink. "I'm right here with you."

She nods. "I just have to walk past him, hope that he asks me to join him, and then find a good time to excuse myself to the bathroom, hope he follows me where we both jump him. I hate hope." She scowls.

"I won't take my eyes off you. You'll be safe." I squeeze her hand one last time watching her head off in the direction of the ghost of her past. I haven't voiced my concerns to her but I'm worried. She said it herself this plan relies a lot on hope, we have no idea how Michael will react.

My nerves are eased ever so slightly when I notice him talking to Everleigh. I can see the anxiety radiating from her as she slides into the booth next to him.

I drink from my water, watching the two out the corner of my eye. I see her tense when he places a hand on her thigh, sitting closer to her, my hand tightens on the glass and it takes every ounce of control to not run over there and cut his hand off for ever touching her.

It's a long ten minutes before Everleigh rises from her seat excusing herself and making her way to the bathroom. We share a nod as she passes me and I wait...

and wait...

and wait.

Michael Knotts never passes me.

I turn back around and it's impossible to miss the smirk plastered on his face staring directly at me, a challenge in his eyes. *This isn't good.* I turn back to the bathrooms but there's no sign of Everleigh. My heart races. *Maybe she's in the bathroom. Don't panic.* I'm about to go find her when the blonde women who were with Michael trap me in place. I politely tell them to move but neither of them do, I'm stuck constantly pushing their hands off my body, my eyes trained on the hallway to the bathrooms. I break free of their grasps rushing to the bathroom. It's been too long.

The hallway is dark as I look around, my eyes catching on the phone lying face down on the floor. *Please no.* I crouch down picking it up, hesitantly turning it around, the collage background one I'm all too familiar with. "Everleigh," I whisper hoping that she's hiding in the shadows. I don't expect an answer yet all of me is hoping I'll get one. I'm met with silence.

My eyes dart around the hallway connecting with Michael's once again, his smirk firmly planted on his face. *Now's not the time. Find Everleigh.* I clench my hands tight, pushing open the bathroom door but before I can enter, my eyes catch on the fire escape.

The open fire escape.

No. Please no! I run out the door into the empty alleyway. Empty except for the simple white shoulder bag laying on the ground, the chain glistening from the single streetlamp at the end of the alleyway.

I pick the bag up, staring at it like it will give me answers. I take the slightest bit of comfort in not seeing a body anywhere. How did this happen? I took my eyes off her for one second and someone took her. I have no doubt that Michael Knotts has everything to do with this. I push away the need to run back inside and force him to tell me where she is by any means necessary, instead opting for calling Camilla using Everleigh's phone.

"Finished already? That was quick." Camilla's chirpy voice is a contrast for how I'm feeling.

"Camilla..."

"Tylan?" Her tone changes immediately, her worry filtering through the phone. "Where's Everleigh?"

"I don't know," I whisper the next part not wanting to make the truth a reality. "She's gone."

"What do you mean?"

"I took my eyes off her for one second and someone took her." My voice cracks despite my best efforts to stay neutral.

"Fuck. Meet us at the basement now." She pauses before adding, "We'll find her Tylan." Followed by silence. We'll find her...but what if we're too late?

Chained

Everleigh

It feels like a thousand pins are stabbing at my head, made even worse whenever I try to open my eyes, my arms and legs are heavy; I feel like I'm paralysed. The grogginess in my head starts to fade as I force my eyes to blink open into a cold dim room, the scent of death making my stomach churn.

I groan, pushing up onto wobbly arms, sitting up ever so slightly so I can look around the tiny empty room, the only thing in it is the single lightbulb hanging above me casting a warm glow in the otherwise freezing room. I try to pull my legs towards me stopping at the sound of chains. My heart races as I call out in a whisper, knowing in my heart that I'm not going to get an answer. "Tylan." Silence. "Tylan!" Silence. "Tylan?" My voice turns into a plea but there's still no answer.

I sit up more crying out at the sharp pain in my side. My head snaps down, my shaky hand touching the dark stain on my dress. It's too dark to see it but I know it's blood. *That motherfucker stabbed me.*

I push through the pain, reaching down to feel the steel cuff locked tight around my ankle keeping me chained to the wall like a wild animal ready to attack. I fumble around my hair searching for a bobby pin, cursing silently when I remember Tylan rushing me before I could put any in. My mind races, filling with doubt. *Did Tylan do this? Did he set me up? Was I stupid enough to let him lower the walls around my heart? What if—No!* I shake the thoughts out my head, pressing one hand tight to the bleeding wound as I push myself to stand shakily, taking a second to gain my balance.

I massage my temple chasing the oncoming migraine away, wincing when flakes of dry blood flutter onto my eyelashes as I do. I take a deep breath my entire body riddled with pain, walking to the door a few steps away. Delusion makes me think it would open but it doesn't stop me from trying.

I twist the handle and push nearly tripping over my own feet when it opens into a narrow unlit staircase. I huff out a disbelieving laugh not thinking as I run out the door. I make it just past the threshold before my ankle is yanked back. I fall hard, agony rippling through my body, my head hitting the hard, luckily blunt, wooden steps. I slowly roll onto my back lying on top of the cold concrete floor staring into pitch blackness, berating myself for ever letting my guard down.

I don't know how long I lay there clutching at my side feeling the warm blood dripping down my legs until I'm lying in my own puddle of blood, granted it's only actually a few drops but this isn't how this was supposed to go – Michael Knotts was meant to be the one lying in his own pool of blood not me.

Anger courses through my veins as I force myself to stand up again, holding tight onto the door frame. "Where are you, you coward?!" I scream needing to see the monster holding me captive. "What are you scared of?!" Even if he's not on the other side of the door at the top of the stairs he has to be watching, there's normally cameras in this situation, right? I squint searching every corner of both the room and the hallway looking for a single red light mocking me, but there isn't one.

I close my eyes, resting my forehead on the door frame as a fresh wave of pain passes through my head. I jump at the sound of footsteps stalking towards me from the darkness, squinting at the shadows lurking a few feet away.

"What's the matter, Doll? I thought you liked being chained up." His dark chuckle echoes in the small space. I stand up straight, glaring at the figure, masking my pain. *You're not weak, Everleigh.* I chant to myself despite how weak my body is, but I've been through worse, I can get through a little stab wound.

He stalks towards me, evil radiating around him, his eyes scanning my body. "You're pretty. I can see why my boss wants you." *Wait. His boss?* My eyes snap up to the man now standing directly in front of me, his menacing smirk etched to his face. A face I don't recognise.

"Who are you?" I wince at how small my voice is.

He doesn't even acknowledge me as he speaks. "You're lucky my boss wants you alive for now." His fingers grip my chin in a harsh grip pushing my cheeks together causing me to pout. "You'll look even prettier drowning in your own blood." My glare doesn't falter. "Cat got your tongue, Doll?" His chuckle is nothing but evil when he lets my face go, flicking my bottom lip with his thumb as he does. I take the opportunity and spit at him. His grin drops as he wipes his chin, his eyes surprisingly calm. My heart races, realisation slowly dawning. That was a terrible choice. My head snaps to the side at the force of his slap, the sound echoing in the empty space. I reach my hand up gently touching the warming skin. "Get some rest. You're going to need it." I watch as he walks back into the darkness he came from.

I need to find a way out and fast.

I'm jolted awake, screaming at the sharp pain coming from my side. I don't know how or when I fell asleep but all of me wishes this was just another nightmare and I'll wake up in Tylan's arms surrounded by his warmth and non-stop kisses...I miss him.

I open my eyes, another scream ripping from my throat as another sharp twinge rushes through me. Staring back at me are the black eyes of my captor, his hand holding a scalpel hovering over the wound on my side. His arrogant smirk forever painted on his face. "You ruined the fun, Doll. But your screams are music to my ears."

"I thought your boss told you not to hurt me." I try to glare at him through the pain that rushes through me as I sit up until we're face to face.

"You're wrong, Doll. He said I could do whatever I want as long as you're alive when you get to him." He traces the scalpel down my cheek, taunting me. "And the best part?" He leans in to whisper in my ear, "No one's coming to rescue you." His evil maniacal laugh echoes around the room.

I don't have time to dwell on the thought that I may be alone in this, I need to focus all my energy on getting out of here. I keep my eyes trained on the scalpel glistening with my blood, I need to find a way to distract the man in front of me. I need him to let his guard down so that I can overpower him, all I need to do is grab the scalpel and turn it on him; it's just like a knife but smaller and I'm a master when it comes to knives. It sounds simple – books and movies always make it seem simple – but this is real life and by the look in his eyes this definitely isn't his first time.

I look into his eyes, masking the fear threatening to overwhelm me. "You're wrong. I have plenty of people who will not rest until they find me." I lean into his face refusing to back down. "You better hope you're not here when they do."

He laughs in my face. "I'm not scared of them."

"It's not them you should be scared of."

"Go on." His face is nothing short of amusement.

"You have no idea who I am." I feel my own lips moving up into a smirk, my mask of confidence refusing to back down.

"You underestimate me." I let out a hiss at the scalpel dragging across my cheek, the metallic taste hitting my tongue as the warm trail runs down my face.

"You're the Polaroid Reaper." I gasp, my mask breaking apart at the seams, his smirk transforming into a mocking pout. "Didn't expect that, did you?"

"H-How—" I make the split decision to change the course of the chat. "Who?"

He rolls his eyes at me. "Don't be cute." He stands up, towering over me menacingly. "Get up." I stay firmly planted on the floor, refusing to give him the satisfaction of following his orders. If he thinks I'm going to do what he says he has another thing coming. I can't work out what he mutters under his breath but the next second his grip on my upper arm is tight enough that I'm pretty certain he cuts off circulation dragging me up, my feet tripping over the chains. I lean my weight on one hip trying to ease the pain in my side. It works...until my arms are yanked behind my back, coarse thick rope bounding my wrists together, cutting into the delicate skin. "Don't even think of trying to run."

That option becomes increasingly favourable when the steel cuff releases my ankle but, even if I did run, I wouldn't get far, not with my hands tied behind my back. I don't fight as he drags me out the room and into the darkness he comes and goes from. I try to look around to get my bearings, trying to find an escape route but I can't see anything other than darkness.

We stop briefly outside a locked door, giving me a second to steady my footing, my eyes focused on the hands of my captor when he pulls a key out of his pocket, turning it in a lock moments before I'm pushed into a brighter room; the overhead light illuminating a small stage-like feature in the centre of the room, a hook hanging from the ceiling, a small couch sitting to the side facing the "stage", a cupboard placed on the other side of the room. I swallow the lump in my throat, anxiety rising within me.

"This is where the real fun happens." I may not be facing him but I can hear his smirk, excitement evident in his voice. "Take your place on the stage." My feet remain planted tight to the spot, my mind racing with solutions, one standing out more than the others. The scalpel is sticking out of his pocket, if I get close enough I can grab it and conceal it in my hands until I have time to cut myself loose. I take my opportunity when he shoves me onto the stage, close enough to me that I can reach in and grab it. My heart races as I close my hands around the warmed metal praying he doesn't notice. My arms are forced up another scream ripping out of me, he hooks my wrists to the ceiling, my shoulders twisting painfully, forcing me to grip my hands tight around the scalpel digging into my hands.

He stands back, that fucking smirk taunting me, his eyes shining with satisfaction as he admires his handiwork. I keep my eyes locked on his refusing to back down and show any more weakness. My screams are already giving him too much but there's only so much pain one can endure in silence.

He stalks behind me to the cupboard I saw when I walked in, I focus my attention on listening to him, hearing the creak of the cupboard door opening, followed by some clanging and what sounds like a knife being sharpened. I take a deep breath mentally preparing myself for the pain about to happen. I hear his footsteps echoing around the room as he makes his way back to me. Shuddering at the cold sharp tip of the knife tracing around my back, silently cursing myself for wearing an open back dress. Is it even still "tonight"? Come to think of it, I have no idea what time or day it is. Has it only been a few hours? Or has it been days?

My thoughts of time are interrupted by the cold knife digging into my back, the blood dripping down from the small wound. "You like stabbing innocent people. Why don't we see how much you like it?"

"They're not innocent." My reply is nothing but a hiss when the knife is struck into my back and yanked back out. There's no break in between the cuts, scratches, sometimes stabs of the knife into my back, none of them going deep enough to scar, just enough for them to sting, the pain overwhelming me. I scream out, struggling against the binds desperate to get away.

A breath of relief escapes me when he steps off the stage in silence. My senses are heightened, my back warm and sticky, blood trailing down into a puddle at my feet, the smell of blood strong in the empty room. I can physically feel my body trying to shut the pain out, tingling as it tries to heal itself. Dried tears stuck to my cheeks. I stare ahead, my arms now a soothing ache compared to my back. I need to find a way out of here and fast. Before I end up dead.

Chapter Twenty-Three

The Basement

Tylan

Why did I take my eyes off her? Why didn't I stay with her? What if I never see her again? It's been four days since I lost her, my mind is racing with thoughts of Everleigh and what she could be going through right now. I feel like I've failed her. I was there to protect her, to make sure nothing happened to her, but that psychopath took her anyway. I let my guard down and now she could be dead.

"I think I know where she is." I'm sat around the poker table in the basement with Camilla and the twins, we all look like zombies having had no rest for three nights, we've spent every second of the past few days trying to find her. The air around us is thick with anxiety, every single person in this room loves Everleigh in some way – I just hope Everleigh knows that. I hope she's hanging on for us, for herself.

"Don't keep us waiting, Camilla." I turn to face her, looking at the map that she passes me. It's full of multiple lines and crosses but one building stands out, circled in red. I recognise it straight away, the blood draining from my face. *Is this my fault?*

"What is it Tylan?" Camilla's voice remains calm but I can see the panic in her eyes.

"It's my father's old office."

"Why would he take her to your father's office?" Her gaze is full of blame.

"Why don't you go ask him yourself?" I leap off the chair grabbing my jacket.

"Before we go you have to tell us why Everleigh is so important to Michael." Callum looks between all of us in confusion.

Camilla wastes no time in replying. "He was her therapist after her family's death and a short while after you killed your parents—"

"Wait, what?" I interrupt her, the information shocking me. All my research implied that Everleigh's foster parents, the twins' real parents, were good people who were killed in a random mugging. "Why would you kill your parents?"

"You'll have to ask Everleigh when we find her." Callum avoids my eyes.

"As I was saying. He helped her for a while but then he started to get handsy with her and started to ask her for favours. She got out, threatened to turn him in but he has money. He said he would ruin her if she ever told anyone. The man's powerful enough that he can make up lies and people would still believe him over one of his victims. But how do you know him?" Camilla directs that question at me.

All their eyes turn to me. "He's blackmailing me." I don't elaborate. I can't. Not until I tell Everleigh the truth, she deserves to hear it first.

"I have a good idea. Why don't we continue this conversation in the car on the way to finding her?" Freddie glares at all of us, anger radiating from him.

"We can't just barge in without a plan," Callum speaks calmly to his brother.

"Like hell we can't!"

"Freddie!" Camilla slams her hands on the table forcing him to look at her. "We don't know how many people he has working under him. If we barge in we could be ambushed and none of us want that."

Freddie closes his eyes. "What's the plan then?" Silence. None of us have any idea what we're up against but we need to come up with a plan and fast.

It didn't take us long to agree to a plan, it may not be the best but none of us acknowledge that fact. We sit in silence as Callum drives us to the secluded office building in the abandoned part of Little Bray. My mind races with the possibilities of what we could be walking into. The hold this woman has on me is crazy. I feel my heart breaking at the mere thought of her injured or even dead all because I failed at protecting her.

Callum stops the car behind the line of trees at the side of the building, out of view from anyone inside. "Where would she be?" Callum whispers looking out the window in the direction of the building.

"Would they be as cliche as the basement?" Camilla is unusually quiet as she flicks through the photos and blueprints of the office building. I hated that basement; I've never understood why it was built when it's just a narrow hallway with a singular room and storage closet. Even so...

"It's our best bet." I step out the car, the others climbing out after me. We all stand together facing the building when a blood-curdling scream rips through the silent night. "Everleigh?!" I sprint towards the house, the sound of my name floating through the air from the others.

"Tylan stop!" I'm about halfway to the building when Camilla grabs my arm, stopping me where I am.

"But Everleigh—"

"I know. But she's alive—"

"She's in pain!"

"But she's alive! And she will be when we get her out but we can't rush it. Remember the plan." Camilla grips my arms forcing eye contact. "Do it for her. I hate that I'm even saying this but she needs you more than ever, Tylan."

I take a deep breath, nodding as the twins reach us, another scream echoing from the building. "Let's stop stalling and get our girl."

We all sneak towards the building, splitting up to take both the front and back entrance. Camilla and I take the back, expecting the door to be locked but instead it opens with ease. We look at each other uncertainty starting to seep in when we're interrupted by thuds from within. I enter first looking around thoroughly only walking further when I'm certain it's clear. Camilla follows behind me, shutting the door quietly, we hear the twins entering from the front just as quietly.

We meet up at the door to the basement, the pained screams getting louder the closer we get. I open the door as quietly as I can onto the old wooden staircase I know all too well leading into pitch blackness.

"I'll go first," I whisper to the others before making my way down the staircase, stopping a few steps away from the bottom at the loud creak that echoes around the hallway. I freeze, anxiety burning me from the inside, my mind transporting me back to one of my worst times here when I was fourteen.

I shouldn't have come here. I thought telling my dad about my good grades, for once, would make him stop treating me like I ruined his life. But no. The second the lift door opened his face was screaming anger. What did I do wrong this time? He stormed towards me, gripping my arm tight enough to leave fingerprints, dragging me down the wooden staircase into the singular room whilst I pleaded with him to let me go. It didn't work.

His new thing is to tie me to the hook in the ceiling, ever since I fought back a couple of months ago. That's where I am now, my arms tied above my head, my dad standing in front of me holding his beloved whip, scowling at me in hatred. "I knew we should've given you up years ago." I breathe through the sharp sting left behind by the whip, I've been through this enough times that I've learnt how to control the pain. "You never learn," he spits out. "You're still a brat. Do I not give you enough money to stop pestering me?" I hiss in a breath at the leather hitting my skin repeatedly.

For the next couple of minutes the only sound in the room is the leather ripping my skin apart but they only get worse when he speaks up again. "Like mother like son. I give your whore of a mother all the money she could want and she still cheats on me." I can't hold back my pained grunts or struggles, each whip harder than the one before. I close my eyes against the pain, waiting for it to finally stop.

The funny thing is, my mother never cheated on him and he knew that.

I snap out of it, the screams having lowered to whimpers, reaching the bottom of the stairs I head through the darkness the cries growing louder with each step.

I stop outside the open door, staying hidden in the shadows. The sight in front of me has my heart aching. A man I don't recognise straddles Everleigh, pinning her to the floor on her front, a knife pressed against her throat. I glance over her body, a mix of dried and fresh blood stains her usually pale body but the sight of her back is what really makes my blood boil, covered in a mix of both deep and shallow slashes, some messily patched up, there's not even an inch of white on her back just multiple shades of red.

I move my eyes up to her face, a singular healing scratch mars her cheek, but her eyes...her eyes are distant. She's in a state I've never seen before, it's almost like she's given up. "Are you coming in?"

My eyes snap to the face of the man causing her all this pain, a smug smirk stuck on his face. Anger courses through my veins – by the time we leave he'll be dead. I take a breath wrapping my hand around the gun in my back pocket, pulling it out and stepping into the light. "Tylan?" Ever-leigh's voice breaks, her eyes focused on me, lighting up ever so slightly.

He presses the knife closer to her throat breaking the skin as I step closer. "One wrong move and I'll slice her throat open." I stop in place listening to the three pairs of quiet footsteps behind me but the soon to be dead man can't hear them.

"Just give me her, alive, and we can all walk out of here no one needs to get hurt even more than they already are."

He chuckles. "That's not going to happen. I have a lot of money riding on this one."

My hand tightens on the gun in my hand when he strokes her hair. "Get your hands off her," I growl, narrowing my eyes at him.

"£50,000 and you have a deal." His hands grip her hair forcing her to look directly at me. She shakes her head as best as she can, so small that I nearly miss it. I don't get the chance to answer. Camilla rushes past me in a blur, wrestling the man off her, causing the knife to nick Everleigh's neck. I focus my attention on her trying to pull herself away from them and I can hear Camilla struggling but I don't even have a choice to make.

I rush to Everleigh dropping down next to her. "Bubbles?"

She turns her head to me pushing herself up onto her knees crying out in agony. I stroke her knotted hair back from her face, tears running down her cheeks as she reaches her hand out to touch my face gently. "Are you really here?"

My heart breaks at how broken she sounds. "I am. You're safe now." I press a kiss to her forehead letting her collapse against me. I hold her close to me keeping my hands away from her back. She cries into my shoulder and I take the opportunity to look over her shoulder to the others struggling with the soon to be dead man, at least until Camilla hits him with a heavy paperweight knocking him out.

Silence.

No one says a thing as I hold Everleigh tight, her silent cries soaking my t-shirt. Camilla looks over at me catching her breath. Freddie is standing over the man looking down at him with hatred. Callum glances at Everleigh's back before storming out the house. "Ready to go home?" I whisper so only she can hear. She nods against my shoulder.

I glance at Camilla and Freddie and then at the man laying between them, unable to stop the anger from rising within when he starts to stir. "Take her to the car. I'll be right behind you." I gently move Everleigh off me so that I can stand up. "Do you think you can stand?" She shrugs, holding her arms out towards me. I hold her hands keeping her steady as she stands, crying out in agony.

"It hurts!" I don't let her stop until she's standing, leaning against me.

"I know, Bubbles. We'll get you to Summer but for now go with Camilla and Freddie, I'll be right behind you." She gives me one last tight squeeze. Freddie walks over to us, letting her lean against him instead. I watch them leave, her face scrunching up in agony.

Camilla follows them, stopping to face me when she reaches the threshold. "What are you going to do?"

"Kill him. No one hurts my girl and lives." A flash of longing passes through her eyes before she follows after the others. The man on the floor groans, bringing my anger to the forefront of everything. I walk over to him calmy, crouching besides him. "You should've taken my offer. And for the record she's worth way more than £50,000." I let myself go, taking all my anger out on him – anger at him, anger at the situation, anger at Michael Knotts, anger at my parents, anger at myself. My fists hit his face and I don't stop until he's unrecognisable, his body still. Once I'm satisfied and have calmed down, I leave the room heading back to my girl.

The walk to the car is short but throughout it all I can't get over the uncomfortable feeling that I'm being watched. I look around but in the darkness of the night I can't see a single thing other than the lights from the car peeking through the trees. I shake the feeling off, opening the back door of the car. Callum is behind the wheel staring out into the distance, Freddie is in the passenger seat typing furiously on his phone, Camilla is behind Callum, stroking Everleigh's hair as she lays across the back seats her head on Camilla's lap, eyes closed.

"Everleigh?" I talk softly to not scare her, watching her eyes flutter open. It takes a minute for her eyes to focus on me but when she notices me she shoots up, wincing at the movement. I quickly get in the car shutting the door behind me. She wastes no time in lying back down, this time with her head on my lap. This is what I never knew I needed in my life, this beautiful woman. I've never felt so honoured or lucky before, but no matter what I feel I know it won't last so for now I hold onto this feeling, treasuring it.

Alone

Everleigh

I don't know how long I've been stuck down here dangling from the ceiling like one of those carcases in a butcher shop, I can feel my body shutting down. My captor hasn't offered me any food or nearly as much water as I need. I've lost count of the number of times he's been down here to rip my back apart, but each time he cleans up the mess on my back placing temporary bandages on them to keep me from bleeding out.

I don't think of my own death often, mostly because I have no plans of leaving this world until I find the man who ruined my life, but with each slash of the knife to my back I find myself wanting to just slip away. It's unexpected but in this moment I'm not afraid of death, I'd be happy to go just so I could escape this pain. I'm losing hope fast that I'll ever get out of here.

I really am alone.

After the first session I tried so hard to get out. I didn't know he was going to come back to stop the bleeding, I thought I was in the clear. I had the scalpel in my hands sawing away as best as I could at the rope binding my wrists. I started to get there when he came back, I thought I was fast enough to hide it but I wasn't. My punishment? He ripped it out my hand and used it to slash deeper into my open wounds.

I felt so helpless.

My plan was working but I let my guard down and rushed it, just like I've been doing a lot lately. Ever since Tylan started helping me. I know in my heart none of this is his fault, he's not the one forcing my hand in these situations, it's me. I'm jeopardising my own life and for what? I realise now that I'm standing at the edge of the cliff, one more step and I'll be falling into the depths below. I was beginning to think I'd have Tylan to catch me at the bottom, to rescue me from myself, but now. Now I'm not so sure. I'm feeling even more alone than I ever have before.

No. I'm not going to do this. I'm not going to give up. I'm not going to let some stranger take my life. I struggle in my binds searching for a way out, ignoring the sharp tugs at my back, with no luck I take a different approach trying to pull my wrists off the hook. I lift up onto my tiptoes until I'm practically floating, further than I managed in the other times I tried. With a few more twists of my wrists I manage to lift them off the hook, I drop them back behind my back, my shoulders drooping in relief. I ignore the pain running throughout my back finding the end of the rope, it takes a lot of effort but eventually I loosen the ties and the rope drops to the floor. I rub my red raw wrists searching the room. I need a weapon. I turn around my eyes drawn to the cupboard. Bingo! I rush over as fast as I can, which isn't very fast at all and then my luck runs out.

The door slams open and I can hear the heavy footsteps running towards me. I try to leap out the way but I'm not fast enough. I'm pinned to the floor, wiggling desperately, trying to buck him off me. "Did you not learn your lesson last time, Doll?" I don't stop struggling not even when the knife in his hand slashes one of my previous wounds but he doesn't stop either, the slashes relentless. He gives me a brief second to catch my breath as I slump into the floor.

I begin to relax and that's when he drives the knife deep into one of my closed wounds, a blood-curdling scream ripping from my throat. He doesn't stop, my screams spurring him on, not until we both hear a creak from just outside the room. He moves the knife to my throat whispering in my ear. "Don't say a word." I don't. The room is cast in silence besides my whimpers as my body is consumed by the pain.

I look towards the darkness, convincing myself I was just hearing things. Trying even harder when Tylan steps into the light. I zone out of what happens next, I think I might mutter something but I'm not sure, my mind's trying to play tricks on me. Is this what death is like? Do you see the faces of the special people in your life? Before I'm aware of what's happening, the weight on top of me is gone and I'm pulling myself along the floor, stopped by Tylan. I lift myself up onto my knees gently placing my hand on his cheek.

He's real.

He's really here.

He saved me.

I collapse against him, unable to stop the tears. I sob into his shoulder, his hand stroking my hair but he refuses to touch my back and that just makes me cry harder at how hard he's trying not to hurt me.

I don't want to leave but when he tells me to leave with Freddie and Camilla I don't have the energy to argue. I know it won't be long until I'm in his arms again. Callum doesn't look at any of us as we climb into the car, he just stares out the window a haunted look coating his face. I lay down on my side, resting my head on Camilla's lap and she strokes my hair in the comforting way she always does when I'm down. I let my eyes drift closed, the need for sleep overwhelming me.

My eyes are only closed for a couple of seconds when there's a soft tap on my legs. "Everleigh?" I sit up immediately at the soft voice, wincing at the pain, but I ignore it, lying back down with my head on Tylan's lap once he's in the car, his scent and body is so familiar that I can't help but to drift off to sleep.

I'm woken up, whimpering, when I feel an arm softly wrap around the middle of my back. "I know, Bubbles. I'm sorry." Tylan's voice is full of guilt as he presses a kiss to my forehead. He carries me through my house to my bedroom, placing me on my feet next to my bed. “Is it okay if I take your dress off?”

“Why?” I wrap my arms around my body, feeling way too vulnerable in this moment.

“Summer’s here to properly look your injuries over. She’s going to need to see all of them.” I can’t stand seeing the sympathy in his eyes as he looks down at me.

“Will you stay with me?” I hate myself for showing this much vulnerability but I don’t have the energy to pretend like I’m okay.

“Of course I will.” I can feel his gaze on my face trying to get my eyes to meet his but I can’t. I give him a small nod and he tugs the straps of my dress down. I guess in a weird way I should be thankful that I picked out this dress, I hate to imagine how much worse this would be if I had any type of fabric dragging down my back right now. I shiver at the thought. Tylan rubs his hand up and down my arm, pulling my dress down my legs, leaving me in nothing but my little red lace panties – they were meant to be a surprise for Tylan, a little thank you for helping me rid the world of one of the men I despise more than anything, but now I just feel exposed. So much so that I cross my arms across the front of my body trying to cover as much as possible.

The room is silent other than Muffin’s soft snores coming from my pillow. It’s so quiet that I can hear muffles from the hushed conversation coming from the guest bedroom next to mine, the blood rushing through my head makes it impossible to hear what they're saying.

Tylan crouches by my feet, my eyes catching on his guilt ridden ones, a pair of my black jogging bottoms scrunched up ready for me to step into. I tentatively place a hand on his shoulder stepping into them and allowing him to pull them up for me. He stays on his knees our stares never breaking apart, he opens his mouth to speak but I place a finger on his lips, as perfect as I remember, shaking my head. I can't do conversations right now. I don't trust myself not to speak my mind, not when the self-deprecating voice is the dominant one. I look away climbing into my bed and getting comfortable on my front, taking comfort from Muffin's purring right by my head.

The bed dips beside me, a gentle hand caressing my hair just as a soft knock sounds from my door, followed by the creak of the door opening. The nauseating bubbly voice of Summer fills the room. "Hey, Everleigh. You know we should really talk more instead of me just having to check up on you professionally. Don't you ag—Oh my god!" She stops at the side of my bed, staring at my back in horror.

"Summer!" Tylan hisses from behind me.

"Sorry." There's a nervous tint to the huff she lets out. "But have you seen the state of your back? It looks like most of these wounds have been sealed, terribly I might add, and then slashed open again. It's entirely re—"

"Summer!" Tylan's voice booms around the room making me flinch. I've never heard him so agitated before.

Summer's eyes open wide. "Sorry. I guess the twins are right, they always say I don't think before I speak." She lets out another nervous huff playing with the ring on her finger. She shakes herself out of it, straightening out and looking intently at my back. "I can't get a good enough look at all your injuries until we clean your back."

"No!" I widen my eyes, shaking my head. Tylan softly strokes my hair trying to calm me down. "That'll hurt."

Summer switches her weight between her feet, twiddling with her thumbs. "Yes, it will. But I can't determine how bad your injuries are with all the blood on your back."

"It will just be for a few minutes, Bubbles. I'll be gentle. Unless you'd prefer Summer to do it for you?"

I mull over his words trying to prepare myself. Eventually I shake my head. "No, I want you to do it."

"Here, use these. They'll help disinfect the wounds as well." I watch Summer pass Tylan a bunch of wipes before diverting my eyes to Muffin sitting on top of the pillow I long to hold through the pain. I'm close to pushing him off said pillow when a cushion from my bay window is shoved into my arms. I look up to see Summer holding a you're-going-to-need-this look on her face.

"I'm sorry, Bubbles." I take a deep breath before I feel the first touch on my shoulder across the first of my wounds. I can't stop the whimpers from escaping, gripping the cushion so tightly that my nails break the cover. It feels like it's been hours by the time I hear the two words I've been waiting for. "All done." I let out the long breath I didn't even realise I was holding, relaxing my death grip on the cushion. Tylan places a soft kiss on top of my hair before I feel him leaving the bed and walking to my dresser, I assume he's throwing the wipes in the little bin but I don't have the energy to turn around and check.

Summer leans over the bed observing my back intently. "It's good news, they're all superficial and should heal by themselves including the one on your cheek and the one on your neck, other than these two that are deeper. I'll stitch them up for you but they will probably scar." Great. That's another couple of scars to add to my collection.

It doesn't take long for Summer to stitch up the wounds she was talking about. "I'm just going to put a bandage on some of the bigger ones just to stop you from accidentally reopening them. You will need to use this dressing and change them twice a day until they're healed." She places the dressing and a load of bandages on my bedside table before placing some on my back. "If you have any pain just take the regular dose of painkillers." She gives me one of her bright smiles before leaving Tylan, who's now back on the bed behind me, and I alone. The silence between us is usually comfortable, relaxing even, but now it's just awkward.

"Tylan?" I whisper, unable to handle the awkwardness for a second longer.

"Yes?" He gently places his hand on my waist, squeezing gently, his thumb rubbing soothing circles careful to avoid any of my fresh scars.

"I want to be alone tonight." As soon as the last word leaves my mouth his hand stops. We sit in silence again but I don't dare turn my head, I don't want to see what he's thinking.

"Are you sure?" He tries to cover it but I can hear the tiniest hitch in his voice. I nod, my energy slipping. His hand leaves my waist just as fast and I feel the weight leaving my bed. "I'll be on the couch. Goodnight, Everleigh." The last thing I feel is his lips against my forehead before I'm left alone to my thoughts. I didn't want to tell him to leave but I needed to. When I was in that cold room I came to a realisation, one that I'm scared to allow to come true and right now I just need the time and space to think about us. About whether love is worth it.

Chapter Twenty-Five

Bonnie and Clyde

Tylan

This isn't how it was meant to go. Everleigh's been different ever since we got her out of that basement. I tell myself it's because of what she had to go through but my gut's telling me a different story. It killed me to see her in pain but it hurt even more when I was causing it even if I needed to do it to help her. I saw a side of her tonight I've never seen before; when I first saw her my fierce tigress was nowhere in sight. She was replaced by a lamb, caught by the wolf. I'll never forget how helpless she looked. I need my fearless warrior back and I will do anything I can to make that happen.

I sit down on the small couch, staring at the full liquor cabinet in front of me. I've never been one for drinking my problems away but that cupboard is looking more and more inviting the longer I stare at it. I've never been more grateful for a distraction than when Callum walks in. At first he doesn't notice me as he walks to the kitchen but he quickly does a double take. "Tylan? Shouldn't you be with Everleigh?"

"She wants to be alone." I go back to staring at the bottle of scotch that stares right back at me, calling to me.

I hear his sigh followed by the sound of a cupboard opening and closing. "She's just being Everleigh." My staring contest is broken by Callum's muscular figure opening the cabinet and pulling out the bottle, pouring the perfect amount into two crystal glasses. He hands one to me. "One drink won't kill you." I take it but I don't drink it, instead I just stare at the amber liquid. I hear the cupboard closing before the couch dips beside me.

"I shouldn't. What if something happens to her?" I continue my latest staring contest, getting increasingly closer to losing it.

"Nothing will happen to her here. She has the four of us to protect her, plus Summer...And let's not forget Muffin."

I turn my head to him, raising an eyebrow. "Muffin would not help in protecting her, he'll roll over for belly rubs."

His drink pauses halfway to his lips. "He hates belly rubs. He's always scratching and hissing at all of us." He lets out a small chuckle. "Even her cat likes you." I try to decipher the meaning behind that statement as Callum sips from his drink. I eventually give up the fight and take a sip from my own glass.

We sit in silence, both of us deep in our own thoughts. I haven't had the chance to think back to that night up until now, but now it comes back in full force, I feel like I'm back in the club all over again. I looked away for a mere second but that was all it took for that vulture to snatch her away. I replay the night trying to find a way I could've prevented it, when in reality the only way I could've done that was to follow her to the bathroom. Yes, she would've been mad at me but it would've been a hundred times better than what actually happened. I never should've agreed to that night, I should've insisted we waited a little longer. I down the rest of my drink in one go.

I place my glass on the coffee table with a sigh, resting my elbows on my knees, my hands clasped together in a prayer position against my lips. "As much as I hate to admit this, you know her better than me. Can I fix this with her?"

"There's nothing to fix." He places his hand on my shoulder. "She might freak out for a bit because she's falling for you but her life is crazy, has been for the past five, nearly six years. I don't know what her life was like before we met, but in the years I've known her the only men in her life to treat her properly has been me and Freddie but now she also has you. No one else can tell you what to do all I can say is that you need to speak to her, and sooner rather than later because I can promise you that she won't hesitate to push you away especially if her dominating voice is her self-deprecating one."

"Her self-deprecating voice?"

"She's always had it. It's the voice inside her that constantly beats her down until she shuts down completely and it's never easy to get her out of that mindset. The first time we noticed was the first time my parents...” He trails off refusing to finish his sentence.

“What did your parents do?”

“I’ll tell you the same thing I told you earlier. It’s her story to tell not mine. Ask her about it.” He gives me a friendly slap on the shoulder, standing up to go back upstairs. “For what it’s worth. You’re good for her Tylan.”

I don’t know when I managed to fall asleep but my body aches as I stand up, stretching from my uncomfortable sleep on the couch. I look towards the stairs wondering if Everleigh is awake, my conversation with Callum playing on repeat in my mind, I need to have a proper conversation with her, but where would I even start? I take a deep breath deciding to bite the bullet.

My knock on her door is answered by shuffles and soft groans, I don’t wait for an answer, pushing her door open and closing it behind me. I turn around to an image I was not expecting – Everleigh standing with her back to the full length mirror in the corner of her room, twisting her body to try to get the bandages off, her face scrunched in pain. I rush over grabbing her hands to stop her. “What are you doing?”

She rolls her eyes at me and I can’t help the miniscule smile forming on my face at the gesture I’m all too used to. “I need to change the bandages.”

"Let me do it." The change in her is instant when she looks into my eyes, her shoulders tensing and her breathing intensifying. "Everleigh. Talk to me." She shakes her head but instead of running away she turns her back to me, moving her hair over her shoulder to give me full access to her back. The awkward silence from last night returns, hanging thick in the air around us. I wish she would just talk to me, but I know I can't just push her or I'll drive her away completely. For now I relish in her trust in me as she allows me to help her.

I carefully peel away the bandages revealing the healing scratches making her back flush red. I take my time applying the cream, her face scrunching with sharp intakes of breath as I do, before placing new bandages on her back. Her face relaxes but her eyes stare at the reflection of the floor in the mirror. I place the final bandage on her back, placing a soft kiss to her shoulder.

"I want to kill him." Her voice is a mere whisper.

"Sorry, Bubbles. I beat you to that." I raise my eyes to her face in the mirror, her eyes widening.

"Why would you do that?"

"Because no one hurts my girl and gets away with it." The silence between us is agonising. I need my Everleigh back. I need the woman who snapped at me in the middle of the street when I nearly ran her off the road. I need the woman who can fight off a fully grown man without even trying. I need the woman who makes my heart race whenever she's nearby.

"I can't do this, Tylan." She avoids my eyes.

"Do what?" I rest my head on her shoulder staring at her through the mirror, slowly her eyes meet mine, silent tears running down her cheeks.

"This." She gestures between the two of us. "Us." She tries to step away from me but I hold onto her waist, careful not to touch her back.

"Why not?" This was not what I meant when I said I wanted her to make my heart race again.

She lets out a half sob, half laugh. "We're never going to work out. The detective and the serial killer? This isn't some silly little romance novel." She pushes my hands off her waist, walking as far away from me as she can. "I'm meant to be in jail. Or dead. Or in hiding. I'm not meant to be here." She stretches her arms out, a waterfall of tears running down her cheeks. "You're changing my story. You're making me into a hero but I'm no hero, I'm the villain."

"You are not a villain, Everleigh." I step towards her but she holds her hand up stopping me.

"I am. I'm the villain in this story and you're the hero. I'm not meant to get a happy ending, but you are. Being with me is just going to hold you back from that." She turns away from me, staring out her window.

I can't handle seeing her so broken, beating herself up over some fucked up thought. "What hero kills men to cover their own back?" I don't even realise what I said until it's too late.

She's staring at me, her eyes wide, tears never ending, her mouth dropped open. "What are you talking about?" she breathes out in disbelief.

"My life isn't all sunshine and rainbows. I already told you I'm not a detective because I want to be. I'm a detective because I need to be. I have a whole mountain of skeletons just waiting to be discovered."

Her eyes drop from mine, tears still falling, shaking her head. "That doesn't change anything. Being with me is just going to ruin your life. My foster parents ruined mine and now I've ruined the lives of every person I love."

"How did they ruin your life?"

She collapses onto the bay window, curling in on herself. "It started three months after I moved in. I thought they were accepting me as part of their family, they seemed like normal loving people. But I will never forget the first night they came into my room, pinned me down to the bed, stripped me, and..." She takes a shuddering breath. "That happened at least once a week, I was too weak to overpower them. The one time I tried they gave me this." She indicates the scar on her collarbone before, realising she's still topless, covering herself with a blanket. "I thought that once the twins killed them it would be over, their ugly truths would be revealed." She shrugs helplessly. "But no. They get painted as loving, wholesome people devastatingly killed in a mugging." She scoffs. "I will never get an apology from the people who made me this monster. So why should I apologise for becoming that monster?"

I walk over to her, crouching in front of her and, after she reluctantly agrees, help her into her favourite baggy hoodie. "Stop calling yourself a monster, a villain, or even a fucking psychopath. You're a survivor who was dealt a shit hand in life but you have nothing to apologise for."

"You don't get it." She looks me directly in my eyes, her tears dried up, her eyes lifeless. "I'm not sorry for what I've done and that's what makes me crazy. I have no sympathy for the men I've killed or for their families. The way I see it is that I did them a favour, I tried to reveal their truths." Her lips curl up in disgust as she looks at me. "But the detectives decided to cover it up, paint them as victims despite what they do. *You* call them victims, Tylan."

"It's not my choice. If it was then I'd shout it from the rooftops. Which is why I'm handing this in." I reach into my back pocket pulling out the folded piece of paper.

She takes it from me, reading it before looking back at me. "You're resigning?" I nod. "Why?"

"Because I want to help you in any way I can and I can't do that as a detective. I'll inevitably mess up somewhere and mess it up for both of us. I would much rather work and hide together, if you'll let me."

"I told you I can't do this and I mean it. I'm the Polaroid Reaper. I'm never going to get my own little bookstore. I'm never going to get my own little family. I'm never going to get that perfect husband. I'm never going to get to live the rest of my life with my friends by my side."

I hold onto her hands wrapped around her legs. "But you can have all that. That little voice inside here..." I tap her forehead gently. "Is making you doubt yourself and you're letting it win—"

"I realised something down in that basement." I look into her eyes, worry coursing through my veins. "You're making me lose who I am. A year ago I set out wanting to rid the world of these men and I was fully focused, but now I make mistakes because I just want to get back to you. I find myself wanting you to be there, killing them with me, not just cleaning up after me."

"Is that such a bad thing?" She lifts her eyes to meet mine and I shrug. "We could be like Bonnie and Clyde."

"You want to be a crime duo?" She tilts her head looking like the adorable powerful woman I know her as.

"If you'll let me. I'm resigning no matter what you say."

She takes me by surprise, uncurling herself to sit on her knees, her hands dragging my face to hers in a soft kiss, softer than all the previous ones we've shared. "As long as you're my Clyde, I'll be your Bonnie." The smile I love spreads across her face as I pull her towards me for another kiss and everything feels right again and that's all that matters in this moment.

Vultures

Tylan

It's been a long two weeks since I handed in my resignation; my superiors insisted that I stayed on the Polaroid Reaper case until my final day and I was more than happy to, after all I had to make sure I threw the team off enough that they'd never discover the truth. I officially handed my badge in fifteen minutes ago and now I'm packing up my personal items, which is nothing more than stationary and a couple of decorative pieces.

I'm interrupted by a knock on the open door. I look up to see Blake closing the door behind him. "We're good friends right, Tylan?"

"I think I'd describe it more as good work colleagues." I shrug, closing the cardboard box with my items in. "Why?"

"Why are you resigning? You're not one to give up." He eyes me suspiciously.

"It's not giving up. We've already spent too long trying to find her, one of us has to take the fall and as the leader that responsibility lands on me."

"I think we're closer than we think. You know that as well." He crosses his arms and a wave of uneasiness hits me. "Everleigh Carlton's alive isn't she?"

It takes everything in me to not react to that statement. I shoot him an amused look. "She's dead. I may have thought she could be a lead but we've seen her death certificate and no one's seen her since. Not one person."

He observes me in silence and I just stand there waiting for my world to come crashing down. But it doesn't. "You have a point." We stand there in awkward silence. "Where are you heading next then?"

"I have a friend who needs my help out in the country." I shrug. *I need to get out of here.* "Speaking of which I better get going before I'm late to my press conference."

"Consider this your warning, they're relentless today." He arches an eyebrow at me.

I pick my box of things off the desk. "Aren't they always?" My final farewell hangs in the air as I make my way to the station doors, the loud buzz of reporters creeping through the closed double doors. I take a deep breath before stepping outside and feeding myself to the vultures.

The space around me is filled with the raucous sounds of relentless questions, microphones and cameras thrust in my face as I make my way to the podium set up in the middle of the steps. I place my box behind me before turning back to face the crowd, holding my hand up to silence them. "I will not be answering any questions today, all you will get from me is what I am about to say." The buzz slowly quietens down. "As of today I am no longer part of the Little Bray police force. This does mean that I am stepping away from the Polaroid Reaper case and you will not be getting any information on that case from me. The Polaroid Reaper has been around for a little over fourteen months, throughout which she has killed a total of six men and we have had very little success in finding her." I take a breath preparing myself for my next statement. "As a detective I could not say what I am about to, but as a member of the public I am free to tell you the truth. Every man she has killed was killed because they were rapists. They had the money or connections to keep that side of themselves quiet but I will not stand for that any longer, their victims deserve justice. So I am putting out this call right now that if you have ever been a victim of a man, or woman, like this who has paid their way out you can reach out to me and I will make sure you get your justice. Thank you."

I turn around to pick up my box catching Blake's eyes. He looks pissed. I turn around pushing my way through the crowd, climbing into my car and making my way back to my penthouse. I drop the box on the floor by the entrance and waste no time in feeding Bailey who happily accepts it. I spend the rest of the day relaxing. Revealing the truth makes me feel ever so slightly lighter. Except now I have to worry about what my old team will find out. Did I make a mistake?

Chapter Twenty-Seven

I Want You

Everleigh

After two weeks of bed rest I'm practically shaking with the need to get out of here, the need to end Michael Knotts once and for all, the need to rid the world of the monsters hiding in plain sight. My body feels like it's going through withdrawal, my hands are constantly clenched trying to find the comfort of my knife that's not there. This whole situation has made me insufferable, I've lost count of the number of times I've snapped at everyone who's tried to help me with anything, I've given Tylan nothing but hell every time he's changed my bandages insisting that I can do them myself, when in reality I know it's not possible.

My mood swings to Tylan probably aren't helped by how sexually frustrated I am. Every night he comes over after taking care of Bailey and curls up in bed with me wearing nothing but a pair of boxers that show off everything. I've tried to initiate things just to get some relief but he shuts me down, insisting on waiting until I'm fully healed, but I'm desperate to feel him again, to be near him every second of the day. There's only so much a girl can control herself.

I've taken the rare morning I'm alone, whilst everyone else is off at work, or in Tylan's case to do a food shop, to catch up on reading. My mind keeps drifting to Tylan. He was hesitant to leave me alone, and deep down so was I, but I eventually got him to agree – it's good to know that my puppy dog eyes never let me down.

The low autumn sun shines through the bay window creating the perfect cosy lighting as I sit with my legs stretched, Muffin curled up on my lap. I feel so at ease in this moment that it puts me on edge, waiting for the bomb to explode but I shake it off for now, distracted by the sound of the door opening.

I tense for a split second before I catch a glimpse of Tylan's car sitting in the driveway and it's not long before he's bent over me, kissing my forehead tenderly. "Hey Bubbles. Did you miss me?"

"Hmm?" I tilt my head looking up at him, shaking my head. "No. I have the only man I need right here." I tap my finger on the book in my hands, failing to hide my grin.

"The only man you need, huh?" My grin widens at the sight of him towering over me, his eyebrow raised and arms crossed.

"Mhm. He really knows how to treat and fuck a woman properly. Real men just don't do it the same." I let out a dramatic sigh, looking away to hide my giggles when his eyes darken.

The weight on my lap disappears as I feel Tylan leaning over me, casting a shadow over my open book, trapping me in between his body and the seat. I lift my head only to be met with Tylan's face millimetres away from mine. "Are you trying to rile me up?"

I bat my eyelashes at him innocently. "Why would you think that?"

"Because," he grips my chin forcing me to look directly into his darkened ocean pools, "you're acting like a little brat who just wants to be fucked."

"Can you blame me? You haven't touched me in weeks." I glare at him playfully watching his eyes soften.

"I don't want to hurt you."

I shiver as his hand lightly runs down my back, running along the two raised scars. "You won't. I can go on top or you can bend me over, I don't care I just need you." I pull his face towards mine until our lips are touching in a frenzied kiss. The kiss is frantic, full of passion and need as our tongues explore each other. I wrap my arms around his neck pulling him impossibly closer to me, his wrapping around my waist. I pull away panting for breath and he takes the opportunity to dip his head, kissing my neck. I bite my lip tugging at his t-shirt until he pulls away for a split second to get it off. I run my finger down his chest, mumbling to myself. "How did I get so lucky?"

"I think you'll find I'm the lucky one," Tylan mumbles against my neck, biting and kissing down to the sweetheart neckline of my dress. I arch my back into him, desperate to get him to continue his trail down but instead all I get is his devilish smirk against my skin.

"Stop teasing me," I growl in frustration but he just chuckles at me.

"I'm not teasing. I'm worshipping my goddess." A flash of something, I can't tell what, flashes through his eyes so fast that I nearly miss it, but it does make me wonder if there's more to that statement than meets the eye. "Now shut up and take what I give you." I squeeze my legs together trying to ease the increasing pressure between them. It feels like forever before he pulls the straps of my dress down, kissing down my arms as he does.

There's not a single inch of my body that he leaves untouched, torturing me with kisses. I whimper when he kisses over my breasts, avoiding touching my hardening nipples. "Shh. I'll give you what you want..." He speaks softly, his kisses barely stopping. "Eventually."

I whine, feeling his smirk against my breasts. He wastes no time in taking my dress fully off leaving me in nothing but my comfy cotton panties, the ones that he's currently running his fingers along the waistband of.

"Fuck. You look so sexy in these," he breathes out.

"All these sexy lacy panties I own and you like my plain cotton ones?"

He looks up at me pressing delicate kisses along the waistband. "I love you in whatever you wear. You can make anything sexy."

"Even a rubbish bag?"

He hides his chuckle against my skin. "Yes. Even a rubbish bag." I hold my breath as his lips move back up to my most insecure part of my body, his kisses continuing along the roll just below my breasts. "Breathe for me baby." I do. I let my breath out. He likes this part of my body, every part of my body, I just hope I can come to love it just as much as he does.

I lose track of how long we stay at the bay window, lost in the sensation of Tylan's kisses all over my body. He places one last kiss on the inside of my thigh before standing up straight, holding one hand out to me. I take his hand letting him lead me to the bed. He sits on the edge of the bed gripping my waist to pull me in between his waist. "I want you on top of me. For now at least."

I grin at him, pushing him back onto the bed and climbing on top of him, straddling his hips, feeling his hard cock pressing against me through his jeans. I waste no time in standing back up and pulling them off, my hands hooking into the waistband of his boxers preparing to pull them down as well when I'm stopped by his hands on mine. I look up at him, pouting, his face breaking into a chuckle.

"I want you here first, Baby Girl." He emphasises by tapping his fingers against his lips. I smile leaning in to give him a kiss when he stops me again. "No, baby, as much as

I love your kisses, I want your other lips." I blush hard as the realisation settles in but it's also mixed with excitement about the suggestion.

I sit up, hooking my fingers into my panties and pulling them off, Tylan's eyes watching every movement. I climb back up his body. "Are you sure? I might suffocate you." I yelp at his hand landing a sharp slap on my ass.

"You won't. I want to taste you, baby. Now get your pretty little pussy up here." It takes a little bit of adjusting but I manage to straddle his face, my pussy hovering just inches above his waiting mouth. He growls moments before his hands are grabbing my ass pulling me down, his tongue licking between my folds avoiding my aching clit. I grab onto the headboard grinding against his tongue and he smiles against me, his tongue swirling around my clit. It still amazes me how fast he learned exactly what I like. It doesn't take long until the pleasure rises within me, exploding in a tidal wave of pleasure.

He doesn't stop, dragging my pleasure out, until I'm pushing his head away, his smug smirk looking up at me. I move down panting for breath until I'm comfortably sitting, my pussy brushing against his hard cock. His hands run over my body as I grind softly against him, leaning over to grab a condom from the draw. I kiss him deeply, it's not the most elegant kiss by far but neither of us care, as I roll the condom onto his cock. I don't let go, teasing my hand up and down a couple of times guiding it towards my waiting entrance.

Neither of us break the kiss, his cock stretching and filling me slowly. I can't help the moan that escapes, captured by his lips on mine. I missed this. Not just the sex, as amazing as it is, but the connection. When he found me I pulled away from him, convinced myself that falling for someone makes me weak, and maybe it does, but I need to be selfish sometimes. I deserve to be happy and the more time I spend with Tylan, the more I convince myself I can be.

I may very well have fallen off that cliff but Tylan caught me halfway keeping me on the ledge safe from losing myself completely. Fourteen months ago I killed the first man, the social worker who handed me over to the people who stole what little innocence I had left, I guess I can give him credit for introducing me to the twins but that's all he'll get from me. I never would've imagined myself falling for any man back then, apart from in my dreams, but now I've fallen for the detective who could've easily thrown me in jail. I'm constantly waiting for something to derail it all, like it's some sort of sick joke.

My thoughts are interrupted by my own moans as Tylan thrusts up into me. "I lost you for a minute, Bubbles. Stay with me." Tylan's grip on my hips is strong but his caresses are gentle. This is all so different to the previous times. For once we're both relishing in the gentle soothing thrusts, focusing on our connection. We work each other up until we fall off the edge of pleasure together as one.

He sits up, his cock seated tightly inside me, my legs wrapping around his waist and my arms around his neck, I hold him like a koala hugging a tree. Our post-sex cuddles are always comforting, always healing. I can physically feel the broken pieces of my heart gluing back together one piece at a time. Maybe my silly little romance books hold some truth. Maybe there is such a thing as soulmates, and I have a strong feeling that this man is mine.

We stay wrapped around each other until we've both caught our breaths, Tylan lifting me gently off his cock and sitting me back on the bed but not without one last soft kiss. "Do you want to join me in the shower?"

I shake my head. "I had one this morning. I'll take a warm cloth though."

I didn't even think it was possible but his soft smile warms my heart even more, I wonder if it's possible that I may be healing him as well, just a little. "That I can do. You just get comfortable." He kisses my forehead before climbing out of the bed and making his way to the bathroom. I move up, leaning against the headboard, wrapping myself in a blanket listening to the sound of running water moments before Tylan returns, cloth in hand.

He chuckles when he notices me, climbing onto the bed. "I'm going to need to move the blanket so I can clean you, Bubbles." I pout playfully as his fingers brush my thighs, pushing the blanket off my legs, goosebumps rising at the contact. I spread my legs a little to help him, sighing softly at the feel of the soft cloth caressing my skin, followed by Tylan's soft kisses. "All done." He sits back, pulling the blanket back over my legs.

"I'm hungry." I bat my eyes at him smiling sweetly, Tylan shakes his head at me but I don't miss the smile spreading across his face.

"Why don't you order something whilst I'm in the shower?" He stands up from the bed walking over to his discarded jeans before he throws his wallet onto my lap, followed by my phone from the bay window. "Use my card and get whatever you want."

I smile at him watching him walk back into the bathroom. I snuggle into the blanket pulling up my food delivery app. After a few minutes I decide on my favourite Italian place adding enough food for the both of us to the cart before opening Tylan's wallet, searching for his card.

My heart stops beating at the sight of an all too familiar picture stuffed behind endless amounts of cards. I pull it out, praying that I'm not seeing what I think I am. *How could you be so stupid?*

Maybe it doesn't mean anything.

Why would he steal the photo of your family then?

The voices in my head battle, I'm unsure of what to think, maybe if I just ask him about it he'll tell me?

My heart stops completely. Behind the picture he stole from me is another photo, the date is the first thing I catch sight of – December 25th, 2010 – I take a deep breath preparing myself to turn it over. I shouldn't have. The photo confirms the one truth I never would've imagined. I want to tell myself that it's not true, that there's some other explanation but how could there be?

The image isn't fabricated, it's real. The people in it are real. The house behind them is real. My healing heart disintegrates, betrayal stabbing me in the back, far worse than the pain I felt a few weeks ago. I can't breathe. I'm suffocating. Last time I was simply falling off the cliff, this time I was shoved, forced over the edge into the darkness below.

I should feel hurt and maybe I will later on, but right now, right in this moment, all I feel is anger. Anger at myself for ever believing he truly cared for me. Anger for being so naive. Anger at the man currently showering in *my* bathroom. I shove the blanket off me marching over to my wardrobe, my eyes landing on the black mini dress from the night of our first time together. Did he know who I was when we first met? My grip tightens on the wardrobe door at the thought, my nails scuffing the paint. I yank the dress off the hanger throwing on the matching black lingerie. It takes me mere minutes to throw on the rest of my outfit from that night before throwing my hair up into two Dutch braids.

I'm staring in the full length mirror besides my dresser, staring at the reflection, the woman who I once was stares back at me. The real me stares back at me. I lost myself for a few months but with one simple photo she's back. Everleigh Carlton. The woman who *will* avenge her family's death. It's been a long five years and eleven months but tonight I will finally get my revenge.

My eyes zone in on my mango body spray sitting on top of the dresser, I spray it all over, my mind souring at the scent he loves. After tonight I'll be finding a new signature scent, one that suits me a lot better. I pick up the decorative paperweight from the dresser walking over to the bathroom door when I hear the shower shut off.

I grip the paperweight tight in my hand as the door opens. "Hey Bubbles. You're going to need—" I hit him hard with the paperweight, his body collapsing onto the floor, unconscious for now. I stand there looking down at the monster laying still on my bedroom floor drawing my eyes away to search for his jeans – I'd rather not have him naked. It's a struggle but I manage to get his clothes back on, wasting no time in dragging him out to his car, my still healing back aching from the effort. It's even more of a struggle to throw him into the back of it, but I manage before I climb into the driver's seat. I send a quick message to Camilla to meet me at the one place I've had ready for my family's murderer for the past three years.

I don't know how long I have until he wakes up so I rush over to the abandoned house I once called home, ignoring every red light and every traffic sign. I park the car, staring out at my childhood home, memories rushing back to me all at once. Why didn't I deserve a normal life? Why did I have to be punished? Why do I have to be this monster? This victim? My eyes catch on the man lying in the backseat. *He's the reason.*

I push the memories away climbing out the car, dragging him with me all the way through to the cellar where I found my twin sister and baby brother tied up and bleeding out on the cold stone floor, now perfectly set up for this exact moment.

I waste no time in tying him up in the chains. I sit back in the chair placed in the shadows. And now I wait.

Betrayal

Tylan

Fuck! My head is pounding. *What happened?* My eyes blink open, the stars clouding my vision slowly clearing to reveal an empty dark room lit by a single yellow spotlight highlighting a small metal table covered with different objects, too far away for me to see what they are. I try to move but I'm jerked back. One simple glance at my wrists and ankles reveals why – shackles binding me to the wall greet me. Where the fuck am I? This definitely isn't Everleigh's cottagesque house. Where's Everleigh?

"Aww, good." My head snaps towards the mocking voice belonging to the woman I know all too well, sitting there in the same tight black mini dress from our first time together, the one that drives me insane, one long pale leg crossed over the over. My eyes catch on her upper thigh where one of my love bites shines bright. My attention moves to her hands watching her take a sip from the glass of champagne in her hand, her eyes shooting daggers into my soul. "You're awake." Her voice holds no emotion, the light reflecting off the knife twirling in her other hand.

It takes me a moment to come to my senses and realise what this is, my mouth tugging up into an amused smirk. "You know, Bubbles, if you wanted to be in charge for once you only had to ask." My smirk falters slightly when she takes another sip rolling her eyes at me.

"Men." She mutters so quietly that I nearly miss it. Slowly, she places her drink on the small table before standing up, staring me down once again, the knife twirling between both of her hands. This situation would be hot if she didn't look so murderous. The room is silent other than the sound of my shackles as I try, once again, to break out of them – unsuccessfully I might add. "Stop trying." I stop struggling at the emotionless sound, shocked as I realise Everleigh, my Bubbles, my love, is staring straight through me, up close I can see straight past the murder in her eyes into the sadness and betrayal.

"Everleigh? This isn't funny. Just tell me what's going on?" False hope takes over me as she gently caresses my cheek but that hope is quickly squashed at the scratch from her claws, her hand moving down to my neck.

"You're all the same." Her soft voice is a contrast to the sharp sting I feel when she pulls her hand away leaving behind a bleeding scratch on my neck. I watch her swiftly turn around, strutting back to the table. "I was stupid to think you were different." I can fully hear the sadness in her voice, I can see the slight tremble of her shoulders before she shakes it off, picking up two pieces of paper.

"What are you—?"

She whips around, a breeze coming from the end of her braids, screaming at me, "I know what you fucking did!" Holding out the pieces of paper at me. I squint quickly realising they're not random pieces of paper, they're polaroids, just like the ones Everleigh has of her victims. I'm confused until I look at the dates. The first one dated December 25th, 2010, shows my biggest regret. The second one dated July 28th, 2006, is of a young family, a mother and father in a loving embrace a baby held in their arms and two twelve year old girls blowing bubbles in front of them.

My eyes widen as I look once again at the twins in the photo...*shit.* "Don't act like you didn't know." Everleigh scoffs, putting the photos down again before crossing her arms, the knife still dangling from her fingers. "Just tell me the truth. That's the least you owe me."

"The twins. They're you and Maya?" I try to play innocent, her hands clenching at the sound of her sister's name. I swallow before continuing, "That's your family." It's not a question. My only response from her is her signature eye roll but I still don't understand why she showed me those photos, or why I'm shackled to the wall...Wait a minute. "You think I killed them?" I breath out in disbelief.

Chapter Twenty-Nine
Revenge

Everleigh

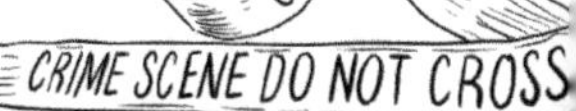

That does it. I practically leap at Tylan chained to the wall of the cellar, my knife pressing deep against his throat, my face close enough to him that one word and our lips could touch just like they have countless times before–*no Everleigh, stop it.*

Pulling back from him I can feel the scowl forming as I stare directly at the man I thought I knew. "I know you did." I press my knife harder against his neck drawing a little blood to prevent him from speaking. "December 25th, 2010, at exactly one am you broke into my family's home and slaughtered my entire family, the only loving family I've ever had. You didn't find me of course because I snuck out, and the next day when it was all over the news do you know what they called me?"

I wait a few seconds for his response and when it doesn't come I move the knife down stabbing it into his broad shoulder, still with no response from him. I can feel my heart clenching, watching the blood run down his chest but I push the feeling away staring right back into the ocean blue eyes I loved to get lost in.

"Lucky," I scoff in disgust, blinking away the tears threatening to fall. "They called me lucky because I disobeyed my parents and left them to their deaths along with my twin sister and little brother whilst I was out getting drunk at some dumb party." My laugh sounds pathetic even to my own ears. "I came home on Christmas morning of all days and do you know the first thing I saw?"

Glancing at my nearly dead phone I look at the blurred numbers trying to work out the time but I ultimately give up, fumbling inside my bag for my keys, not even attempting to climb up and sneak back through my bedroom window in my drunken state. My parents don't need to know I disobeyed them, yet alone a hospital trip on Christmas Day...I need to apologise to Mum in the morning, I still can't believe I told her I hated her. After what feels like hours I finally mange to open my door and, somehow, quietly close it.

I hang my coat on the coat rail, catching a glimpse at my disastrous reflection in the round mirror. I look like I've been attacked by a hundred cats. Now that I think about it...where is Muffin? "Muffin," I whisper quietly turning around searching for our newest kitten, my eyes catching on something strange sticking out from the corner leading to the kitchen. Before I can think twice about it, I stumble unsteadily towards the kitchen but not without stubbing my toe on a book sitting in the middle of my path. Okay...that definitely doesn't go there.

I quickly sober up, my eyes scanning the room noting the messy state the living room is currently in. Blankets and cushions thrown around, the vase with my grandparents ashes lays broken on the ground, broken glass from picture frames are scattered all around. I continue moving onto the kitchen, a newfound urgency rushing through me, not realising just how much I would regret that choice until it's too late.

Turning the corner I see that the "object" I saw isn't an object, it's my mum's hair sticking out as she lays unmoving on the kitchen floor in a pool of blood forming from a stab wound straight through her heart. I don't move. I don't scream. I don't cry. I just stand in shock staring down at the woman who's always there for me, who holds me when I cry, tells me she loves me even when I'm screaming at her, the only woman who will ever truly love me. It takes me a few minutes until my senses come to.

I grab my phone from my pocket needing to call 999 but throw it to the ground when it won't turn on. I look around frantically for another phone, my eyes landing on Mum's sticking out of her jeans pocket. I know I shouldn't touch anything but I need to call someone. With as little movement as possible, I pull my mum's phone out and with it comes a polaroid picture. I turn it over and that's when I break. The picture of my family four years ago. The reminder of everything I've lost.

I wipe a rogue tear off my cheek, mad at myself for showing any type of emotion. "I came home Christmas Day and I found my mother lying in a pool of her own blood."

"Everleigh, listen to me. I promise you I wasn't the one who killed them."

"I don't believe you."

"Everleigh please," he pleads. "I'm sorry for everything that's happened to you but I'm not the reason. I-I love you."

That's my final trigger. I yank the knife from Tylan's shoulder before letting all my anger and heartbreak out of him, my knife stabbing him repetitively. "You don't love me!" Stab. "You." Stab. "Made." Stab. "Me." Stab. "An." Stab. "Id-iot." Slash. I pause for a moment watching him bleed out. "The last thing my mum ever heard from me was me telling her that I hated her. She didn't deserve that..." I grip the knife tighter in my hand. "But you do." I stare directly into his drooping eyes. "I hate you, Tylan Blaese." I jam my knife into his stomach.

I drop to my knees, my throat closing up, my heart clenching so painfully that I can do nothing but scream and cry until my throat is raw. I finally avenged my family but it cost me everything. My future. My sanity. My love. Some small part of my brain tells me that it wasn't worth it – my revenge wasn't worth it – but I shut it out, the tears flowing like a waterfall. I cry so much that I half expect to be swimming in a puddle of tears soon.

My tears eventually dry out but I stay here on my knees, on the floor of the cellar looking at the one man I've ever truly loved. I should feel relief, I caught him, but I don't. All I feel is betrayal and heartbreak, like this is some horrible nightmare that I can't wake up from no matter how hard I try.

I'm still kneeling, staring up at him when I hear a proud whistle behind me. "You got him good." I don't have the energy to turn around as Camilla's footsteps approach me stopping abruptly. "Oh, Everleigh." I hear the sympathy in her voice, her arms wrapping around me.

I don't hug her back, my arms hanging loosely at my sides. "I can't believe I was so stupid." My voice is barely audible.

"You're not stupid. You're just a girl who fell in love."

I abruptly push out of her arms, leaping up, my walls coming back up in full force. I never loved him. *Keep telling yourself that.* "Clean this up." My voice is emotionless once again, just as it should be. I turn around walking out of my childhood home, closing the door on the worst chapters of my life. I make it far enough away when the explosion happens, with both Tylan and Camilla trapped inside. I glance down at the photo in my hand, the one taken on December 25th, 2010, the two of them kissing outside this house with blood all over them, both holding bloody knives. I scrunch it up, throwing it on the ground. Now my revenge is complete...

After all. How was I supposed to know it wasn't? Not yet at least.

Chapter Thirty

Vengeance

Dear Miss Reaper.

Beware, beware, the ghost of past.

Prepare, prepare, to say goodbye.

Despair, despair, you've made a mistake.

I can't believe my eyes. Tylan Blaese being dragged into your, my dear Reaper, childhood home was shocking enough, but watching you walk out alone, blood splattered over your pale skin a few hours later is the biggest shock of all. My fingers click intensely on the camera shutter, snapping every bit of evidence against you. My grin plasters my face as I stay hidden in the bushes, not that you would've noticed. You're broken.

But, my dear Everleigh, you've just signed your own death certificate.

Part II

Chapter Thirty-One

Run

Tylan

My body is tingling. Blood pouring out of me. I'm struggling to stay awake as Camilla undoes my shackles. The only thing she says to me as she drags me out a secret entrance is, "You're going to need to run."

I look down at my broken body. "How do you expect me to do that?" Fuck. Even speaking hurts. She rolls her eyes gripping tight onto my hand, dragging my limping body behind her as we run into the woods. We're just past the tree line when an explosion sounds behind us. I turn around to see the house we were just in is nothing but smoke and flames. "How did you know there was a bomb?"

She shoots me a look that screams are-you-an-idiot? "I helped her set it up." She glances down at my chest. "Come on, we need to stop all of that." I limp after her through the trees, my body slowly shutting down, every step nearly impossible. We make it to a small shack – inside is nothing but a small kitchen, bathroom, and two bedrooms. I follow her through to one of the bedrooms. "Sit." She points to the bed and I practically collapse onto it. She rushes to the bathroom coming back with a small medical kit. “This is going to hurt and I’m probably going to need to give you some of my blood.” I look at her, questioning. “I have O-negative blood.” She answers my unasked question.

Nothing can hurt more than the pain I felt when I saw the betrayal written in Everleigh’s eyes. Why did I take that stupid photo? *Why didn’t you just tell her the truth?* I curse my conscience for the stating the obvious. I know I probably deserve to die tonight but I can’t. I need to stay alive for her. I need to stay alive so that she can get her truth.

I’m saved from my overthinking, hissing out a breath, when Camilla cleans my wounds. It takes a solid thirty minutes before she’s cleaned and bandaged all of them. I close my eyes against the spinning in my head, taking a deep breath. “Sleep.”

I don’t object, laying back against the pillows, but there’s one question I need to ask first. “When are we going to tell her the truth?”

“Never.” My head pounds as my head whips towards Camilla standing in the door frame. “When Everleigh sets her mind to something it’s incredibly hard to change her mind. She’s convinced we did it and, in case you’re forgetting, we didn’t kill them but we know who did.”

Chapter Thirty-Two

Darkness

Everleigh

Twenty Two Months Later

Day six hundred and seventy five. One year, ten months, five days since my life fell apart completely. I didn't even think that was possible after my family's death but being betrayed by your best friend who you've known for eighteen out of your twenty three years of life, and by one of the only men you ever trusted and loved...? Well that's just the cherry on top of the cake. Throw killing both of them by your own hands into the mix and, well, that's enough to kill, no pun intended, any addiction to killing you may have.

Two months after that night I moved out of the city and into a safe house in the countryside, I couldn't exactly trust that Tylan wasn't building a case against me and that I wasn't minutes away from being arrested, plus I needed to move away from my past and the ghosts who haunt me every day.

Little Bray has always been my entire life. I wanted to be alone but the twins insisted on moving in with me claiming I was too unstable to live alone. For once, they were probably right. If unstable means having no idea what you're meant to feel in a situation like this then put my name at the top of the list.

It's funny how dreams works. Here I am on my former best friend's birthday, living in my dream house, a secluded cabin surrounded by nothing but nature, but I'm not living with the family I've always wanted, I'm living with the only people I have left in my life…and Summer.

It turns out that Jason Richards, the man they pulled out the river, was actually Summer's fiancé. I may have been hurting but how could I say no to the twins begging me to let her join us, claiming that she needed their support as well? I may be a monster but I'm not *that* big of a monster. I had to agree.

There's only one part of my life that hasn't changed and that's my love for books. Yes, I may have gotten a little more animated when reading, especially if there's a happy ending, but they're my only distraction from the numbing pain coming from the hollow space where my heart is meant to be.

It didn't take long after we moved for me to find my reading spot – a swinging seat placed strategically between two trees so that it looks as though the trees are holding it up. The wooden awning protects the seat from all the elements making it a perfect getaway, even in the infamous British rain. I decorated the awning with a bunch of fairy lights and added comfy cushions to the seat, as well as a waterproof cabinet to keep a couple of blankets inside.

"Everleigh?" My peaceful reading time is interrupted by Summer's bright voice, a beacon of sunshine through the darkness in my life...and I hate it. I don't want sunshine in my life, sunshine represents hope and hope is the last thing I need.

"What do you want, Summer?" I hope she can hear the annoyance in my voice. I don't take my eyes off my book – a dark Alice in Wonderland retelling – not even when she sits next to me, the seat swinging back and forth as she uses her feet to push it.

"I wanted to check on you." I glance at her out the corner of my eye, her sweet smile plastered on her face.

I flick my eyes back to my book. "I'm fine."

I tense at the feel of her hand on mine which she quickly retracts. "It's okay not to be okay. We all know what today is." *I don't need your pity.* I bite my tongue against saying what I really want to, uncurling myself from the seat. "Where are you going?"

"I'm hungry." I walk off leaving Summer on the swing seat. The walk from the lake to the house is simply a set of steps up a small hill, the steps are old stone laced with weeds growing through the cracks but they're still practical. I step up onto the wraparound porch, pushing open the sliding glass door that leads into the modern kitchen.

I'm greeted by the sight of Callum cooking what smells like bacon on the stove, he hasn't noticed I'm here, I wonder if I can sneak past him to hibernate in my room. I lose any hope of that when he turns around reaching for the bread bin. "Hey Cap. Want a bacon sandwich?" He knows my weakness.

"Okay." I wrap my arms around my stomach, a comforting action I've been doing for the past two years, I can't do hugs from other people most days anymore. I look away from Callum, unable to stand seeing the sympathy laced in his eyes, walking over to the dining room sitting down at my favourite spot at the head of the table, facing the floor to ceiling window that overlooks the lake. You could say the lake has become my comfort place; I was drawn to it ever since we moved in, so much so that the other's happily let me have the master bedroom that faces it. It's the calm in the raging storm of emotions constantly running through my mind. One look at the lake and everything goes silent.

Callum places my sandwich in front of me, taking the seat to my left. We eat in silence, me getting lost in my thoughts. "Everleigh." I blink, turning my attention to him. "Don't hate me but I've been thinking." He takes a deep breath, my face remaining neutral as I stare at him. "What if they didn't do it?"

I suck in a breath, looking away from him. "There is no 'what if'. They did it." I take my final bite, standing up abruptly, walking to the sink and dropping my plate into the pile of dishes waiting to be cleaned.

"I know you want to believe that but it doesn't make sense—"

"Callum!" I spin around to face him. "Not now. Please." My voice cracks and I waste no time sprinting up to my room, the tears falling down my cheeks. I'm so tired of the tears, of crying every single day. I would've thought they'd have stopped by now, that I would've used up every last tear in my body but somehow more escape every day.

I slam my door behind me taking in shaky deep breaths, trying to stop the tears. I make sure my door is locked before I walk over to the curtain next to the window, pulling it back to reveal the pin board behind it, covered with news articles, photos, notes, and more, just like the case board Tylan used to have. The truth is, I have considered the fact that my family's murderer is still out there somewhere.

I've been trying to piece together everything that happened that night, desperately needing to prove they did it, and why they did it. I know I'd feel a lot better if I knew for certain that it was them and that I didn't get it wrong, that I didn't jump to conclusions like I always do, than if I found out they didn't. I couldn't deal with the knowledge that I ruined my own happiness because of a lie.

I know I'm getting close to the truth but I'm missing something and I can't work out what. Camilla was always the one who did the research and I admit that I underestimated just how hard researching people is. I stare at the board looking for something to jump out at me but I have no luck. I grip my hair letting out a frustrated scream, pulling the curtain back over it, if I can't see it then it's not there. Why is it so hard to get my answers? All I need is the truth so I can move on, is that really too much to ask for?

My thoughts are interrupted by a knock on my door. I sigh walking over and opening it. "Is now a bad time?" Freddie stands outside my door, his hands tucked casually in the pockets of his jeans.

"Depends what you're about to say." I step aside, closing the door behind him.

"I might have a lead on Michael Knotts."

I perk up whipping my head in the direction of his, a small smile gracing his lips. We've been working together for the past year and a half trying to find Michael Knotts. I always said that my last kill would be my family's murderer but I refuse to let the man who abused my trust, and countless others, get away with it. "Where is he?"

He raises an eyebrow "How did you—Never mind. He's an hour's drive away."

"That's the best news I've heard all day." I sit on my bed, inviting Freddie to sit next to me. "We'll get him this time, right?" My back tingles at the memory of the last time we tried to do this.

Freddie reaches out, touching my hand gently. "Of course we will."

Chapter Thirty-Three

What If

Tylan

"Are you sure this is going to work?" I glance over at Camilla in the passenger seat, who's staring out the window, twirling a black curl around her fingers.

"My plans never fail." Her answer is robotic, her stare never breaking from the window.

"They did once. Or did you forget what happened the last time we tried to face Michael Knotts?" I know it's a low blow. I know it's nearly been two years since that incident but that was the night I felt everything starting to go wrong, the night I started to lose Everleigh. I have to stop thinking about her. I've tried so hard to forget about her, to move on, but she just keeps filling my every thought. I know she probably hates me, she said as much the last time we spoke *"She didn't deserve that but you do. I hate you Tylan Blaese"* they're the words I keep hearing over and over again to the tune of the heartbreak in her voice.

"Let's not talk about that right now." I turn back to Camilla who's staring back at me, her eyes narrowed. She snaps her head back to the window, a signal that the conversation's over, it's not the first time she's done this over the years. I know in theory our plan is foolproof, we've been working on it long enough, but I can't stop my mind from wandering back to last time – Michael Knotts is smarter than we give him credit for – what if he's on to us? What if we walk into a trap? What if—

No! No more what ifs, this plan will work. I need to get Michael Knotts where we need him and then I can get Everleigh back. I know she's my soulmate whether she likes it or not, and I will do everything I can to make her mine again. I'm not ashamed to admit I've been following her every chance I get. I've spent numerous nights hiding in the woods by her safehouse, watching her. It breaks my heart seeing the extent of her emotional pain.

She's lost herself; Her beautiful smile is non-existent, I haven't seen even the slightest hint of one, not even when she's sitting by the lake with one of her books – she always had the biggest smile when she was reading, she said it was a reminder that every hero gets a happy ending. *She thinks she's a villain.* She always said that, she focuses on her vices, blocking out all the good parts of herself, and now she thinks I've betrayed her and taken away her happy ending. I've made her biggest statement true. I have to prove to her that we have a future, that she can have her happy ending...I just need her to willingly talk to me.

The twins caught me sneaking around a couple of months ago, they didn't seem surprised to see me though, it's almost like they knew I was hanging around there often. It took a lot of talking but eventually I managed to convince them to help me – Callum came around a lot sooner than Freddie did. I know they probably don't trust me yet but Everleigh means everything to them and I know they'll do anything to make her happy. I snap out of my thoughts, parking the car a couple of streets away from our destination. "We'll have to walk the rest of the way."

Camilla turns her gaze to me, uneasiness written in her eyes, a contrast to the rest of her facade. "When we get there, I knock on the door offering some new Wi-Fi service and whilst he's distracted you break in the back, attack anyone else in there and then sneak up on him—"

"And then we kill him." We share a look of indifference. After tonight Michael Knotts will cease to exist.

"Let's do this," she whispers, climbing out the car as I do the same. We walk in silence to the end of the street staring at our target. "If something goes wrong, I'll offer him a discount and that's your cue to get out. Don't go rogue on me, Blaese."

"Nothing will go wrong. He won't get the best of us this time." I can see the uncertainty written in her eyes but all she offers me is a simple nod. She takes a deep breath, straightening her cream blazer before heading off in the direction of the house. I wait until she's reached the driveway before making my way around to the back walking along the fence outlining the modern town house searching for a way in, I think about climbing over but the barb wire sitting on top is a strong no. There has to be a way in somewhere.

I continue along the perimeter searching every panel until I come across one with a keypad. I roll my eyes at myself. Of course it's locked. *Think, Tylan, think.* What would someone like Michael Knotts use as a code? He's a self-entitled prick, maybe his birthday? No, he's smarter than that. The day he started his company? No. *Think, Tylan.* I can physically feel the blood drain from my face as the realisation dawns on me. I turn to the keypad and type in four numbers. 3213 – February 3rd, 2013 – the day he assaulted Everleigh. The green light flashes at the same time the sound of the mechanical lock moving fills my ears.

My visions fills with red as I push the gate open. *Reign it in, Tylan.* I close my eyes, taking a deep breath. shoving my anger to the back of my mind, for now at least. I need a clear head for this. I close the gate behind me leaving it the slightest bit ajar. I take a look around the garden I'm now standing in, staying behind the bushes as I sneak my way to the back door, stopping just outside to sneak a glance through the window for any signs of any of his guards.

"It really won't take that long, just a few minutes of your time and I'll be out your hair." Camilla's voice drifts around the side of the house, her voice sounding just like those fake customer service voices you hear from all salespeople. Confident the coast is clear, I crack the back door open cringing at the creak from the hinges. I pause, listening for any movement from within. When there's no reaction, I open the door the rest of the way, sticking to the darkness within the open plan kitchen. I can hear the faint sound of Camilla and Michael's voices as I move within the shadows towards the two men sitting around the dining room table.

I crack my knuckles trying to work out the best way to handle this. My struggle is broken when one of the men glances at his phone, rushing to the front door. I look around one last time double checking I'm alone with the other man before making my move. Catching him by surprise, I wrap one arm around his throat tightly, my other hand clamping his mouth shut. He struggles against me trying to reach for the gun sitting just out of reach on the table next to him, but I have him pushed tight enough between me and the table that he can't. He doesn't stop struggling until he loses consciousness, but I don't release him for another thirty seconds, just to be sure he's dead.

I glance around, noting the open laptop full of video feeds from every room in the house. I examine each room carefully, looking for anyone else who may be in the house but there's no one other than me in here, and Michael, Camilla, and the other guy in the hallway. That works for me. If I can get Camilla's attention then we can overpower both of them. I quietly creep into the hallway, the two men don't see me but Camilla catches my eyes subtly shaking her head.

Ignoring her warning, I turn my attention to the men talking together in hushed tones, feeling Camilla searing holes into the side of my head, the man showing Michael something on his phone. I can't make out what they're saying but Camilla can, made obvious by her next statement. "If you sign up today I can offer you a twenty percent discount." Her face lights up with a fake smile, her eyes widening ever so slightly when they catch mine, urging me to get out, but I can't move. Michael turns his attention back to her and I just stand there watching, her smile dropping when she catches sight of something hidden in his hand.

Everything that happens next happens so fast that I don't even get the chance to blink. Michael Knotts yanks Camilla past the threshold, slamming the door closed behind her, holding her tight to him, she struggles but he's too strong for her. I take one step forward before two sets of hands are twisting my arms behind my back followed by a sharp prick to my neck. My head goes dizzy as I try to focus on Camilla but all I can see is Michael's smirk as he holds her limp in his arms. *What have I done?* The world goes black.

Chapter Thirty-Four

Raw

Everleigh

I've tried everything I possibly could to distract myself today. Reading? Nope everything reminded me of Tylan. Cleaning? There's only so much a person can clean in an already clean house. Meditating? That one's a joke. I've never meditated a day in my life. Bathing Muffin? My arms are now covered in scratches. Online shopping? I need money I don't have for that. Movie marathon? I'm pretty sure I've watched the entire catalogue of the streaming services we pay for by now. Baking? That's what I'm doing now. I wouldn't necessarily call it a disaster...

"What the fuck?"

I turn to Callum, never stopping my mixing of the brownie batter. "Hey, Cal."

"It looks like a bomb exploded in the flour in here." He looks around the kitchen, stunned. He's not wrong...maybe I should've left cleaning until after baking.

"I'm making brownies." I show him the batter in the bowl before placing it on the side. "There's some muffins over there." I point to the sad looking lemon muffins gracing the kitchen island. “There’s a marble cake in the oven. Oh, and there’s some Oreo mini cheesecakes in the fridge.” He raises his eyebrows at me, opening the fridge to the twelve ramekins full of cheesecake as I pour the brownie batter into a square tin.

“What’s going on Everleigh?” He sighs, closing the fridge and taking a seat at the island, picking up one of the muffins.

I’m taking the cake out the oven when I hear him spit out the muffin. “They’re not that bad.” I roll my eyes, placing the cake on the cooling rack, closing the oven.

“They’re raw.” He hesitates.

“What?” I spin, marching over to see for myself and they are in fact, raw. “Just throw them away, everything else is fine though.” We both know I’m not talking about the sweet treats. He looks me in the eyes but I break his stare, heading back to the brownie batter. I crouch down to put it in the oven when my hand knocks against the oven door causing the tin to go flying out my hands, brownie batter splaying everywhere. I collapse onto the floor, my eyes filling with damn tears once again.

Callum rushes over to me, taking the now empty brownie pan out of my hands, turning the oven off. “Hey, it’s okay. It’s just a little brownie batter, you can make some more.” He sits beside me, engulfing me in yet another hug.

“No it’s not.” I can’t stop the tears that fall. “This whole day’s a disaster.”

"We all have off days. Your life's not going to be like this forever." He holds me tighter, pulling me close to him until my legs are resting over his. I hate to admit it, but Callum really does give the best hugs, he's just a big giant teddy bear.

"It feels like it will be," I mumble against his shoulder.

"Wait until you get rid of Michael Knotts. I already know your life is going to change for the better."

"Or I could end up in jail."

I can feel his eye roll against my head. "Okay negative Nelly—"

"My name's Everleigh." I look up at him.

"It's a saying." He ruffles my hair and I glare at him. "Now, can I finish?"

"Will you stop using phrases from the 1960s?"

He glares at me playfully. "Your self-doubting stops today. Right now."

"That's not how that stuff works, Cal. You can't just wave a magic wand and it will all disappear, trust me I tried." I roll my eyes.

"It stopped the tears though." He points at my face and I push him away, pulling myself out his arms. "Come on. Not even a tiny smile?" He says it playfully but I still feel the ache in my chest at the question. "We need the old Everleigh back tonight." This time his voice is serious.

"And you'll get her back. But I can only promise it will be temporary for now." I shrug, crossing my arms.

He simply nods, standing up from the floor and walking the few short steps to pick something up from the kitchen side. “Here.” He holds the item out to me – a kitchen knife. My heart races, my breathing intensifying.

A knife.

I killed Tylan with a knife. Why is he offering me a knife? Images flash through my mind of that day. My knife plunging in and out of his chest, his fresh crimson blood covering it more and more with each stab—

“Everleigh!” I’m brought back to the present, Callum’s hands shaking my shoulders gently, no sign of a knife is present. “We should’ve tried this earlier.” He sighs. “You can’t go into that house unarmed.”

Did I mention it’s been a long two weeks since Freddie discovered where Michael is? “I won’t be. I have these.” I hold my fists up to him.

He shakes his head. “We both know you’re not strong enough to overpower him with just your hands.”

He’s right but... “I have an idea...” I look away from him, taking two deep breaths. In. One. Two. Three. Out. One. Two. Three. Repeat. “Follow me.” I stand up from the floor, leaving the oven open so I can clean it later. I lead Callum to my bedroom, walking straight over to the loose floorboard in the corner of the room.

“A loose floorboard?” He raises his eyebrows at me. “That’s such a cliche.”

"Mm-hmm," is my reply as I pry it up. I reach in pulling out a box I've kept hidden ever since we moved in. I never thought about it until today. I sit back on my heels, placing the box in front of me.

Callum crouches beside me. "What's in it?"

I look at him, emotionless. "The Polaroid Reaper." That's what I like to call the part of myself that publicly lasted a total of fourteen months, really she lived for six years. The Polaroid Reaper started with Tylan but she also ended with Tylan. I take another deep breath before opening the box, setting the lid next to it. I pull out the polaroid camera that I used to carry around everywhere, even before the Polaroid Reaper made her first kill. I gently place it next to me, shuffling past the polaroids of mutilated men, pulling out the object I really came here for.

"Is that the knife you used to kill him?"

"Them." I admire the knife, the leather bound handle fitting perfectly in my hand.

"You're not freaking out over this knife?"

I look at him, my voice monotone. "Why would I? This one protects me."

"I didn't realise how creepy this Everleigh was." He tilts his head at me and I glare at him.

"I am not creepy."

"You have the wide eyes, emotionless expression."

"Do you want us to kill Michael tonight or not?"

"We need to." His urgency gives me the feeling like he's hiding something from me but I brush it off.

"Then I'm using this knife." I place the knife on the floor, packing the polaroid camera back in the box before replacing the lid, hiding the box beneath the floorboard again. I straighten looking at Callum. "Let's do this."

Bruises

Tylan

My eyes slowly peel open, my head refusing to open them fully, I'm squinting but all I can work out are support beams and a set of old wooden steps in the corner of the room. A basement. It's always a basement. I try to move but don't get very far. I look down noting the wooden chair I'm tied to, as well as the fact that I'm only in my boxers. *Shit. Where's Camilla?* Right on cue I hear a small feminine groan behind me, turning my head I see a head of raven black curls. "Camilla?" I whisper.

"Tylan?" She groans back. "Where are we?"

"If I had to take a guess, I'd say Michael Knotts' basement."

"Fuck." She swears under her breath. "We need to get out of these." I can feel her tugging at the rope tying our arms together, shortly followed by an offended gasp.

"What is it?"

"I'm in my underwear." I can hear the scowl in her voice.

"Don't worry, so am I."

"That doesn't fill me with much confidence." Her raised voice catches the attention of two other people in the room.

I can't see them from where I'm sitting but I'm pretty sure Camilla can based on how she tenses, leaning into me.

"You're a pretty one." I recognise the voice as the man who was with Michael Knotts.

"Don't touch me," Camilla hisses, struggling against the binds.

"I'll do whatever I like." I can feel her struggling against me, followed shortly by what sounds like her spitting at him. I sigh inwardly. *This isn't going to be good.* Smack! The sound reverberates around the room followed by silence. "Am I clear?" I can hear her audibly swallow, able to turn my head just enough to catch her tiny nod.

The other man walks over in front of me. I don't recognise him from earlier, at least I assume it was earlier. He smirks down at me, smugness written across his face. "This is going to be fun." I choke on a breath at his surprisingly strong punch to my stomach. I'll give it to him, he's good...and he has me completely bare and open for his punches. This is *not* going to be fun.

It wasn't. He didn't stop until I was coughing up my own blood. The other man didn't show Camilla any mercy either, except he used a knife, claiming that he "doesn't hit women". At least the man has some morals. I can't speak for Camilla but I have no doubt we both had our confidence knocked down after only one day. Or should I call it a session? We have no way of keeping time down here.

The second time they came down they switched. I thought for certain I'd get a couple more stab wounds to add to my collection but no, they made it pretty clear that day that I would be their punching bag and Camilla would be their stress reliever. That part makes sense at least. It's common knowledge that stabbing can be seen as a sexual act for most men, given the intimacy of it.

The next time they came down they weren't alone, Michael Knotts was with them, but they gave us a reprieve, sticking to an interrogation this time. Neither of us said anything, why would we? We're both a lot stronger than he gives us credit for. Not even when he tried to taunt us, even revealing my biggest secret. The same one that got me involved with the bastard in the first place. Camilla remained silent even after we were alone again.

The same cycle repeated for what I'm guessing is days, maybe even weeks, sometimes there were long gaps that felt like they could've been entire days. I feel like I'm going crazy with no sense of time. They give us minimal amounts of food and drink, just enough to keep us alive, I'm sure if they wanted to they could just let us starve to death, it probably wouldn't take too long when it's combined with the beatings.

My body is black and blue, bruises forming everywhere – I'm not sure there's a single inch they haven't touched. I can physically feel my body shutting down, I'm not sure how much longer I can last, Camilla's not in any better shape.

It's been a while since our last interrogation and apparently Camilla has had a new burst of energy, if her shuffling is anything to go by. "What are you doing?" I whisper to her.

"I'm tired of not fighting back," she whispers back.

"We'll get out of this another way."

"How?" She huffs out a laugh. "No one knows we're here Tylan."

"I thought Dean knew." Dean being Camilla's fuck buddy, as she calls him.

"I never told him where we were going." The silence between us is deafening. We really are alone. Camilla struggles again eventually letting out a relieved gasp.

"What did you do?"

"I got one of my legs free."

I roll my eyes. "What are you going to do with one leg?"

"I have no idea. But if you stop questioning everything and actually help me try to find a way out of these arm binds that would be a lot more help. Your sweat against me is making my skin crawl."

I don't respond to that last statement, this isn't particularly pleasant for me either. "I've been trying to come up with a plan."

"And how's that working for you?" Silence descends around us again and then we're both trying to undo the binds again but nothing is working. Both of us stop struggling at the sound of the door opening.

The two men stalk towards us, the smaller one walking straight past me to Camilla. "Ready for some more fun?" Even I can hear the smirk in his voice, despite not being able to see him. She lets out an ear piercing scream. *Shit. They're getting more aggressive.* Our time's running out.

The other man walks past me towards the corner of the room where he works on some sort of device. This isn't good at all. It's not long until he stalks back to me, his fist clenching. This one loves to pay special attention to my face, maybe he's jealous? My head snaps to the side as his fist connects with my cheek. I spit out the blood filling my mouth, the metallic taste strong. He gets in a few more punches, this time on my stomach, before we both hear a grunt from the man behind us.

"You bitch," he hisses. I manage to turn my head just enough to see him, blood running from his nose. He grabs her free ankle, wasting no time in twisting it hard. I wince at the crack echoing around the room accompanied by her gut-wrenching scream followed swiftly by her pained whimpers and the creak of the door opening.

The men share a look, the smaller one holding his hand over Camilla's mouth, silencing her whimpers. The bigger one stalks over to hide in the shadows by the stairs. I watch as the mysterious intruder makes their way down.

Wait a minute. Is that?...There's no way.

The light flickers on casting the figure in a spotlight. What is Everleigh doing here? I can do nothing but watch as the two men advance on her, for a split second I worry that she won't be able to overpower them, but then she shows me just how wrong I am, easily gaining the upper hand, stabbing the smaller one straight through his heart.

I struggle against the binds desperate to get out and help her as the larger one pins her to the floor directly in front of me, his hands around her neck until he lets out a single grunt collapsing on top of her and the whole room goes still. She pushes him off her, sitting up directly into my eye line. I can't stop staring at her dull olive green eyes – God I've missed those eyes. I watch as she pushes up onto her knees until she's kneeling directly in front of me I lean into her hand tracing my cheek, her face an image of disbelief. "I'm okay, Bubbles."

Art Therapy

Everleigh

I can't believe I agreed to this. Callum drives the three of us to Michael Knotts' house, my senses hyper aware of the knife currently strapped to my thigh, whilst my mind wanders back to the last time I faced him – the scars on my back burning at the memory. I don't know if I can go through that again. If this all goes wrong there's a good chance something worse could happen. "What if he's not there?" I voice my concern.

"He will be. We've been keeping track of him." Freddie passes me his phone, a red tracker flashing on a map unmoving at Michael's house. The same house he tried to force himself on me in. The memory still angers me to this day, knowing that he got away with it and who knows how many other girls he's assaulted.

"I don't know about this." The knife burns against my skin, making its presence known. "I haven't picked up a knife since that night."

"We'll be with you, nothing is going to happen to you, Cap." I lift my head at the nickname, meeting Callum's calming hazel ones in the rear view mirror.

I can feel the muscles in my jaw trying to force a smile but that's just another item in the long list of things I lost forever. "He won't be alone."

"That's why there's three of us." Freddie winks at me. I remain silent for the rest of the journey, staring out the window, my blood racing through my body, the anxiety rippling through me.

It's another twenty minutes before Callum pulls up behind the heavily gated town house, my eyes catching on the CCTV cameras. "What are we doing about those?" I point at them.

"I've already dealt with them." Freddie turns around in his seat to face me. "We can just walk past them and all they'll see is footage from this time last night.

I raise an eyebrow at him. "When did you get so digitally smart?" The twins share a look. "Best I don't ask?"

"It's always best you don't ask, Pixie." I offer him a tiny nod, whipping my head back to the window, taking a couple of deep breaths to calm my racing heart. *You can do this. You're the Polaroid Reaper.*

I turn back to the twins sitting in the front, determination written on my face. "Let's do this."

We step out of the car, quietly closing the doors behind us. I take the lead, walking casually to the back gate, cautious of any prying eyes that may be lurking from the neighbouring houses. I input the code I still remember into the keypad. A red light flashes. I hit the keypad letting out a small frustrated huff.

"The code's 3213, Pixie." I tense up. *That son of a—Deep breaths, Everleigh, deep breaths.* I type the new code in which is swiftly followed by a green light and the gate swinging open ever so slightly. I give up with taking it slow, needing to get my hands on Michael Knotts. I rush to the back door, ignoring the hushed yells of my name coming from the twins behind me not stopping until I'm standing in the middle of the open plan kitchen. It's too quiet.

"What are you thinking—" I put my hand up, silencing Callum's whispers.

"It's too quiet," I whisper back, the heat from the two men flush against my back.

Freddie leaves me and Callum, walking over to the dining room table where a tracker lays beside an open laptop with multiple video feeds. "Fuck," he whisper-shouts, picking up the tracker.

"Let me guess." I cross my arms. "It's the tracker you planted."

"Yeah." He's barely paying attention to me, instead opting to observe the video feeds. "It looks like we're alone but—"

"Callum you go upstairs, Freddie stay here, and I'll go to the basement." I can feel the buzz coursing through me, the need to kill coming back in full force. I pull my knife out the holster, the leather handle sitting perfectly in the contours of my hand – a familiar comforting friend. One that reminds me who I really am on the inside. The me who is slowly becoming unburied. I stalk my way over to the basement door, doing a double take when I pass by the pin board, hanging next to the basement door.

My blood boils at the sight of the multiple random drawings, nothing but scribbles of crayons forming vague shapes. My eyes catch on the only one that's not covered by any others, the one showcased like some sort of trophy. The one I made the day he put his hands on me. I'm transported back to eighteen year old me.

"Everleigh, I'd like to try art therapy with you this session." My therapist, Michael Knotts, interrupts my daydreaming. My social worker insisted I see one claiming it would be good for me to talk to a professional. One month later I was signed up to see Michael twice a month at his home office. The first time I saw him I thought I was at the wrong place, I thought he would be some old professor guy, but he's actually a twenty-eight year old, mildly attractive man, honestly, I'm surprised he's not married yet, he seems like he'd be a family guy by now.

I shocked myself that first session, I never thought I'd open up to anyone but it's surprisingly freeing to open up to someone, or maybe it's the fact that I know anything I say won't go any further than the two of us. "Everleigh?"

I blink. I must've zoned out again. "Sorry." I clear my throat. "What's art therapy?"

"Follow me." I stand up from the leather couch, following him to the dining room table where a new box of multiple coloured crayons sits along with a couple of sheets of paper. "I want you to think of this as a healing exercise." He pulls the chair out for me and I happily accept it. "I just want you to draw."

"Draw what?" I look up at him, confused at what he's saying.

"Anything. Don't think just draw." He pushes my chair until I'm a comfortable enough distance away to draw.

I pick up the box of crayons, carefully peeling the tape away. "What's this meant to do though?"

"It's a way of expressing the emotions you can't verbally explain."

"Please tell me we're not going to analyse this after," I groan.

He sighs. "Everleigh..." He places a hand on my shoulder. "We've been meeting for two years and you're not showing any signs of improvement."

"Has it ever occurred to you that it's because they still haven't found him? Who's to say I'm not next?"

He squeezes my shoulder gently, looking down at me sympathetically, a look I'm all too familiar with. "Take those feelings and draw. Let your hand lead."

I take a deep breath, emptying the packet of crayons onto the table, picking up the three colours I'm drawn to; red, black, blue. Anger, nothingness, sadness. It takes me a while to get into it, hesitating with every touch to the paper, but eventually the movements flow. The page filling with scribbles from all three colours,

Michael's hands gently massaging my shoulders. Weird. *I brush off the feeling, focusing on the task at hand.*

It's only when I pick up the blunt black crayon, placing it on the paper, that his hands start to drift, wandering over my shoulder and down across my collarbone. I ignore it for now but then his hands drift further down, tracing the top of my bra through my shirt. "What are you doing?" I try to shake him off but his grip remains firm on my breasts.

"It's okay. Just keep drawing." He hands move to the buttons of my shirt, playing with them.

"Stop touching me." I reach up to pull his hands away but he pins my hands to my lap, using his other hand to unbutton my shirt. "No. Stop." I struggle, desperately trying to shake him off me but he pins me between the chair and table.

"Shh. It's okay." He lets go of my breasts for a brief second to stroke my hair in what he must think is a comforting manner. His hand drifts lower, the other one keeping my hands pinned, I beg him to let me go but he doesn't. He makes the mistake of letting go of my hands when he struggles to undo my trousers with one hand. I use all my strength, placing both hands on the table and pushing back, knocking him off balance just enough for me to escape his hold. I run back to the couch grabbing my phone from my bag. "I wouldn't do that if I was you." I turn around to Michael leaning against the wall, smirking.

"Why not?"

He pushes off the wall, stalking towards me, but I step further away from him, buttoning my shirt back up in the process. "Who do you think they'll listen to? A misbehaving teenager, or a successful businessman with money to spare?" His predatory gaze stays trained on me as I process what he's saying.

"I'm not going to let you get away with this." I sprint towards the front door but he grabs me, pulling me into his chest.

"You let this get out and I'll ruin you," he whispers in my ear. The thing is I don't doubt that. I break out of his arms, rushing out the house. "I'll see you in two weeks, Miss Carlton." I offer him a simple middle finger, if he thinks I'm coming back then he's in for a big shock.

My vision fills with red as I rip the drawing down, tearing it in the process. I don't turn back to the twins, gripping the basement door handle tight. "No matter what. He doesn't get out of today alive." I yank the door open, forcing myself to take careful steps down into the darkness.

Why is it so quiet? I get to the bottom step feeling along the wall for a light switch. The room illuminates in a warm yellow glow, my eyes blinking rapidly at the sight in front of me. My mind has to be playing tricks on me. There's no way the two people currently tied to two wooden chairs in nothing but their underwear are Tylan and Camilla. They're dead. I killed them.

I don't get the chance to take a second look. Two men are striding towards me, murder written in their eyes. I drag my eyes to them, gripping my knife tight in my hand. *You know how to do this, Everleigh. You're the infamous Polaroid Reaper.* I straighten my back, rolling my shoulders out. I've taken down grown men before, surely two of them at once can't be so hard...right?

The smaller of the two leaps for me but I manage to dodge out of his way just in time. He lands hard on the wooden steps and I take the short opportunity whilst he's recovering from the shock to deal with the other man. He reaches for my arm holding the knife trying to knock it out of my hands, but it fits so well that it's practically impossible. It takes a lot more effort than I care to admit but I manage to gain the upper hand, driving my knife straight through his chest. He releases me, dropping to the floor but I don't get the chance to breathe before the smaller guy wraps his arms around my waist, pinning my arms to my side. I struggle against him, twisting and kicking, feeling his grip slowly loosening, just enough for me to knee him in his most prized possession. He drops me onto my knees right next to the other man and I waste no time in yanking the knife out, jumping back onto my feet slowly stepping backwards as the smaller guy stalks towards me, a murderous grin plastered on his face.

I trip over the uneven floor, falling backwards, he takes his chance, straddling me his hands tight around my throat. I claw desperately at his hands struggling to get any air into my body. *Don't panic. Don't panic.* I don't. Instead I manage to keep my arm steady and drive the knife deep into his back, followed by one through his heart for good measure. My breathes come in quick and short, his body collapsing on top of me. I shove him off, dragging my knife out in the process.

I sit up, my eyes meeting the ocean blue ones I used to love. My heart pounds as I stare at the broken and battered ghost of my past, bound to the chair in front of me. Neither of us speak. We just stare at each other in stunned silence. I push up onto my knees, moving between his legs, my eyes never leaving his, reaching out my shaking hand, running it down his bruised cheek. I'm enamoured by the memories of how he made me feel. Alive. Happy. In control. I stand up, leaning over until our foreheads are touching, shutting my eyes, finding comfort in the familiar moment, unable to resist the invisible pull. *I just want one ki—* "I'm okay, Bubbles."

I jump back a good two feet, snapping out of it, reality settling in. I whip around sauntering up the stairs, straightening my dishevelled clothes, ignoring the need to run. I'm two steps away from the door when the twins appear in the doorway, seconds before the door is slammed in my face. I push on the door but it doesn't open, almost like something, or someone, is blocking it. I scream, pounding on the door. "Let me out!"

"No can do, Pixie. You two need to talk." Freddie's smug voice floats through the door. I try it again but eventually give up. I sulk back down the stairs until I'm in front of Tylan again.

"Speak." I cross my arms, glaring him down.

"I'll tell you everything when we get out of here." He looks up at me, silently pleading, his voice barely there.

I scoff. “Give me one good reason why I shouldn’t leave you here to rot.”

“Because you need—deserve answers and I’m close to bleeding out.”

I should just leave him here to die. He killed my family. *Didn’t he?* That damn question keeps coming up, doubt constantly creeping in. The longer I stare at the man in front of me, the harder it is to believe he really did it. I let out a frustrated sigh, slicing through his bounds. I help him up, resting his arm around my shoulder, dragging him up the stairs.

“Let us out!” I shout. Silence. “Unless you want him to bleed out.” The door is flung open, quickly followed by a frantic set of twins taking Tylan from me, all of us rushing out the house. I look back, the feeling that we’re forgetting something is strong. I shrug it off, walking a little bit behind the three men, lost in my own mind. I snap out of it when I see the twins trying to get Tylan in the car. “What do you think you’re doing?” I’m met with three equally confused stares.

“We can’t just leave him here, Cap.” Callum blinks at me like I’ve gone crazy.

“Let me talk to him first.” None of them bother arguing with me. The twins climb into the front leaving me alone with Tylan outside the car. “There’s only one question I want you to answer.”

"I didn't kill them Everleigh." He stares directly in my eyes, saving me the job of trying to determine if he's lying. He's not. His pupils always widen if he's lying, it's a subtle tell, but his pupils remain the same size. He may not have lied about that but I can still see the guilt written in his eyes.

"You know who did," I mutter, his reply being a simple nod. I straighten up, shaking my head. "You saw how much my family's death haunts me and all that time you knew?"

"Everleigh I—"

"I don't want to hear it." I open the back door. "I'm done with you Tylan Blaese. Never speak to me again."

"But what about my injuries?"

I shrug. "You healed just fine last time." My breath catches, my heart skipping a beat at the tattoo of three bubbles on his shoulder, covering up a scar. *Did he do that for me?* I snap myself out of it. "I'm happy you're alive." I close the door, shutting it on my past. "Drive."

The car ride back is silent. I'm still in shock. None of this feels real. They're alive. Camilla and Tylan. The two people who have been haunting me for the past two years. The same people I left to burn. My chest tightens to the point of pain. My lungs struggling to gain any oxygen. The second Callum places the car in park I leap out, running to my room. I don't have the chance to lock the door as I sink down to the floor, the wall supporting my back. Hugging my knees to my chest,

I bury my face in my knees trying desperately to gasp in breaths, never getting enough air. I'm transported back to nearly two years ago and the helplessness I felt after killing the two people who betrayed me, at least I thought I killed them.

I don't know when the tears started but they soak my leggings making breathing nearly impossible. I can hear the twins talking but it's all muffled, my ears ringing, my mind racing. I can barely feel the two sets of hands lightly touching my arms. I feel nothing but everything all at once. It's all too much. Memories rush back, swimming around each other. Memories of how special I felt with Tylan. Memories of Camilla making me smile even when I didn't want to. All of them tainted with betrayal. My breathing changes to panicked sobs, the hands tightening their grip against my aching body.

"Everleigh!" I can just about make out my name as Callum grips my face, forcing me to look directly at him. "I need you to breathe with me." It takes a lot of effort but I copy his breaths. In. One. Two. Three. Out. One. Two. Three. Each one of my breaths is shaky, Freddie's hand rubbing my arm comfortingly. Eventually my breathing becomes normal again, only to be replaced by my agonising sobs. I fall forward into Callum's arms, letting every emotion I've been keeping hidden out. He holds me tight, rubbing my back softly as I soak his shirt. Freddie moves closer to me, wrapping around me until I'm the meat in an Archer twins sandwich.

They hold me, my sobs echoing throughout the room for what feels like hours. My sobs eventually slow to sniffles, my head resting on Callum's shoulder. I stare at a random spot on the floor, my mind racing with thoughts of Tylan and Camilla. How did they survive? Do they hate me? Do they really know who killed my family? I know I should've just asked him earlier, but the longer I stayed with Tylan the harder it was becoming to not fall back into our old rhythm. I hate whatever invisible force is bringing us together. But I hate myself more. They didn't kill my family, that means I'm the one who destroyed my own happiness over a mistake. I'm the one who ruined everything.

"Hey. Is everything okay?" I don't break my staring contest with the floor when Summer's summery voice breaks through the silence. I feel Freddie unwrapping himself from my body and moving over slightly in time with the sound of soft footsteps padding across the floor. My stare breaks at the sound of shuffling, my attention turning towards the sound.

Summer is sitting in Freddie's lap, her arms wrapped around his neck as he holds her close to him by her waist. I feel the tears burning my eyes. I always loved when Tylan held me like that. They all share a look seeming to read each other's mind, and probably mine in the process. Callum pulls me closer to him, pushing my head gently to rest on his shoulder. I unconsciously bring my hand to my lips, biting at my nails.

"What happened?" Summer shuffles on Freddie's lap.

There's another uncomfortably long pause before Freddie speaks up. "They're back."

"Who?"

"Camilla and Tylan," I speak up, my voice small and hoarse from my dry throat.

"How?!" Summer's eyes widen and I have no energy to do anything but shrug. The twins look at each other but I know them well enough to know when they're hiding something.

"What are you hiding?" I sit up straight looking between the two, both of them avoiding my eyes. I let out a sigh. I don't have the energy to deal with their games today. "Spit it out."

"Camilla dragged him out the cellar door before the explosion," Callum tells me.

I stare at him. "How do you know this?" Silence. Neither of them want to give me an answer but I don't need one, I know what they're hiding. "You knew they were alive before today." I push myself up to standing, walking away from them, my heart racing again.

"We didn't know how to tell you."

I let out a laugh in disbelief. "How long have you known?"

"Just a couple of months. We found him lurking in the woods."

"You found him what?" I rush over to the window searching the darkness for any sign of life. I come up empty but I can feel more than three sets of eyes on me. Come to think of it, I've felt eyes on me before tonight, only I thought I was just imagining things but...Has he really been watching over me? And why do I not feel disturbed by that thought? I take a deep breath.

"Get out. I need to be alone right now." I keep my gaze out the window, hearing the three of them walk out my room, leaving me alone once again. I can still feel a set of eyes on me even though I know I'm alone. I pull my curtains closed, coating my room in darkness, changing into my pyjama top and shorts before climbing into the comfort of my bed.

I can't sleep. No matter how hard I try I can't stop tossing and turning, today's events playing on a constant loop in my head. I can't help but wonder if he's still out there, watching and waiting. I roll over glancing at the time on my alarm clock. 2 am. I'm not getting any sleep, not if I keep thinking about the man outside my window. I climb out of bed throwing a jumper on and slipping my feet into my sliders. I tiptoe my way down to the kitchen door stopping to look out into the darkness of the night. The only movement noticeable are the trees swaying in the breeze. My eyes catch on a hint of lightly tanned skin hiding between them. Taking a deep breath I slide the door open, stepping out into the cool autumn night. I walk towards his hiding spot, tugging the sleeves of my jumper down. "You stalking me now?"

"I wouldn't call it stalking." He turns to me with a smirk. I take the opportunity to observe him in the moonlight, I can't see his chest anymore since he's now dressed in clothes that don't fit quite right but I can see his face. One of his eyes is circled with a blackening bruise, a small cut coating his bottom lip. I reach out touching his cheek softly. "It's not as bad as it looks."

I snap my hand back, wrapping my arms around myself, shivering in the cold. "We have a couple of spare bedrooms. You and Camilla are welcome to stay until you're healed." Okay I admit it, I overreacted earlier, I shouldn't have left him to heal by himself, not when we have our own doctor.

"I'd rather stay with you." He looks into my eyes, tucking a strand of hair behind my ear. My eyes drift down to his lips, my body leaning closer—

I snap back, "No. I need answers, Tylan." That part's true at least. Maybe after I get my answers I can tell him to never speak to me again and actually mean it.

"Ask and I'll answer."

"Not tonight." I turn and walk back to the house, feeling Tylan's presence behind me. I'm halfway back to the house when I realise there's only the two of us. I stop abruptly, Tylan gripping my waist as he bumps into me. "Where's Camilla?"

I look over my shoulder when he doesn't answer, his eyes full of panic. "Did you untie her?"

"No. I was a bit distracted." I point at him emphasising my point. We stand in silence.

"So you left me to die? Again?" I jump out of Tylan's arms, turning to face my former best friend.

"You got out?" I stare at her, stunned.

"Thankfully, this one also worked out where we were." Her face softens ever so slightly as she points at the man standing behind her, holding onto her waist. Also known as Dean Murphy. The two of them have a complicated relationship, Camilla, the commitmentphobe she is, likes to call it a fuck buddy situation.

A shiver rocks my body as we stand there, none of us knowing what to say. "We should get inside before you freeze, Bubbles." Tylan tries to wrap his arms around my waist but I brush him off.

"Don't call me that," I mumble, leading the group the rest of the way to the house, Dean carries Camilla in his arms and I can't help but wonder why, locking the door once we're all inside. I turn around, letting out a gasp as I see the full extent of both of their injuries. "I'll get Summer to look over you both tomorrow. But for now, there's one bedroom down here and one upstairs with the rest of us. Who wants which?"

"Camilla can barely walk. She can have the downstairs one with Dean." For the first time since she appeared I notice her ankle wrapped in a makeshift bandage, guilt running through my veins.

"It's just down the hall last door on the left." I point in the direction of the bedroom, waiting until Dean and Camilla are out of sight and I'm left alone with Tylan. "Your bedroom is next to mine." I lead him upstairs stopping outside his door.

"Everleigh—" I put my hand up stopping him.

"Not tonight. Goodnight, Tylan." I turn around heading back to my bedroom, craving the comfort of my bed. I slip my sliders and jumper off, throwing it into the darkness, and pull my duvet up to my chin. Tomorrow is going to be a long day, one that I'd rather not deal with.

Vengeance

Dear Miss Reaper.

Beware, beware, the ghost of past.

Prepare, prepare, to say goodbye.

Despair, despair, you're too late.

My dear Everleigh, you got away. They saved you again. It was close. They scurried out the building mere seconds before it ignited. But even before you moved you always had a twin with you wherever you went. Do you know I'm here? Do you know I'm watching you?

Then you moved to this hidden cabin, almost making it too easy for me...if it wasn't for Tylan. I saw him. I saw him watching you just like I was. I know now that I should've just got rid of him but I can't, not until you're gone. But don't worry, I know patience is key.

Count your days, Miss Reaper.

Chapter Thirty-Eight

Jealous Of Water

Tylan

CRIME SCENE DO NOT CROSS

I jerk awake, sweat dripping down my body, my heart running a thousand beats per minute. I look around the room. *Where am I?* It takes me a second to feel the bed I'm sitting on, my heart returning to its normal rhythm, the memories of last night rushing back in full force. Everleigh saved me. The ruthless, tough Everleigh I fell in love with was back last night. Gone was the girl who was a mere shell of her former self...at least until she arrived back here at the safe-house. My heart tightens at the memory of how I watched her through the window. She was broken because of me.

I need to convince her to give me another chance, I am not ready to give up on what we could be. I drag myself out of bed and into the ensuite bathroom. I'm about to turn on the shower when I hear a faint noise of what sounds like singing drifting through the walls. I swear she has me under some sort of a spell because I must look like an idiot pressing my ear against the wall just to hear her voice better. Granted, I definitely wouldn't describe her singing voice as angelic or even good, but it still does something to me. Her voice mixed with the sound of running water stirs up images in my mind of what she must look like right now, with the water running down her perfect curvy body. That should be my hands. Am I really jealous of water?

I back away from the wall pulling my clothes off, wincing from my injuries. I face the mirror, tracing over my year old tattoo – three bubbles covering the scar from one of her deadly stabs, I couldn't imagine anything else covering it, the biggest one has her name written inside, and I intend to fill the other two with the names of our future children, if I need to get more then I will, but two feels like a good start.

I step in the shower, setting it to the perfect temperature, my cock standing out desperate for some attention. I don't hold back, wrapping my hand around my hard cock, jerking off to thoughts of the goddess who's standing on the other side of the wall. Nothing's as satisfying as her though.

It's not long after I've stepped out the shower when there's a knock at my door. I open it, leaning against the door frame to admire Everleigh in her leggings and off the shoulder jumper, her wet hair thrown up into a bun on top of her head. She looks so casual and images flash through me of the two of us living in this house together. Her eyes run up and down my body stopping at each of the scars scattered on my chest before her eyes meet mine.

"Summer's here to check you over. Throw on some pants."

I admire her round ass in the leggings that hug her perfectly as she struts away from me down the stairs. A little cough to the right of me draws my attention away. I look over to my right where the petite red head stands dressed in a ridiculously yellow summer dress and a massive smile on her face.

"Hi. It's been a while." She holds her hand out to me to shake which I pensively take. The one thing I noticed from when we first met is that her name perfectly matches her personality.

"Watch it, Blaese." I break my stare from Summer to meet Freddie's glare. He walks over to us wrapping an arm around Summer's waist and places a kiss on her neck as she giggles. How does a girl like Summer get stuck with a guy like Freddie?

"You're winding him up," she whispers to him and suddenly I'm feeling like a third wheel, despite the fact she's here to check me over.

"But it's fun winding him up, Sunshine." Callum appears from nowhere, wrapping his arm around her waist but this time he places a kiss on her lips. I raise my eyebrows. Both of them? Callum meets my gaze. "Is there a problem?"

"No. No problem here. But your girlfriend's here to check me over not you two."

"Oh, I'm not their girlfriend." She pulls away from the twins, waltzing into my bedroom.

"Put some pants on, Blaese." Freddie glares at me.

"Scared your girlfriend won't be able to resist me, Archer?" I wink at the twins, swiftly closing the door with a grin. "I'm just going to put some pants on in the bathroom." I leave Summer to set up her stuff, grabbing a pair of boxers and jogging bottoms on my way to the ensuite.

I sit on the bed letting Summer look over all my injuries, wincing every now and then. She pays particular attention to my face seeing as that's where the worst of my injuries are. "You'll be fine. Just take some painkillers if you need to and don't do too much exercise for a few weeks." I do nothing but offer her a small nod in response, my mind having wandered back to Everleigh. It feels so strange to be so near her again. "You two will be okay." I blink, turning to face Summer who's now leaning against the desk in the corner of the room, watching me.

"What?" I ask, still half dazed.

"You and Everleigh. I may not be close to her but I've still seen up close how badly you affected her."

"It doesn't matter." I shrug. "She hates me."

"No she doesn't. Not in her heart. She hates herself more because she knows what you mean to her."

"She won't believe anything I say."

"Then show her." She rolls her eyes at me. "Girls love it when a guy shows his love for her so what's your plan, Romeo?"

I smirk, I know exactly how I'm going to win her back, and I plan on starting tonight. "Thanks Summer. You can go back to your boyfriends now."

"They are not my boyfriends." Her bright smile slips ever so slightly, my eyes zoning in on the ring attached to her necklace that she can't stop playing with. Her smile returns. "Besides, I have to deal with Camilla now and she never reacts well in these situations." I huff a laugh, that's something we can both agree with. "Good luck, Tylan. I hope it works out for you two." She closes the door behind her and I waste no time in throwing a t-shirt on. My first step today is grabbing supplies from the shack.

Thankfully Callum is the only one in the kitchen when I enter. I want to speak to Everleigh but I have a couple of things I need to do first that she can't know about – not quite yet at least. I also have a strong feeling that Freddie's not quite back on team Tylan, but Callum seems like he just wants everything to go back to normal. "Can I borrow your car?" He's pouring salt into something that he's cooking but he pauses in mid-air.

"Why?" The single word is dragged out in suspicion.

"I need to grab a couple of things from the shack but I don't have a car around here."

He blinks at me once. Twice. Three times. Snapping out of it, he stops his pour, probably having already ruined the dish. "How did you get here last night without a car?"

"Twenty minutes of walking through the woods and you'll end up right at Michael Knotts' backyard." I point towards said woods.

"Wait, really?" Callum's eyes widen.

"Yeah. It's an hour by car though. I had to wait twenty minutes before you showed up last night." I shrug nonchalantly.

"How did you find out?" His face curls into disgust at the taste of the dish.

"I had to find the easiest way to get here and that was one of the routes I took."

"I—" Callum shakes his head, leaning against the kitchen side. "Word of advice." He crosses his arms. "Don't let Everleigh know you've been stalking her. Keys are next to the door." He nods in the direction.

"Thanks. I owe you."

"You owe me a lot Tylan."

"I'll help you get Summer!" I shout over my shoulder, chuckling as I walk out the door, grabbing the keys on the way.

The shack is a good hour and a half drive away, closer to the town centre than the safe house. I gather as many clothes and toiletries as I can, making sure to also grab Camilla's, as well as what I really came here for, safely locked away in my mother's old jewellery box. I make sure everything is in the car before doing one final check around the shack, stopping in Camilla's room to grab her most prized possession and also to grab Bailey, he wouldn't stop whining at me when I first got here, and for good reason.

I fed him and let him out to do his business. Thankfully I assume Dean looked after him whilst we were trapped in the basement given how lively Bailey was. I lock the shack behind me, placing him in the passenger seat before hopping in the driver's seat and making my way back to the safe house. I only stop twice along the way to buy the final pieces for my plan.

It's mid-afternoon when I arrive back at the cabin, parking the car back in its place. Everleigh steps out of the house just as I step out the car. She jumps back when she spots me.

"What are you doing?"

"I went back to the shack to grab some essentials."

"Why?" She glares at me. "You'll be going back there soon."

"Not if I can help it, Bubbles." She rolls her eyes at me, placing one of her ear buds in her ear, it's only now that I realise she's dressed in the tightest sports bra that pushes her voluptuous breasts up, paired with a pair of running shorts that hug her ass, both of which leave her midriff exposed. That was always my favourite part of her to kiss and I can't wait until she lets me do it again. She's about to put the other ear bud in when I stop her. "Have dinner with me tonight."

She raises an eyebrow at me. "Excuse me? Why would I do that?"

"I'll answer anything you ask. I'll give you your truth tonight just meet me on the dock when the sun starts to set." I'm close to getting on my knees and begging her but she spares me the humiliation with a small nod before she swiftly jogs past me. I walk around the car opening the passenger door, picking Bailey up, it's not as easy as it used to be considering he's now a fully grown golden retriever, but I don't fancy adding cleaning him to my to-do list for today.

I've only just stepped in the house when Bailey starts barking and wagging his tail like crazy. It doesn't take me long to realise why when I have three faces staring at me all with different expressions. Freddie looks like he literally has steam coming out his ears, Callum is nothing but shocked, and Summer looks like a little kid at the zoo. "Oh my gosh!"

"What is that?"

"No way!" Their voices all overlap.

"What do you mean no way?" I'm shocked by Summer's glare at Freddie who glares right back at her but she doesn't back down.

"Why do you have a dog?" Callum leaves the other two to their glaring contest, walking over to me.

"I was not about to abandon my dog." I hold him closer to me.

"Let him keep him. Please." We both turn to Summer who's broken her stare with Freddie and is now looking at us with the exact puppy dog look that Everleigh's mastered.

Callum shrugs. "I'm okay with it." We all turn to Freddie who still has the same glare plastered on his face. I don't miss how Summer increases her pout at him, even adding in a few bats of her eyelashes at him.

"Fine," he relents, quickly followed by Summer's squeal as she hugs him tight.

"What's his name?" Callum asks, scratching behind Bailey's ear.

"Bailey."

"Aww. You're such a good boy, Bailey." Summer races over to us her smile as bright as ever, she joins Callum in showering him in hugs. I place him down only for him to leap at Summer knocking her down as he licks all over her face, her response is a load of giggles as the twins rush over to her.

"Bailey. Sit." He listens to me, panting happily, his tail wagging none stop. "Do you mind watching him whilst I unload the car?"

"Not at all." Summer grins at me, petting Bailey. I leave them in the house, making a couple trips back and forth until everything is unloaded.

"Where's Camilla?" I ask, dropping the keys back on the table by the door. The trio have moved onto the couch, cuddled up watching what appears to be a chick flick, Bailey resting on Summer's feet.

"In her room with Dean. She can't really walk right now." Callum nods towards her bedroom. "I'd knock before entering if I was you."

"It's nothing I haven't seen before." I wish that was a lie, but when you live in a tiny shack with two people who are fuck buddies, as Camilla likes to call it, you see a lot of stuff you wish you didn't. I pick up the bags with Camilla's items in and walk down the short hallway to her door. I knock just in case, I would rather not see either of them naked again if I can help it.

"Come in," Camilla's voice calls from the other side of the door. I open the door to the pair cuddled up in bed watching Ratatouille on the TV. *Why is everyone so loved up?*

"Thought you might like this." I throw her the battered teddy bear she's had for as long as I can remember.

"You went back to the shack?" She unwraps her arms from Dean opting to hold the teddy bear tight in her arms instead, it's always been her comfort, there was no chance I was leaving the shack without bringing him back for her.

"Thanks Tylan." Dean glares at me.

"Your cuddle time's up for today, babe." Camilla grins tapping him condescendingly on the chest.

"I also brought you your clothes." I hold up the bags before placing them on the floor.

"Thank God. Summer's nice and all but she really needs to sort out her wardrobe." We all glance at the pale yellow jumper she's currently wearing. A smiling sun sits in the middle with the saying "Don't worry, be happy" written underneath it. I throw her one of her plain red jumpers she always wears and she wastes no time in swapping the two. "That's much better." I go to sit at the foot of the bed. "Not there!" I raise my eyebrow at her. "I don't want you breaking my ankle even more."

"It's broken?" I sit further up the bed to make sure I avoid her ankle.

"Just sprained. But still..."

"Got it." I mock salute her.

"Have you spoken to Everleigh yet?" Dean asks.

"Briefly. She agreed to have dinner with me tonight."

"How the fuck did you manage that?" Camilla raises her eyebrows.

"I promised her the truth." I shrug.

"And are you going to tell her everything?" She plays with the silver ring on her thumb.

"I have to Cami. She deserves it."

She nods. "I know."

"She'll forgive you." I place my hand on hers.

"I lied to her for nearly six years, longer than that really. You were only in her life for five months, my betrayal hits far worse than yours. I saw the effect that her family's death had on her in real time. I lost my best friend that night and I tried to make it all better out of guilt. I wouldn't be surprised if she doesn't forgive me." She shrugs Dean off when he tries to wrap his arm around her shoulders.

"I won't allow it. She'll forgive me and she'll forgive you once we tell her the truth." I give her hand one last squeeze before leaving the two alone.

I spend the rest of the afternoon putting all my clothes away and setting up a picnic on the dock. Once the base is set, I head back to my room changing into one of my three piece suits. I finish off by cooking the last of our meal, packing it all away in the picnic basket, making sure I include her surprise. I search around the kitchen for a couple of bottles of champagne but I can only find one. One is better than none I suppose.

It doesn't take long to finish setting up our dinner, the last thing I do is light the candles sitting in the middle of everything else. And now I wait. I have to keep reminding myself not to lean against the handrail, I do not trust them at all, given how precariously they wobbled earlier when I was decorating them.

I don't have to wait long before Everleigh is walking towards the dock, unable to contain the smile gracing my lips, her hair is thrown up in a messy bun, paired with a baggy t-shirt and old jogging bottoms. I can take a hint. She clearly doesn't want me thinking this is a date but she's failing because she still looks as sexy as ever. I take a deep breath. Here goes nothing.

Picnic

Everleigh

What was I thinking agreeing to this? *You deserve answers.* That's all this is. My chance to get the answers I've been fighting for, for the past eight years. The weather is unseasonably warm, the low afternoon sun reflecting off the glistening lake creates a calming atmosphere, it's a clear contrast to what I'm feeling inside.

I have a strong feeling Tylan thinks this is a date, probably thinking that I'll hear him out and everything will be magically resolved but it won't. I refuse to give myself any more false hope in my life. I throw on my baggiest t-shirt and comfiest pair of black jogging bottoms, throwing my hair up in the messiest bun you've ever seen. I chance a glance in the mirror and I definitely do not look like I'm going on a date, we're just two people talking, that's it, there's nothing more to it. I close my eyes and breathe in. One. Two. Three. And out. One. Two. Three. I stare at myself in the mirror. *You can do this Everleigh.*

The dock looks completely different than it normally does. There's fairy lights tangled around the handrails, two lanterns sitting on the end posts, there's a tartan picnic blanket sitting near the end of the dock, on top of which sits two sets of plates, cutlery, and champagne glasses finished up neatly with a lit candelabra in the middle. Some might say this is romantic but all I can think of is the candelabra tipping over and this entire dock going up in flames. I tentatively walk the few short steps to the end of the dock, feeling Tylan's eyes on me but I avoid his, I don't have the strength in me right now to not fall into his ocean blue trap.

We couldn't look more different than we do right now. Here I am dressed like a hungover teenager who's just been heartbroken, whereas Tylan's dressed in one of his signature three piece suits like he's about to meet with the King.

Wait a minute. I avert my eyes away from the picnic set up, taking in his full outfit. I recognise this suit. Then I see it. The embroidered "TB" on the shirt collar, and on the lapel of his jacket. It's the same suit he was wearing when we first met. The manipulative bastard. If he thinks he can get all sentimental and I'll come crawling back to him then he's in for a big shock. "You look beautiful." I scowl at him refusing to speak as I go to sit at one of the place settings. He stops me, placing his hand gently on my arm. "This one's for you." He indicates the other setting.

"Why does it matter?" I shrug his hand off, my glare intensifying.

"Everleigh, just humour me." His usual playfulness is gone, replaced by a version of Tylan I've never seen before.

I bite the bullet and look into his eyes, drawn to the dark circles beneath them. He looks exhausted. I should know, I looked like a walking zombie for at least the first year after we last saw each other, but why would he look like one? I was only a game to him...right?

I relent the slightest bit, taking a seat at the other setting. I don't even bother trying to fight the urge, I lean over blowing out the candle. Tylan raises an eyebrow at me taking his seat opposite me. "I don't exactly trust the wood we're surrounded by." Why I felt the need to explain myself is beyond me. His lips lift up at the edge ever so slightly as he watches me, butterflies flutter in my stomach. Wait no, not butterflies, hunger. That's all this is.

I can't take the eye contact. I break it looking around for food. My eyes land on the wicker picnic basket just within my reach. I perk up reaching over and pulling it towards me. I close my eyes, moaning at the delicious smell that escapes when I open it. I waste no time in pulling out the multiple homemade dishes, not failing to notice they're all my favourites: Chicken Caesar salad, chicken alfredo, red velvet cake, cinnamon rolls, and even a bowl of watermelon and honeydew melon. I look towards Tylan, speechless.

"I could never forget what you like, Bubbles." He gives me that damn wink that always makes me weak in the knees, at least I'm already sitting down so I can cover it up pretty easily.

"Speaking of… where's the bubbles?" I ask, scooping a couple spoonful's of the alfredo and salad onto my plate.

"Right here." He reaches behind him to an ice bucket I never noticed, inside sits an unopened bottle of Dom Perignon. He really did think of everything. I watch silently, stunned, as he opens the bottle, pouring a little into both of our glasses. "I know you don't like sharing your champagne but I only saw one bottle in the kitchen." That's not surprising, there may have been a little champagne induced incident when we first moved in that ended up with me taking a trip down the stairs, and the twins taking it in turns to clean up puke whilst I sobbed in the other's arms all night. After that night they both decided to stick to one bottle in the house at any time. It was definitely not my finest moment at all.

"What is this Tylan?" I twirl my glass in my hand, careful not to spill any.

"I figured I kinda owe you for saving my life last night." He seems so calm and casual as he piles his plate up with food that it actually annoys me.

"That's not the reason I'm here." I push the food on my plate around, suddenly not feeling hungry at all.

"I know." He sighs, placing his fork full of food back on his plate. "I'll tell you anything you want, Everleigh, anything to get you to stop hating me."

I don't hate you. I bite my tongue refusing to admit it but the smile that graces his lips moments after I think it… "I said that out loud didn't I?"

"Not if you don't want me to know." He winks at me again and I can't help the smile that graces my lips. I haven't smiled in forever but here Tylan is waltzing back into my life and bringing that side of me out again. I don't want this with him though. I lose my smile, taking a bite of the food. I wish I could say it's horrible but it's not, he's always been a good cook.

"Who did it?" I blurt out, needing a distraction.

"Did what?" he asks, taking a bite of his food.

"Don't play dumb." I roll my eyes, scowling at him.

He sighs, dropping his fork. "Ezra Blaese." He looks away from me in defeat.

"Ezra Blaese..." Why does that name sound familiar? "Who's Ezra—" I gasp realisation hitting me like a bullet. "Your dad?!"

Tylan avoids my eyes offering me nothing except for the tiniest of nods. My heart races like crazy. Tylan's dad killed my family. Why? How? How does Tylan know? Why didn't he tell me? My mind races with unanswered questions, each one constantly blocking out the ending of another. I feel like my head is about to burst from all the activity. They stop when a gentle hand lands on my arm. Everything is calm. Tylan makes everything calm. No. No he can't.

"Why?" My voice is nothing but a broken whisper.

"They owed him money." Tylan's voices matches my own.

I raise my head slowly, glaring daggers at him. “Money,” I spit out. “They died because of fucking money?” my voice is low, full of venom as I force the words out.

“My father wasn’t a good man, Everleigh.” He avoids my eyes, his voice betraying how broken he is.

“No shit.” I let out a disbelieving laugh. “What kind of man kills people for money? Kills innocent kids for money? My sister was sixteen, my brother only five!” I’ve never felt so angry in my life. Money? My life was ruined over something grown on fucking trees?

“The same man who beats his own kid.” I physically jerk back at his admission, my anger simmering ever so slightly. The scars on his body...my eyes widen. It all makes sense but one thing still doesn’t sit right with me.

“When did you know he did it?” I have a feeling I really don’t want to know the answer to that question.

He looks me in the eyes, guilt swimming through them, mixed with distress. “That night. He came home covered in blood and told me everything. He threatened to beat me if I didn’t help cover for him.” He shrugs sadly. “I would’ve taken that beating but Camilla was with me at the time—” Camilla? Of course, the picture.

“How did you know Cam—”

“We were together. She wanted to keep our relationship a secret.” He smiles sadly. “You two have that in common. When my father saw us together he threatened to pin it all on her and with the money he had—”

"He would have done it," I finish for him. I can understand how they may have felt trapped. Money is a wonderful thing until it falls into the wrong hands.

He nods. "So we helped clear any evidence of him...until you interrupted us. We got out the house where my father was waiting for us, he forced us to take that picture as black-mail."

"The footsteps I heard...I thought I was imagining things but it was you." It's not a question. "Why didn't you kill me?"

He looks me in the eyes. "I wasn't a killer back then. Plus I would never hurt an innocent person, yet alone a child."

"You should've killed me," I mumble quietly, looking down, playing with a loose thread on my t-shirt.

"Don't say that." He places one hand underneath my chin lifting my head to meet his eyes. "I never would've killed the girl I love."

"You don't love me." I shake my chin loose from his hold. "You never have and you never will." I shrug. "No one will, I'm unlovable."

"That's crazy, Everleigh. You're the most lovable person I've ever met. This little voice..." He taps my temple softly just like he did two years ago. "Is just refusing to let you believe it."

"I can't do this Tylan. We're never going to be what we were two years ago so stop trying." His hand on top of mine stops me from running away like I really want to.

"Don't you have more questions?" He looks at me, hope shining in his eyes.

"I do. But I don't know if I can handle any more of the truth right now." I pull my hand away from his.

"I'll tell you everything you need when you're ready." He promises, standing up. "At least enjoy the food I made for you, I'll leave you alone for now. But Everleigh," I look up at him, "I will never stop fighting for you." I watch his retreating form, waiting until he's back inside before I release the breath I didn't realise I was holding.

I turn back to the lake. The sun is now setting casting the sky with hues of orange and red. I pull my phone case off, unfolding the picture of my family I now keep there. "I did it. I know who killed you. Are you proud?" My voice breaks, a drop of rain landing on the old picture. Wait, it's not raining. It's my tears, again. There hasn't been a single day in the past six hundred and ninety two where I haven't shed at least one tear. I'm tired of crying. Will I ever stop being so pathetic? I wipe the tears away, folding the picture again, placing it back in my phone case where it's safe.

I finish my plate of salad and now cold pasta, basking in the peace of nature. For once I feel hopeful that everything is going to be okay and I don't try to banish the thought. Maybe I really have made it through the storm and now I just have to piece everything back together again.

I reach back into the basket pulling the cake out. I take off the protective lid revealing the small four-inch cake, on top of which sits a white rose, my favourite flower, with a small scroll tied to it. I pick the flower off, sniffing it, sighing at the floral scent. I delicately untie the scroll and open it, revealing a letter.

20th December 2016

Dear Bubbles,

Happy Birthday! I know it probably doesn't feel very happy but it's only customary, right? I know you're probably wondering why I'm sending a letter in this day and age, but I wouldn't be surprised if you've blocked me on everything. Plus you think I'm dead, a text message from a ghost is probably the last thing you need right now. Camilla and I are both safe. I know you probably hate us but I promise I will tell you everything when you're ready. You might feel like you will never be ready, but I know you Everleigh. You're stronger than you realise. It's a lot to ask but you have to trust me. I never killed your family, but I do know who did, I just need to work out the exact reason why and then I will give you the closure you and your family deserve.

I won't give up on us, Bubbles. We have something special and I will prove it to you. I will prove it to you every day until you take me back, until you have my ring on your finger, until we move into that cabin, until you open your bookstore, until we have mini versions of us causing havoc, until the die I die. I love you Everleigh Carlton.

Your Tylan
xx

Tylan wrote me a letter a few weeks after I tried to kill him? A letter explaining that he wasn't going to give up on us? What does he think this is going to prove? I scrunch up the letter, walking over to the edge of the dock, holding both the letter and the rose over the water...I can't do it. I let out a frustrated scream storming back to the house. Tylan can tidy up his picnic for all I care. I'll entertain his little games but there's no way I'll fall for them. Not again.

Chapter Forty

Roses and Letters

Tylan

The picnic last night didn't necessarily go the way I was expecting. I'm not stupid, I knew she wasn't going to forgive me just like that but I thought she would at least give me something to work with. Part of me was worried she wouldn't even find the rose and the note, the tension eased inside me slightly when I went back to clear up later and there wasn't any sight of a rose or a letter. I know her reaction can't have been good though considering the amount of food that was left over.

I tidied up the dock as best as I cold, leaving the cake and cinnamon rolls in the kitchen for everyone to have if they wanted. Part of me is starting to doubt that my plan with the letter is going to work but I'm not giving up just yet.

It's currently seven am but the pain running through my body made for an uncomfortable and restless night. I give up with sleep, opting instead to get on with the day. I take a quick shower, still feeling the dust crawling over my body from that basement, despite the numerous showers I've already had. I change into a pair of jeans and a simple black t-shirt, picking up a single white rose from the bouquet sitting in a vase by the window. I gently place the rose on top of the bedside cabinet, reaching into the bottom draw to pull out my box containing the letters.

I run my finger over the etching of my mother's name, I never found out if she knew what my father liked to do with me, she died before I could ask. I want to believe she didn't, I want to believe that she didn't leave her only child to suffer but they both had no problems in telling me how big of a mistake I was to them, maybe she really did turn a blind eye. I push those thoughts away rifling through the letters until I find the one I'm looking for, scanning it quickly before rolling it up and tying it to the stem of the rose.

I sneak down the stairs trying not to make too much noise and wake up the entire house. I top up both Bailey and Muffin's food and water bowls before grabbing a cinnamon roll, topped with extra icing, and placing it on a plate. I take the sweet treat upstairs, stopping at my room to grab the flower, before stopping outside Everleigh's room.

This could be a bad idea, she doesn't tend to sleep a lot and when she does she's a light sleeper. I take a deep breath, pushing the door open slowly. I peek inside noting the sleeping figure curled up under a mountain of blankets, tiptoeing inside, quietly placing the snack and rose on her vanity. I pause at the sound of sheets rustling, sneaking a glance over my shoulder. She's still asleep.

I know I should get out of here but I can't fight the urge that's making me stalk over to her bed. I crouch down admiring her sleeping figure, she always looks so peaceful when she's sleeping, almost like it's the one time her mind shuts off and she can relax. I hope she realises one day soon that she doesn't have to wait until her eyes are shut, drool pooling on her pillows, and her dreams take over, for her to be at peace. I place a soft kiss on her forehead, tucking a piece of hair behind her ear, savouring the softness that I've missed, before forcing myself out of the room.

The sun is only just starting to rise so I decide to take Bailey on his walk early, grabbing his favourite toy as well as a couple of bags before throwing on my coat. I lead him out the house, his collar jiggling with every step, it's not long until he's racing ahead of me, finding a new tree to do his business at. I wait for him to finish before cleaning up after him. I can't help the smile at the memory that this was the exact reason Everleigh got a cat instead of a dog. "*They walk and clean themselves. Plus all you have to do is change their litter box.*" That was the exact reason she gave me...whilst she was in the middle of changing said box.

The sun has fully risen by the time we've completed the circular walking route back to the house, the last stretch is the most beautiful part, walking alongside the lake. I can see a figure in the distance, sitting on the end of the dock, looking slightly distressed. My heart races, a smile widening on my face at the thought that it could be Everleigh. My smile drops as I get closer and can make out the red tones and petite body dressed in workout gear. I try to sneak past but Summer's bright voice stops me. "Tylan!"

I turn around, smiling at her waving me over to join her. I open the door to the house, cleaning Bailey's paws before letting him free, closing the door behind him. I make the short trip back to the dock, sitting beside Summer. "You okay?" I ask.

She nods. "I always do this in the morning. I go for my morning jog and then sit here to watch the sunrise. It's really so beautiful isn't it? Not just the sunrise I mean this whole area. It's like something out of a movie." I simply look at her as she rambles on. "I mean for starters the house is quite something, I can't believe the twins own something like it. And then there's this lake, surrounded by the towering trees and nature. I mean this dock could use some repairs but—" She lets out a nervous laugh when she catches my eyes on her. "Sorry. I tend to ramble. I don't like silence."

"I get it." I offer her a tiny smile before turning my attention back to the lake. I can sense her fidgeting next to me desperate to break the silence that's descended on us.

"Can I say something?" she bursts out. The only thing I offer her is a nod. "You love her right?" I glance at her, curious to see where she's going. "I'll take that as a yes." She sucks in a breath. "Don't push her away."

"She's pushing me away." I shrug.

"No you're driving her away with your pushiness." I raise my eyebrows at her. "I just mean a girl like Everleigh doesn't take well to obsessiveness. Stop breathing down her neck and give her the time and space she needs—"

"You don't think two years is enough time?" I narrow my eyes at her which she responds with an eye roll.

"She thought she killed you Tylan. And now you've waltzed straight into her life without giving her even a second to process it all." Her face is serious. I swallow, unsure of what to say. She's right. "Listen." She plays with her necklace. "I, more than anyone know what it's like to want more time with someone. I would do anything to have more time with Jason." She stares off into the distance with no sign of the summery girl we all know.

"Who's Jason?"

She offers me the tiniest of smiles. "He was my fiancé. He killed himself a month before our wedding." She takes a deep breath wiping away a couple of tears trailing down her cheeks. "What I'm trying to say is that love takes time. If you really are meant to be together then you will be. Fate will draw you two back together when the time is right, so stop trying to force it to happen sooner than it's meant to. Understood?"

I nod. "So I should stop with the roses and letters?"

"You wrote her letters?" Her mouth drops open, eyes shining with awe.

“Yeah. They stopped me from racing in and facing her before she was ready.” I shrug nonchalantly.

“Whatever your plan is with them now, don’t stop that. I think I would die if a guy ever wrote me letters. Anyway this isn’t about me, what I’m saying is wait for her to speak to you, don’t chase her around. If you’re really meant to be, then you will be together again.” She offers me one final smile before leaving me alone to my thoughts. She has a point. Everleigh hasn’t exactly reacted well to me begging to talk to her. I told her I’m willing to wait as long as it takes, now it’s time for me to show her.

Chapter Forty-One

You're Not Him

Everleigh

I never thought I would say this again but I miss Tylan. He hasn't said a single word to me over the past one and a half months other than a simple "hi" in passing. That's not to say he's been silent, we've been messaging every night for the past three weeks, and I still find the odd rose and letter every now and then. The first one came the day after our picnic.

I woke up to the addicting smell of cinnamon and sitting on my vanity was a cinnamon roll with a white rose lying next to it, the second letter tied to it. I guess my dream that night may not have been a dream after all. I sat at the vanity eating the little slice of heaven, reading through the letter.

1st January 2017

Dear Bubbles,

Happy new year! I don't know about you but I wouldn't call this a "happy" year, not with you hating me. Maybe I can change it around. Maybe it won't be too long until we can meet again and I can give you your answers. Camilla thinks I'm crazy for writing letters, especially since I didn't even send the first one.

I see you've gone into hiding, if the news stories of the Polaroid Reaper are anything to go by. I can't help but wonder why that is? I miss seeing the clippings of my girl's latest victim. You were always braver than I was. You weren't afraid to do right by their victims, even if it wasn't in a conventional manner. I don't think you should give up on that. I see you every now and then and it breaks my heart, I see the bags under your eyes and the tear tracks on your cheeks. I'm so sorry I did this to you Bubbles but I promise I will make everything right again, soon. I never break my promises.

Tylan
xx

I still remember the anger that rose within me with that letter. I stormed out my room, searching for him but I couldn't find him anywhere. Maybe that's a good thing though because if I had, I would have lit both of the letters on fire right in front of his eyes, I would've shown him exactly what his words meant to me. He called me brave in that letter when I'm anything but. A brave person doesn't waste away because of a guy. Alas, I didn't find him and I still have them.

The next letter I received was a week later. This one was sitting on top of Muffin's food bowl, with it was a bracelet with a tinker bell charm, and it wasn't a cheap one.

17th May 2017

Dear Bubbles,
It's been a while since my last letter. I didn't send that one either and honestly, I doubt I'll send this one. Anyway, don't freak out but I found your safe house. It's taken four months and I couldn't believe it when I did, it takes all my strength to not knock on the door. It's the house you've always dreamed of. A modern cabin in the woods with glass walls overlooking the lake? It's perfectly you. You look so at home in it, I only wish it were me you were living with, please promise me one day it will be? How can the twins afford it anyway?

I saw you at your family's graves earlier today. Of course I know why, it's your mum's birthday...my heart physically broke even more for you. It hurts seeing you like this, even more so knowing that I'm part of the reason. I miss the feisty Everleigh I fell in love with and I know you miss her too. She's still inside you, Everleigh, and you will see her again, never give up hope of that.
I wanted to tell you this in person but I think it's time you know who killed them. Writing it in this letter is probably the coward's way out but it's not time for us to meet again. It was my father. Ezra Blaese. I still don't know why yet, but I promise the second I find out you'll know.

Your Tylan
xx

That was the first one I cried at. In that moment I realised that he's been my shadow for the past nearly two years, too afraid to step out but always there watching over me. I thought that day would be the day I'd speak to him again but it wasn't. I searched the entire cabin and woods but he wasn't there. That was when Freddie told me he'd moved out but he had to leave Bailey here. I considered messaging him but I passed by his temporary bedroom and I just couldn't.

One week later and the next letter was sitting on my reading bench sitting on top of a new book. I wasted no time in reading the letter.

5th February 2018

Dear Bubbles,

It's taken me nine months but I finally know why my father did it. I didn't think it was possible for me to hate him even more but I do. He gave your parents £50,000 for a procedure to help them have another child. Only he failed to mention it was a loan. He expected them to pay them back but they refused. They were in the right but I for one know how important money was to my father. He really was a horrid man.

I know sorry won't mean much to you, so how about a promise that I will give you whatever you want and need for the rest of your life? Too much?

Last year was the hardest year of my life. I'm miserable without you, Bubbles. I walked past Forever & Ever yesterday. Do you remember when we first met? I do. I could feel your eyes burning into my skin. I couldn't believe my luck when I turned around. I had the most beautiful woman in the world staring right at me. I may have seemed confident but the truth is my heart was racing like crazy with every step I took towards you. I know now that you were probably just setting your plan in motion, but can we agree to let me believe it was real? That was the day I knew I was in trouble. I couldn't let you go after that night.
Are you ready to give me a second chance, Bubbles?
Your Romeo
xx

Of course I remember that day, I'll never forget it. He's not wrong, in that moment I was setting my plan in motion, form a bond with the detective in charge of my case solely so I could try to get an insight into the investigation. The truth is, that day I had butterflies in my stomach, it was almost like my heart knew something my mind didn't. I read over the final question five times, the rest of the letter was written in black ink, that question in blue, almost like it was written at a different time. I want to give him that second chance but I don't know if I'm strong enough just yet.

I unwrapped the new book he left me – a Romeo & Juliet retelling – the type of romance book I love. I read it in one sitting. *Your Romeo.* That's what he signed off this letter with. It suits him, he really is a hopeless romantic. I caved that night. I couldn't sleep, I was just tossing and turning, so at exactly four am I messaged him, I didn't expect anything back for a few hours but he proved me wrong.

I remember that procedure

I was ten

My parents had been trying for years to have another child but they couldn't get pregnant

They were so close to giving up

September 28th 2004, they came home and told Maya and I we were going to be big sisters

It was a miracle

It wasn't until Ethan was 3 that they us about the procedure

Your father told them they didn't owe him anything...

He was like that

He was a wicked man

He was

You're not him, Tylan

Does this mean you're giving me my second chance?

I don't know if I can

Let's stick to messaging for now

We messaged every night at exactly four am, sometimes they were short exchanges with simple check-ins, sometimes they were longer talks about our past. It took two weeks for the next letter to show up. This one was sitting on the kitchen counter with a fresh iced caramel latte, extra caramel. Callum was cooking when I walked in. "Tylan left that for you."

I couldn't stop it. For the first time in two years a small smile spread across my lips, I missed his letters. I sat at the kitchen island, sipping my coffee.

11 August 2018

Dear Bubbles,

I've been writing letters to you for the last six months, but none of them were right to send to you. You've become my imaginary diary to write my every thought into. I'm going crazy for you, Bubbles. I should've been able to get over you by now, right? Surely this is a sign that we're meant to be together. That's what I keep telling myself at least. Would you believe me if I tell you I now love caramel lattes? I've been making them every day just to feel closer to you. Camilla's not really a fan though. She doesn't say it but she misses you as well, Bubbles. We both do.

We've been tracking down Michael Knotts for the past year and a half. We think we might be getting somewhere. Don't worry, I'll leave him alive long enough for you to get your revenge on him. I promise. The moment we have him, I will come get you. I just hope you don't hate me.

Your Romeo
xx

"Are you going to speak to him yet?" Callum was still cooking away when I finished reading the fifth letter.

"I still have another two months of letters to go through yet." The truth is I was ready to speak to him properly. The fact that he was willing to risk everything just to give me a chance of getting my revenge...that means everything to me, but it still doesn't change the fact that he lied to me.

Before I knew it, it was four am again.

You like caramel lattes now?

When I make them, they're pretty good

Right?

It's not the worst one I've ever had

You always know how to humble me

It's my talent

It's been another long week but the sixth letter was sitting on my bed waiting for me after my shower, along with a matching knife I used to kill the men with, except this one has my initials embroidered on the handle. This one's dated a little over two weeks before I saved him.

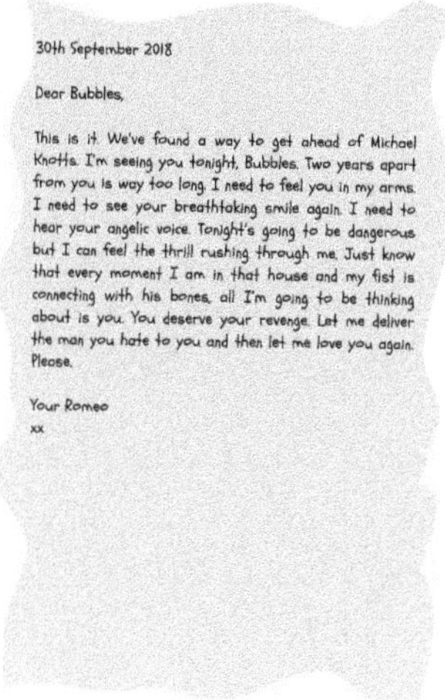

30th September 2018

Dear Bubbles,

This is it. We've found a way to get ahead of Michael Knotts. I'm seeing you tonight, Bubbles. Two years apart from you is way too long. I need to feel you in my arms. I need to see your breathtaking smile again. I need to hear your angelic voice. Tonight's going to be dangerous but I can feel the thrill rushing through me. Just know that every moment I am in that house and my fist is connecting with his bones, all I'm going to be thinking about is you. You deserve your revenge. Let me deliver the man you hate to you and then let me love you again. Please.

Your Romeo
xx

I wipe the tears I didn't even know had started off my cheeks. I think I'm finally ready to speak to him again. Am I ready to let him love me again? I'm not sure. Am I ready to forgive him? Yes. I strip out of my towel, changing into my cream turtleneck and black skater skirt, the same outfit I was wearing when we first met. I'm looking in the mirror when my eyes catch sight of a picture on my bed.

I walk back, picking up the picture I missed earlier, a smile gracing my lips. It was taken on my twentieth birthday, we all went out partying the night away. I had a few drinks too many, but what else are you meant to do when you're not the one paying? One of the twins must've taken it, me and Camilla giggling away on a patch of grass, our hair and clothes a dishevelled mess. We look so happy. I hold the picture close to my heart. I need to speak to Tylan but there's someone else I need to speak to first.

Chapter Forty-Two

Two Left Feet

Everleigh

I wander downstairs looking for either Camilla or Tylan. Camilla never moved out but Tylan visits every day to feed and walk Bailey, I'm guessing his new place doesn't allow pets. I'm tired of holding grudges and I'm ready to forgive both of them, I'm ready to get my life back on track...I just need to find them first. I hear the clatters of pans in the kitchen so I decide to head there first doing a double take when, for once, Freddie's the one cooking, not Callum. "Since when do you cook?"

He turns to me holding a pan with what looks like a burnt omelette inside. "I thought I'd treat Summer."

I press my lips together to suppress the giggle wanting to escape. "Do you want some help?"

His eyes narrow at me. "No."

I hold my hands up in mock surrender. "I'm just asking." He turns back to the stove, pouring in a second omelette. I walk over, leaning against the counter next to him. "Have you seen either Camilla or Tylan?"

He raises an eyebrow at me. "Depends why you want to know."

I roll my eyes. "I just want to speak to them. Clear the air."

His shoulders physically relax. "Camilla's outside on the swinging seat."

"And Tylan?"

"Camilla's outside on the swinging seat," he repeats.

I narrow my eyes at his back. "That's not what I asked."

"Speak to Camilla first. Just trust me, Pixie."

"Fine," I mumble, already making my way to the back door.

I spot her immediately, her raven curls thrown up into a bun, wrapped up in one of my blankets, it's a little chillier today than it has been the past few weeks. I approach the seat, taking the empty spot next to her. Neither of us speak as I push the seat with my feet. "I hate this, Cami."

She looks over at me. "I hate this too."

I sigh. "Where did it all go wrong?"

"Probably the day I started dating Tylan." She huffs out a laugh.

"Why did you never tell me about him? You're the same age, it's not like anything bad was happening."

"I think a part of me, even back then, knew that I'm not cut out for relationships. Feelings are too complicated." I hug my knees to my chest as she speaks. "For me." She corrects herself. "Feelings are too complicated for me. What was the point in introducing you to someone who would be gone soon after?" She shrugs.

"I can understand that." I swallow, scared to ask the next question. "Did you only stay friends with me out of guilt?"

"No!" She turns her full body to me, gripping my hands. "Everleigh, no. I stayed friends with you because you're like a little sister to me. Always have been, always will be."

"But how could you just sit by and watch my whole world change? You watched and held me through my countless breakdowns. You're the one who stopped me from ending it all, all whilst you knew what happened." I don't even try to stop the tears racing down my cheeks. "I want to forgive you, Cami. Just tell me the truth."

"I've been searching every day since that night for a way to turn back time and change it." She uses her hoodie sleeve to wipe the tears from my cheeks. "I broke up with him that night and I raced back to tell you the truth but you were so broken that you collapsed in my arms. You just lost your family and I couldn't let you walk away from our friendship. Not that night."

"And every night after?"

"You became set on killing the person who killed them. What would you have done if you found out your best friend had a part in it?"

I sigh knowing exactly how I would've reacted. "I would've reacted the same way I did two years ago."

"I know sorry doesn't fix anything but you can't hate me any more than I hate myself."

"I don't hate you." I uncurl my legs, wrapping my arms around her. "I'm not saying our relationship's fixed just like that. Tylan's betrayal hurt but yours shattered me. It's going to take a lot of work to fix it, but I'm willing to try if you are." I offer her a small smile.

"I can work with that." She squeezes me in a hug. It's not often that she lets anyone see this soft side of her but it always reminds me just how much I mean to her.

"Do you remember how we first met?" I rest my head on top of hers on my shoulder.

"Of course I do."

"Maya." We say at the same time, sharing a smile. We were in nursery and my sister pretty much dragged us to each other, we clicked immediately.

"What do you think she would be doing if she was still alive?" Camilla asks.

I'm surprisingly relaxed despite the topic of the question. "She always loved ballet. I have no doubt she would've become a professional ballerina but would've retired to teach the kids of today...Maybe I should take up dancing."

"You?" She huffs a laugh.

I look at her in mock defence. "I can dance."

"You, Everleigh Carlton, have two left feet." She sits up. "Do we need to relive prom?"

"Please no," I groan, dropping my head in my hands at the memory, to a chorus of her laughs.

"Your date couldn't believe his eyes. What was his name again?"

"Charlie? Wait, no. Connor? No, that wasn't it. It was something beginning with C."

"I didn't realise you were drunk enough to forget his name." She shakes her head at me in fake disappointment.

"You knew me back then." I shrug. "You know I was a rebel."

"What do I keep telling you?" She places one hand on my shoulder, talking to me like I'm a little child. "Sneaking out and getting drunk three times is not rebellious."

"You're just saying that because I wouldn't get matching tattoos and piercings with you." I point towards her face, indicating where the piercings used to be. As she grew up she took them all out apart from the nose and tongue ones. We lose track of time, reminiscing over our past. It definitely helps me to bring some closure to the whole situation. It's still going to be a long time until that wound is fully healed but I'm more than happy to work on mending it.

"I should probably find Tylan." I stand up from the swing seat, folding the blanket that was wrapped around me, back into the waterproof holder.

"What are you going to say to him?" She stands up, copying me with her blanket.

"I want to give him a second chance...but he's going to have to work to get that out of me." I grin at her mischievously.

"You are evil sometimes." She shakes her head at me.

"I know." I shrug one shoulder with my most innocent smile. "Do you know where he is?"

"The room next to mine. At least that's where he said he would be."

We walk back to the house together. "Why do I feel like he's got you all involved in some sort of plan?" Her answer is nothing but a wink, leaving me alone in the kitchen. I slip my boots off slipping into my comfy slippers, picking up a freshly made pain au chocolate sitting on the island. I stop outside the room Tylan's supposedly in, my hand frozen on the door handle. *You can do this, Everleigh.* I push the door open, stepping inside.

Chapter Forty-Three

Permanent

Tylan

I thought after nearly two years of silence I wouldn't have to suffer through any more with Everleigh. I was wrong. She hasn't said a word to me in one month, other than our four am messages, and it's torture. I'm running out of letters to give her. I have noticed a change within her though, even spotting a couple of smiles gracing her lips. I snuck into her room earlier whilst she was showering and left her the next letter and gift, but I also left her a photo of her and Camilla. I don't think they've said a word since the night she rescued us and I can see the effect that not talking has on both of them.

It may be positive thinking but I'm praying she takes the bait and speaks to Camilla before she finds me. It gives me the chance to set up my surprise for her. I do have a bit of help from everyone else in the house. Camilla was the first person I spoke to and she was more than happy to distract Everleigh, even offering me a hug. The other three were easy to find considering that they're nearly always together and, once again, they were more than happy to direct her to Camilla first. I finish setting up the projector and take a seat on the pull-out bed waiting for Everleigh to join me.

My eyes spring open at the sound of the door opening. I sit up straight meeting Everleigh's eyes but mine automatically drop to her outfit. My heart beats faster. She's wearing the same outfit as the day we first met. Is she trying to torture me? Because it's working.

She leans against the open door. "Hi."

"Hey." I smile at her, holding my hand out to her, inviting her to join me.

She smiles back, shutting the door behind her. She walks over to the bed standing awkwardly beside it. "What is all this?"

"I thought we could have a little movie night. Just the two of us." I shuffle over to give her more space.

"I think we should talk first." She sits on the edge of the bed placing, what looks like, a pain au chocolate, on top of the rest of the snacks laid out.

"I'm all ears."

She lays down on her side, resting her head on one of her arms. "I don't like liars." I open my mouth to speak but she holds her hand up making me stop. "But I understand why you never told me. I wasn't exactly in the right head space two years ago. I was falling for you but I was also so close to my breaking point."

"What are you saying?" I lay down on the bed, mirroring her, brushing a wave of hair behind her ear.

"We rushed things two years ago. I believe in soulmates and I believe that if we really are meant to be then we will be. But I need to go slow. Let's just have a fresh start as friends and see how it goes from there."

"I want to say yes but I promised you no more lies, and I will not be able to keep my hands or lips off you." I grab her waist, emphasising my point.

"I didn't say anything about no touching." She reaches up, wrapping her arms around my neck, scratching my head soothingly. "I just don't want any labels just yet." She smiles at me sweetly. "What movie are we watching?" I don't say a word as I press play, watching her face for the moment of recognition to hit her. Her eyes and smile widen, her head whipping to me. "*Tangled*? That's my favourite!"

"I know, Bubbles. You're just a little kid at heart." I press a kiss to her forehead, moving her gently so that she can rest her head on my chest. Here right now I can confidently say that I'm the luckiest man alive. It may not have been the answer I was hoping for, but it wasn't a never. I'll take it.

I'm woken up by a soft kiss to my tattoo peeking out of my t-shirt. Wait when did I fall asleep? "You set all this up just to fall asleep on me?" I look down into two narrowed eyes, but the smile gives away her playful nature.

"Sorry, Bubbles. I just haven't been sleeping very well lately." No matter how hard I try I can't wipe the smile off my face...not that I try very hard.

She presses another kiss to my tattoo, her eyes widening. "Why is my name on your chest?"

"Because you're my future." I look down into her crazed eyes.

"Tylan this is permanent!"

"So are you." I shrug at her and her mouth drops open.

"I—" She closes her eyes, taking a deep breath. "What are the other two bubbles for?"

"Our children. I can always get more if I need to."

"I-I..." She stammers, speechless. "I don't even know what to say." She stares into my eyes seconds before her lips hit mine.

It takes me a split second of shock until I'm leaning into the kiss. Her lips are just as soft as I remember, and I don't miss the slight chocolate sweetness coating them. I let her take the lead not wanting to push her past her limit. Not when I'm so close to her being mine again. I shiver as her sharp claws drag down my back, wasting no time in tugging my t-shirt up my chest. We break our kiss for a split second so she can get it off, our mouths finding each other immediately after. I can feel the passion and desperation coming from her, but I can also sense her wanting to pull away.

"Are you sure about this?" I whisper against her lips.

"Yes," she whispers back with a nod. I gently push her down until she's laying on her back, hovering over her to admire her the way she deserves. I've missed this. Having this goddess laying on my bed impatiently waiting for me to touch her...I can feel my cock hardening. I crawl up the bed taking my time to kiss up her legs, savouring the feel of her skin against my lips, making sure to not leave a single inch of her skin un-kissed.

I make my way up to her thighs, pushing the hem of her skirt up in time with my kisses, slowly uncovering more and more of her perfect body. The closer I get to her centre, the more I can feel the heat coming from her but I don't touch her there just yet. I continue my way up her hips, taking my time to leave my marks on her pale skin.

Her hands tangle in my hair trying to push me towards her soaking centre but I bat them away, pushing myself up to look in her dazzling eyes. "Let me take my time with you baby, I've waited too long to get you back in my bed I'm not wasting this opportunity." I visually see her swallow followed shortly by a little nod. I waste no time, leaning back down and kissing along her stomach, she sucks in trying to hide it but I simply look at her with a raised eyebrow and she relaxes. "I missed you baby," I mumble against her skin.

Her only response is a whimper as I bite and suck along her stomach and up to her chest, lifting her top as I do. I kiss along the underside of her bra, taking my time on my favourite part of her body. "Breathe for me," I whisper and she does.

I crawl up her body until I'm hovering over her, staring into the emerald pools of her eyes. "Is something wrong?" Her eyebrows furrow.

I shake my head. "I thought I'd never get to see you again." I silently curse myself for revealing that truth. I was willing to go to the grave with no one knowing that but seeing her here beneath me in all her beauty makes me forget everything.

"Tylan." She places her hand on my cheek, her thumb wiping against my cheek which I'm only just realising is wet with a single tear. "I can't promise this is going to be more than just sex."

"I'm okay with that." *I'll take you any way I can.* And it's true. I'm obsessed with this woman. I pull her clothes fully off, leaning down to capture her lips in another kiss before moving back to her chest, placing delicate kisses all over her upper body. I reach underneath her, her back arching up to allow me to undo her bra. I sit up, tracing my fingers gently up her arms to her collarbone down to her breasts, following the line of goosebumps forming on her skin.

I have no idea what happens next but one second I'm taking my time appreciating her body, and the next I'm the one lying on my back with her straddling me, her hair tickling my face where she hovers above me. Her soft lips trace from my lips to my ear. "Do you think you can give up control for once?" she whispers in my ear, nibbling softly.

"I'd do anything for you, Bubbles." My hands move to trace up and down her sides. It's impossible for me to keep my hands off her. She kisses down my neck, her hands wasting no time in tugging my jogging bottoms off. I groan at the feeling of her hand palming my hard cock through my boxers whilst her lips kiss over my chest, each one delicate over the scars she gave me, it's almost like she's apologising with each individual kiss.

She takes her time and it takes all my strength to not just throw her onto her back and have my way with her. It feels like forever before she's tugging my boxers off, her soft warm lips teasing my tip. I close my eyes taking deep breaths as she takes me deeper into her mouth. Fuck! I forgot how amazing her mouth feels. I have no idea how I survived two years without this, without her. I reluctantly pull her off, I am way too close and I don't want to let go unless I'm inside her. She pouts up at me. "I thought I was in charge today."

I smirk, flipping us over. "You had your fun, baby. Now it's my turn." I rip the tiny scrap of lace off her body, pushing her legs wide apart, ever so gently tracing a finger between her slit. "You're so wet for me."

"It's not for you." She avoids my eyes, biting her now swollen lip.

I raise my eyebrow, my smirk widening. There's the brat I know and love. I lie between her open legs placing a delicate kiss to her natural mound, her sweet and musky scent driving me crazy. I'm done with taking my time. I lick and suck her clit bringing her right to the edge, her sweetness coating my tongue, her moans and whimpers filling the room. I slide in two fingers, both of them easing in without a fight. It's not long until her back is arching off the bed, her pussy tightening around my fingers.

I work her through it, prolonging her pleasure, before crawling back up her body, allowing her to taste herself on my lips whilst I drive my aching cock into her. "Fuck," I curse into the kiss. I'm not rough with her, needing to show her how much she means to me. To show her that this is more than just sex for me even if she disagrees. I thrust deep into her slowly until we both reach our climaxes together, neither one of us wanting to break the kiss.

We eventually pull apart, both panting for breath. I look over her body flushed red, sweat glistening all over her. It takes a lot of effort for me to pull out when all I really want is to stay buried inside her. My eyes widening in panic when I realise I forgot to put a condom on. I look back at her expecting to see matching panic but instead I'm greeted with a dazed smile. "It's okay. I have the implant, and I'm clean."

I lay down beside her, pulling her into me until her head is resting against my chest. "You're a lot more chill about this than I thought you would be." She just shrugs at me, her eyes closed. "And for the record I've not been with anyone since you."

"I know," she mumbles sleepily.

"What do you mean you know?"

"There's no way you were writing those letters and fucking someone else at the same time. You, Tylan Blaese, are obsessed with me." She pecks my lips. "This is still just sex though."

"I have one more letter for you. Maybe that will change your mind." I softly tap her ass to get her to sit up.

She rolls her eyes, stubbornly sitting up and giving me the space to get off the bed. "Another one? I think six is enough."

"They were the only thing that kept me sane for the past two years. This is the last one, I promise." I reach over to the side table picking up the final letter. I pull my hand back when she reaches for it. "Be patient Bubbles. You know the drill by now." My tap to her nose is met with a scowl.

I chuckle at her, making my way over to the window where the vase of white roses sits. I take one out, tying the letter to the stem just like the previous ones. When I turn around I'm met my Everleigh's eyes zoned in on my lower half. I can't help the chuckle that escapes when she quickly averts her eyes. "Enjoying the view?"

She shrugs, lifting her head back up to face mine. "I don't know what you're talking about."

I smile at her, shaking my head and sitting next to her on the bed, handing her the rose. She takes it from me, sniffing the flower before unrolling the letter, the one I wrote yesterday.

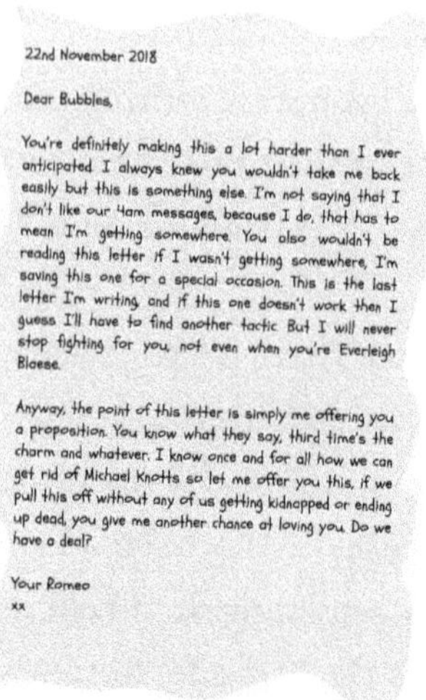

22nd November 2018

Dear Bubbles,

You're definitely making this a lot harder than I ever anticipated. I always knew you wouldn't take me back easily but this is something else. I'm not saying that I don't like our 4am messages, because I do, that has to mean I'm getting somewhere. You also wouldn't be reading this letter if I wasn't getting somewhere, I'm saving this one for a special occasion. This is the last letter I'm writing, and if this one doesn't work then I guess I'll have to find another tactic. But I will never stop fighting for you, not even when you're Everleigh Blaese.

Anyway, the point of this letter is simply me offering you a proposition. You know what they say, third time's the charm and whatever. I know once and for all how we can get rid of Michael Knotts so let me offer you this, if we pull this off without any of us getting kidnapped or ending up dead, you give me another chance at loving you. Do we have a deal?

Your Romeo
xx

I watch as she twirls the rose in her hand avoiding my eye contact. My heart races waiting for her answer. It feels like an eternity before she looks into my eyes. “Deal.”

Games

Everleigh

I'm sitting on my bed watching Tylan rummage through my closet, trying to find the perfect outfit for our plan tonight. We spent a week, in between making up for lost time, talking through our plan, and arguing about whether we should tell the others or not, an argument which I surprisingly lost – I never lose our disagreements. Although in hindsight, given our track record with Michael Knotts, maybe his idea to tell the others was the best option...I'll never admit that to him though.

"A-ha!" He grins, turning around to me with one of my black mini dresses with a high slit in his hand.

I observe the dress before nodding. "I like it." He turns back, rummaging through my underwear draw and grabbing a pair of my most revealing panties. I roll my eyes at his cheeky grin watching him casually stalk over to me. He stops in front of me, pulling my towel away from my body. He stands back admiring his view before I hit his arm. "Give me my clothes."

"I could. Or I could put them on for you." He crouches in front of me.

"You could definitely rock that dress." I nod, giggling. He rolls his eyes shaking his head at me with one of the smiles I love plastered on his face. He lifts each of my legs easing them into my panties, pulling them up my legs.

"I'm looking forward to ripping these off you later." He presses a soft kiss to my pantie-clad pussy.

I push him away. "You're like a horny teenager." I roll my eyes at him...again.

"I think we both know I don't fuck you like a horny teenager though." He leans over me, pecking my lips as I wrap my arms around his neck.

"That is very true." He stands back up taking me with him until I'm also standing.

"Arms up." I lift them, allowing him to slip my dress on, thankfully there's enough support that I don't need to wear one of those torture devices known as bras. "Turn around." I do, goosebumps rising on my skin at the ghost touch left behind from his fingers pulling the zipper up. "Sit." I turn around sitting back on the bed, my eyes widening as he gets down on one knee in front of me.

He rolls his eyes. "I should be offended you look so scared when I'm on one knee." He lifts my right leg, the one with the slit, sliding my knife holster up, pushing my dress up ever so slightly, until it rests perfectly on my upper thigh before handing me the knife he gifted me. I take it from him, admiring how perfectly the handle sits in my hand whilst Tylan slips my heels onto my feet. He places a soft kiss on my ankle before standing up, offering me his hand. I slide the knife into its holder, adjusting my dress to cover the weapon, allowing Tylan to pull me up, all my playfulness gone.

"Let's do this."

We have to take two cars for a change, seeing as we have to use Summer to distract Michael's friends. She's the only girl out of the three of us that Michael Knotts doesn't know so, hopefully, he won't be expecting us. Tylan and I are in the van with Callum driving, whilst the other three are in Freddie's car. We drive in silence, contemplating tonight's events. My leg unconsciously starts shaking, stopped only by Tylan's hand gently squeezing my thigh. I look over at him and he gives me a reassuring smile. "Everything's going to be okay, Bubbles."

"Can we go over the plan one more time?" I squeeze Tylan's hand and he nods back.

"Of course. I'm going in first, sticking to the shadows, to stake him out. Once I lay eyes on him I'll shoot a message to the group chat and that's Summer's cue. Once she's distracted the guards I'll send another message and that's your cue. Freddie will guard the back entrance and Camilla will cover the front. Callum's parking the van round the side and he'll keep an eye on all the cameras, in case we miss something when we're inside."

"And when I'm inside?"

"You head straight to Michael, flirt with him a little, tell him you made a mistake." I tense a little but Tylan rubs his thumb over my knuckles soothingly. "Lead him out of sight where we can knock him out. If flirting doesn't work pull out your knife. I'll be right behind you the whole time; you will never be alone with him."

I nod, taking a deep breath. "Okay." I shake my head, shaking the doubts out. The Polaroid Reaper back in her rightful place. "He dies tonight."

Tylan smirks. "There's the girl I love." My heart skips a beat, he's been saying little stuff like that a lot lately, truthfully both of us have, but neither of us have said the three words, I think we're both scared. He reaches into his pocket pulling out a bracelet. "I want you to wear this. It has a tracker in it, just in case anything goes wrong."

"Okay." I hold my breath, watching him slide it on. He types away on his phone before turning it to me so I can see the red dot flashing on the map following us.

"I've sent the link to Callum as well." He holds my hand tight as we stare at each other. He tries to hide his nerves but I can read them in his eyes, the unspoken worries that he keeps trapped in his own mind.

We pull into the parking lot a couple of streets away from the club, parking next to the others, making eye contact with them through the windows. The tension in the van makes it almost impossible to breathe. I turn to Tylan, squeezing his hand followed by a curt nod. He takes the cue, climbing out the car and walking down the street. I watch him for as long as I possibly can, silently hoping that he'll send me one last look for reassurance but he doesn't.

"Everything will be okay, Cap." I turn my attention to Callum who's offering me the tiniest of smiles.

"I know," I lie. "Do you think Summer can do this?" Call me crazy but that's the thing that's making me the most worried about tonight. Summer's the only one who's never done anything like this before. I'm worried she'll freeze and fuck everything up for us.

"She's a pretty good actress. I think you're underestimating her." He looks away from me but my eyes focus in on his hand clenching and unclenching on the steering wheel. I play with my new bracelet, internally debating what I'm about to do. I take a deep breath, rolling down the window and indicating to Freddie to do the same.

"What's wrong?" Freddie asks, concern evident in his voice but I ignore him, handing him the bracelet.

"Summer put this on."

She takes it from Freddie, observing it. "Why?"

"Just put it on." I wait until she's put it on before rolling the window back up.

I can feel Callum's eyes burning into the side of my head. "Why did you do that?"

I turn to him. "She's the most vulnerable tonight. She needs it more than me." Before he can reply both of our phones ring out with a message, we both look down reading the message from Tylan. My head snaps back to the window at the sound of car doors slamming closed and I watch the other three walk off in the same direction Tylan went. I turn back to Callum but his eyes are trained on Summer and his brother holding hands. "She'll be okay. Tonight the plan's going to work."

"If we keep saying that it'll come true?" His smile doesn't quite reach his eyes.

"Exactly." I reach out, squeezing his hand in reassurance.

We sit in silence for what feels like hours, but in reality it's more like ten minutes, before we get the next message. My turn. I climb out the van closing the door behind me. I close my eyes, taking a deep breath of the polluted London air. I definitely haven't missed this. I don't take a second glance back, making my way to the club. I walk around the side of the club and into the alleyway where Freddie is waiting at the back entrance. I hand him my coat, shivering in the cool winter air, but I don't waste any more time. I open the door, skimming the knife strapped to my thigh, slipping the Polaroid Reaper mask back on. I get my revenge tonight.

I strut inside heading straight to the bar. I order a water, subtly glancing around the room, catching sight of Summer talking and dancing with two men who seem fully focused on her. I continue around the room catching sight of movement in the shadows, Tylan. I've nearly done a full circle when I spot Michael Knotts sitting at one of the booths with two scantily dressed women on either side of him. I straighten my spine strutting over to the booth, adding an extra sway to my hips, his eyes connect with mine instantly.

I stop in front of his booth, one hand on my hip, smiling sweetly at him. "Hey, Handsome." I underestimated just how hard it would be to hide my disgust but I manage it, never letting my guard down. I turn my attention to the two women looking at me. "Thanks for warming him up for me ladies, you can leave now." I wave them off and they reluctantly leave.

My skin crawls at the feel of Michael Knotts' lingering eyes on me. I slide into the booth sitting right next to him so that our thighs are touching. Thank God I strapped the knife to my other thigh. "Where have you been Everleigh Carlton? It's been what? Two years?"

"Too long if you ask me." I trace my finger up his arm slowly, keeping eye contact with him. "I've been thinking and I was a fool all those years ago." He cocks his eyebrow at me and I have to force the bile threatening to escape, back down. "I should've taken your offer." I pout at him. "I reckon you know how to treat a woman in bed. What do you say we change that tonight?" I lean closer to him until our faces are nearly touching. It takes everything in me to keep this fake facade up.

His lips turn up into a taunting smirk. "How's your back?" I suck in a breath, my mask slipping ever so slightly. He leans his head closer to my ear to whisper in it, "I know your games, Everleigh." He grips my waist, dragging me towards him and I can't help it. I tense up. "But I'll take you up on your offer whilst your pretty blood is pouring out of your little body." I try to pull away but he keeps me tight to him. My eyes catch on Tylan's peeking out of the darkness a few tables down. I subtly shake my head at him silently telling him to stay put.

I reach my hand to my thigh, gripping the leather handle. "Do you want to rethink that answer?" I press the knife tight against his jeans, placing just enough pressure for him to feel it.

He chuckles in my ear. "You never did play nicely with others." I snap my head back when his fingers trace my cheek. "You can't win this Everleigh. I have my men and you're all alone."

I smirk at him. "Am I?"

"I'd do as the lady says." Michael jumps at Tylan's whispered words.

I press my knife harder, cutting the fabric of his jeans ever so slightly. "Follow me." I walk out the booth, turning back just in time to see Tylan pushing Michael Knotts out of the booth. My hair whips around me, my smirk straightening out, as I lead the final ghost of my past straight to his demise.

Chapter Forty-Five
Oops

Tylan

It was surprisingly easy to get Michael to follow Everleigh. Too easy. I keep my eyes trained on his every move as we follow her towards the back entrance. The moment we hit the darkness out of sight of prying eyes, he reaches out wrapping his hands around Everleigh's neck. I internally roll my eyes. *Idiot.* My hand reaches out for the iron bar Everleigh hid back here on her way in wasting no time in striking him on the back of his head with it, just hard enough to knock him out but not enough to kill him just yet.

Everleigh rubs at her neck, catching her breath. "Did he really think that would work?" She shakes her head, giggling in disbelief making her way to the door. She holds it open for me as I drag Michael out to the waiting van. Callum climbs out the driver's seat to help me get him in the back whilst Freddie and Everleigh talk, him helping her put her coat back on.

I close the door just as they join us. "You two find the girls and get back to the house. Tylan and I can finish this alone." She offers me a small smile. The twins waste no time in racing inside to find Summer. I help Everleigh into the passenger seat, making my way round to the driver's seat.

She looks at me breathless. "Did we really do it?"

I squeeze her hand. "Nearly." My eyes catch on her empty wrists, glaring at them. "Where's your bracelet?"

"I gave it to Summer." She shrugs nonchalantly, like what she just said isn't a big deal. She reaches out holding her finger to my lips before I get the chance to speak. "She was alone in there. I knew you had my back no matter what." How can I be mad when she says that?

We sit in silence, the air in the van buzzing with excitement, our hands entwined together on the gear stick. I park at my parents' old warehouse, leaving Everleigh to make her way inside and find the perfect spot whilst I get to work dragging Michael out of the van, grabbing our bag of equipment on the way. I find her placing an old chair that looks like it could give way at any moment, in the middle of the room. "You might want a different chair, Bubbles. He's going to be moving a lot when he wakes up."

She considers it for a second before nodding. "You're right." She places the chair back where she found it, coming back with a sturdier chair. I drop Michael onto it, digging in the bag for some rope. I hold it out to her but she shakes her head. "I don't know how to tie rope."

I smirk at her. "I need to teach you." I get to work securing him to the chair, pulling the ropes extra tight.

"Careful or I might think you want me to tie you up." She winks at me when I catch her eyes.

I shake my head at her. "You're crazy." I finish with the last knot, walking over to join her a few feet in front of him.

"You love it though." She shrugs at me, her arms crossed against her chest,

"I do." I wrap my arm around her waist, pressing a kiss to the side of her head. I press my nose against her hair. "Why do you smell like mango?" She doesn't say anything, just looks at me with a soft smile. I can't fight my own smile from forming. She's wearing it because it's my favourite. I was getting used to her new vanilla scent, but I love the mango more. It suits her better. My smile widens as everything hits me at once. In a few hours she'll be officially mine again. A deal's a deal after all. If it was up to me, I'd kill the man in front of us right this second, but I'm not going to take this away from her.

It's only been about five minutes when Everleigh drops her hands, walking over to an old large water bottle in the corner of the room. "I'm bored. Let's wake him up." She carries the full bottle with no signs of struggle, always surprising me.

"What are you going to do with that?" I raise my eyebrows.

She winks at me before throwing the water at the man tied in front of us. He jerks awake, struggling in the ties until he notices us watching him. Everleigh cocks her hip, wiggling her fingers at him in a wave. "Wakey, wakey."

"You bitch." He spits at her but she just giggles.

"Why so hostile? You made me into this." She shrugs, taking a step closer to him.

"You're crazy."

"Yes. Yes I am." She pulls the knife out through the slit of her dress, twirling it in her hands as she walks up to him. "It's time for me to have my fun." She drags the knife down his cheek. I silently curse myself at the feeling of my cock hardening at the sight, now is not the time. She pouts. "You have far too many clothes on for my liking." In just a couple of flicks of her knife his clothes are nothing but scraps. He hisses as the knife nicks the skin on his chest. "Oops." Her grin is close to terrifying.

I can't help how drawn I am to her, especially when she turns to me, beckoning me over. I stand at her side looking down at the pathetic excuse of a man in front of us. "Look I-I'm sorry for what I did to both of you. B-but if you let me go I won't say anything," he stammers out, his body shaking.

"I didn't think he'd start begging this soon," I whisper in Everleigh's ear but it's loud enough for him to hear.

She turns to me, pouting. "I didn't either." Her terrifying grin returns when she leans down to his eye level, trailing the tip of her knife over his bare skin. "Why would I let you go Michael?" She plunges the knife into his arm. "Why would I let you hurt another unsuspecting girl half your age?" He whimpers as she pulls the knife out at an agonisingly slow pace.

"I won't," he pleads causing both of us to laugh.

"The thing is Michael..." She plunges the knife into his other arm in the exact same spot. "We don't believe you." He struggles but it's no use, he's never getting out of the rope. "Don't worry I won't kill you just yet. Tylan still needs to have his fun." She winks at me as I stand back letting her have her fun. She shows him no mercy, plunging and slashing the knife against his skin, the blood pooling around their feet, splattering over her in return.

I've never seen her like this before, I should probably be terrified but I'm not. Seeing her take charge and having complete control over herself...it's beautiful. She finishes by slicing his cock clean off, dropping it to the floor before strutting back over to me adding a little extra sway to her hips. "He's all yours." She pecks my cheek, taking a seat just off the side to watch, one of her legs crossed over the other, the murderous look ever so present in her eyes.

I turn my attention to the mess of a man in front of me. He looks nothing like the powerful money-hungry man he normally is, there's not much space on his skin that's unmarked...except for his face, which I am more than happy to destroy. I don't hold back as my fists connect with his face over and over again. I take all my anger out on him letting it all go. The anger from letting him control my life. The anger towards my father. The anger towards whoever controls this wicked world. The anger towards anyone who thinks they have the right to lay their hands on others. I throw one last punch to the unconscious broken man in front of me, stumbling backwards. My chest feels lighter than it ever has before.

He's still alive. Barely. I hold my hand out to Everleigh who stands up to stand beside me. "Finish him, Bubbles." I hold her knife that she dropped out to her. She glances down at it and then back at me, but I can't read what goes through her mind. With a blink of an eye she's running off towards the staircase at the far end of the room. I waste no time in running after her.

Chapter Forty-Six

Living In Fear

Everleigh

I burst through the emergency door straight onto the rooftop overlooking the Little Bray skyline below, needing to clear my head. My heart is threatening to burst as I climb onto the worn edge to admire the view. In my head I know this is a bad idea but for the first time ever I feel lighter. I feel free. The pounding is so loud that I barely hear the heavy footsteps behind me. I glance over my shoulder to see the panicked expression on Tylan's face, a contrast to the broad smile stretching across my face. I reach my hand out to him. "Join me, Ty."

The panic in his voice is clear as he talks to me calmly. "Everleigh get down. Now."

I let out a little giggle. "Live a little, Ty." He tries to conceal it but I can see how he's looking at me...Like I've finally hit my mental break he was waiting for, that everyone's been waiting for.

He takes another step forward, tentatively reaching his hand out to me. "Come on, Everleigh. You're one step away from plummeting to your death."

I'm still looking at him over one shoulder as I give him a one sided shrug. "So? Everyone dies eventually and if fate says it's my turn today then so be it." I turn back around to overlook the skyline, buzzing with energy. "I'm done living in fear. I won't let fear control my life anymore." I'm not sure when the truth truly hit me. Maybe it was when Michael Knotts had his grimy hands around my throat, or maybe it was that day Tylan cornered me with my truth back in the shooting range, it may have even been years before when I walked into that bloody crime scene. But what I do know is that in this moment I finally have the strength to admit the truth to myself.

I'm living in fear.

Fear of the unknown.

Fear of losing control.

Fear of myself.

And I nearly lost that battle. I nearly lost myself within the need for vengeance. For so long I thought that my need to rid the world of predators was an addiction – an itch I needed to scratch but it wasn't. All of it was just a means to an end, something I needed to do to past the time. Some may even say it was a part of my grieving, and maybe it was.

"What about your family?" I can feel Tylan's presence against my back.

"I found their killer." I shrug. "They'll be proud of me." Another smile graces my lips. "But he is not going to control another second of my life."

Tylan's hands rest on my hips, it almost feels like it's a ghost touching me, his head resting on my shoulder with a soft whisper in my ear. "They deserve real justice."

I nod, my voice matching his. "They do but I'm going about it all wrong." I grip his hands resting on my hips. "I need a professional."

"Who were you thinking of?"

I turn my head our lips brushing softly. "You were a detective. If you truly love me you'll reveal the truth." He closes his eyes, tightening his grip on my hips just a little as I rest my cheek against the top of his head, watching the sun set, my mind drifting to what my future could look like. Me, Tylan, living in the cabin, my dream of owning a bookstore come true and to top it off...two sets of small footsteps running around us. For once I believe it might come true. My smile widens as I realise what I have to do to make sure it does. I mutter so quietly that I'm certain Tylan misses it. "I have to stop killing."

It takes him a couple of minutes before he's looking into my eyes. "What changed?"

I turn in his arms and cup his face. "You did. You came crashing into my life two and a half years ago and you changed it. For better or for worse? Who knows? But what I do know is that you showed me what it feels like to be loved again." I take a deep breath to calm my racing heart. "When I lost my family I lost the only people who ever truly loved me despite all my flaws."

"What about—"

"I may have Camilla and the twins but they'll never truly understand me. They may help cover for me but that's because they have to or I could ruin their lives." I blink away the tears threatening to escape. No more tears. "But you, Tylan Blaese, I lied to you when we first met, you could've easily thrown me in jail by now. You could've ruined my life forever, and I don't care if you haven't out of guilt or for whatever reason. Because instead you chose to give me a chance. You chose to love me."

"You're worth it, Everleigh Carlton. You're worth every damn risk in this world." Our lips press together in a passionate kiss but behind it I can feel the love Tylan pours into this one kiss.

I reluctantly pull back so I can whisper another truth to him. "I still want to hurt them though. We should ruin their lives and make them live with it." My smile widens. "We need to set their world on fire, burn them to ashes." I pull away, walking along the edge until I reach the end where two corners meet, I turn to see the calming view again but my foot catches on a crack meant to send me tumbling over the edge. A strong arm wraps around my waist tugging me back into the hard chest I know all too well, saving me from falling off the edge.

"You're going to give me a heart attack one day." Tylan breathes heavily in my ear, holding me tight to his chest, far away from the edge of the building.

"You always catch me." I giggle softly.

"I always will." His lips press a soft kiss in the spot just below my ear. "You and I, Bubbles...we're going to burn this world down together. But only if you're alive and breathing."

I turn around in his arms, kissing him fiercely, it takes him a second before he's kissing me back just as intensely, his arms wrapping around my waist pulling me impossibly closer. For the first time in my life my heart feels light, providing me with that much needed hope. I never thought I would ever trust a man, but Tylan Blaese came barrelling into my life wanting to take away all of my burdens and he did. I've fallen in love with him and, against my better judgement, I don't ever want to stop.

Neither of us break the kiss until we're forced to by me dragging his t-shirt off. Without missing a beat I kiss my way down to the spot on his collarbone that I know drives him crazy. My ears are filled with his groans as I suck and bite hard enough to leave my mark right next to his tattoo. Guided by his tight grip in my hair, I work my way down his chest tracing every scar with either my lips or tongue. I'm already kneeling, kissing teasingly along the waistband of his jeans when I feel a sharp tug on my hair forcing me to look up into the darkened eyes of my lover.

"Yes?" My innocent voice is a full one-eighty from the neediness within me currently forcing my hands to tug his belt off.

"Quit the teasing." He traces his thumb of the hand not currently holding my hair, along my lips and I can't help but run my tongue along it keeping my lust filled eyes locked on his whilst my hands work his jeans down his powerful legs.

"Make me." Two words are enough to flip the switch within him. Before I can blink Tylan's forcing his cock down my throat hitting my gag reflex without giving me a chance to adjust. I know I could pull back, tell him to slow down, but I don't want to. I love his dominating nature. I love having a chance to give up my control in a space where I feel safe. I watch his eyes roll back in his head when I swirl my tongue over his tip, tasting the drop of precum resting there. His taste is so addictive that it urges me on to please him until I can taste his release.

Tylan clearly has other plans though. He pulls out of my mouth, dragging me up by my hair to kiss me hard, tugging my dress up to my waist. Pulling away, his eyes travel down my body. "You're so beautiful."

His eyes track down my body, testing my patience as I wait for him to just pin me down and remind me who I belong to. "Take a picture it'll last longer." Before I can take another breath he reaches into his jacket pocket whipping his phone out and snapping a picture. I cross my arms playfully, standing there in shock.

"I think this will be my new home screen." I take the time to admire his body, even though it's permanently seared into my mind by now.

"You're such a deviant." I roll eyes playfully before he drags me back to the edge of the building.

"You love it."

"I do." I hum my agreement as his hands drag my panties down my legs. My view changes from his lust filled ocean blues to the view of the city as he bends me over the ledge I was standing on mere minutes ago.

A small squeak escapes me when his hand connects with my ass, whispering in my ear, "I'm going to fuck you like the good little slut you are and you," his hand tugs my hair back, creating that spark of pain I desire, "you're going to look over the city you rule." His teeth pull at my ear at the same time he slams into me.

The combination of his rough hands squeezing and stroking over my body, his soft kisses peppering my back and neck, mixed with his consistent rough thrusts send my body into overdrive. The sound of the wind dancing around us is drowned out by my desperate moans and whimpers and his low grunts of pleasure. "Come for me, baby." And I do – the pleasure ripples through my body as I explode around him, my screams filling the air around us. It only takes a couple more thrusts before he freezes, his seed spilling inside me as he bites down on the back of my neck.

He slowly pulls out keeping his hands on my waist to keep me steady. As soon as he releases me I collapse back against his chest. He pulls me into him allowing me to curl into him as I treasure his warmth, remembering the times when I'd be hesitant to let him cuddle or take care of me after sex but now I crave it.

I'm deep in my contentment that I don't even realise I'm shivering until he speaks up softly. "Let's get you warmed up." I mewl my disagreement, his chuckle echoing my response, pushing me up until I'm standing. I pout at him giving him my best puppy dog eyes whilst he pulls my panties back up, readjusting my dress, and re-dresses himself, leaving a peck on my lips. "When we get home I'll fuck you until you're begging me to stop."

I bite my lip, a mischievous glint in my eye. "Promise?" He shakes his head at me placing an arm around my shoulder guiding me back to the door. I stop him, placing my hand on his chest forcing him to look down at me. "Let's burn this son of a bitch."

Your Legacy

Tylan

My heart dropped when I saw Everleigh precariously wandering the edge of the rooftop. I wanted to drag her home and lock her away so she wouldn't do anything reckless like that again, but I also saw how life had come back to her, something I've never seen before. She looked free. I may never know what changed for her today, but I will be forever grateful for it. Unluckily for Michael Knotts here, it's bad news for him.

I finish pouring the line of gasoline around the room, draining the last of it on top of him before lingering by the door, watching as my sexy girl looms over his broken body tied tightly to the chair. His head is nothing more than a bloody bruised mess imprinted with my fists, his lifeless eyes staring helplessly at the woman in front of him. I can't help but stare at her beautiful round ass as she bends over at her waist to his level. I subtly shift myself to ease the ache forming in my jeans, leaning back against the wall. Everleigh's claws hook under his chin forcing him to look her in the eyes.

"You're pathetic." He lets out a low hiss as she digs one into his chin.

"You bitch." I nearly miss what he hisses but I don't miss it when he spits in her face causing her to jerk back. I see red. In the blink of an eye my pocketknife is out and I'm stepping around Everleigh. She's partly distracted wiping his spit off her cheek, but I waste no time in pulling his tongue out, slicing it clean off, throwing the useless thing on the floor.

"No one disrespects my woman," I hiss in his face.

Everleigh's soft hands tug on my arm her warm breath touching my face. "Let's get out of here." I turn my head to look down at her beautiful face staring up at me, looking entirely innocent and nothing like the woman who kills men for a hobby. I can't resist kissing her lips, she's a drug I can't get enough of.

I pull away handing her my lighter, her fingers squeeze mine gently taking it from me. "Finish him, Bubbles."

She smiles, flicking the lighter on but stops just before she lights the gasoline. "I nearly forgot."

I raise my eyebrow in question as she practically runs over to her bag in the most adorable way, she turns around and my face gains a small smirk at the camera in her hands. "I don't think the photo's going to survive the fire."

"I know. The photo's for me." She shrugs, snapping a photo of the predator tied to the chair in front of us. She places the camera and photo in her bag now hanging on her shoulder before crouching down and setting the gasoline on fire.

I watch her for a single second as she appears transfixed by the flames building around us.

I snap out of it, wrapping my arms around her waist. “You can watch from outside, Bubbles.” That snaps her out of her daze as if she’s only just realising the situation we’re in. I grab her hand, leading her towards the back entrance of the building. We don’t stop until I’ve led her down a dark alleyway far enough from the burning building to keep her safe but close enough that she can admire her work whilst staying hidden from any wandering eyes.

She stands at the corner mesmerised by the thick cloud of smoke billowing out of the window. I pull her to rest against me, my arms wrapped around her waist, my head resting on her shoulder. “Enjoy the show my queen.” She lets out a contented sigh, resting more of her body weight against me, her smile growing at the first sight of blazing flames emerging from the window. I take the chance to admire her beauty in the soft orange glow illuminating her pale skin splattered with crimson.

I place a soft kiss to one of her rosy cheeks, the ones that add to her innocent exterior, before trailing my kisses down her neck. Her head tilts to the side giving me better access to the tempting expanse of skin, her eyes fully focused on the scene in front of us. I nibble softly on the spot I know drives her crazy, inhaling her delicious mango scent driving myself crazy, making me bite harder leaving another mark on her. Nothing can stop me from worshipping my girl, not even the piercing sirens or the flashing blue and red lights racing down the road in front of us, instead I simply pull her further into the shadows, refusing to stop my trail down her neck.

Once I'm certain we're out of view, I move one of my hands up to her plunging neckline, teasing my fingers across it, watching the goosebumps forming on her skin. I don't wait long before I reach my hand under her dress, cupping her breast, massaging but avoiding her nipple currently a stiff peak. "Tylan." I move my other hand from her waist up to wrap around her throat, squeezing with just the right pressure.

I continue squeezing both of her breasts never touching her nipples that I know want attention. I hide my smirk in her hair at the long moan she lets out when I finally squeeze and pull on them, tightening my grip on her throat.

"Quiet or I'll stop." Her soft whimpers are music to my ears. I remove my hand from her chest, trailing it over her soft curves down to the hem of her dress. She squirms against me, her ass rubbing against my growing cock causing me to stifle a groan. I can see her small smirk as I nudge my knee between her legs silently telling her to spread them and she does. "Good girl."

I don't miss her quiet squeak or how she squeezes her thighs around my leg currently squashed between them. I temporarily remove my hand from her throat using it to smack her ass in a silent warning. She bites her dark red painted lip, my leg remaining trapped between her powerful soft thighs. I smack her ass again, harder, and this time she spreads her legs allowing me to continue my path up the inside of her thighs to her panties soaked from our earlier activities up on the rooftop. I brush my finger lightly over her panty-clad clit watching her beautiful olive green eyes close, her head resting against my shoulder, soft moans escaping her lips.

I move my hand away, whispering in her ear. "Be a good slut and watch your legacy as I make you come." One more whimper and her eyes flutter open shining with desperation, her head tilting up to watch the burning building in front of us. I move my hand back to her throat the other one pulling her useless panties to the side. I can feel her racing pulse against one hand as the other traces her dripping pussy, exploring everywhere but where she really wants.

She bucks her hips trying desperately to get what she wants and I take pity on her, pressing my thumb against her clit and rubbing slowly, nowhere near the pressure she thrives off of. Her whimpers and quiet moans are music to my ears, her ass grinding against my cock. "Please." Her whispers are so quiet that I nearly miss her desperation. I increase the pressure on her throat, pressing harder on her clit giving her what she wants. I let her grind against my hand for a little until I push two fingers into her tight hole, her moans getting louder forcing me to move my hand from her throat up to cover her mouth.

"Mmhmm." I feel her lips moving against my hand but can't work out what she's saying.

"I warned you to be quiet." I watch her to make sure she's not trying to tell me to stop but her relaxed body and rolled back eyes tell me that she wants to keep going. I nip at her ear, stroking my fingers against her G-spot, pressing my thumb harder against her clit. Her breathing grows heavier the closer she gets to her climax until she shudders and explodes at the same time the building in front of us collapses. I continue rubbing her softly until she stops shuddering against me, removing my hand so I can kiss her hard. It takes her a few seconds until she kisses me back with a dazed smile.

I readjust her panties and dress, never breaking our kiss. "You two make me sick." I reluctantly pull my lips away, turning my head to view a scowling Camilla standing at the other end of the alleyway behind us.

Everleigh relaxes against me with a dazed smile. "How's Dean doing?"

I watch Camilla's eyes widen in annoyance. "Why the change in MO?" Refusing to let go of the relaxed woman in my arms I turn us both around to face her.

"He deserved to burn for his crimes." Everleigh shrugs.

Camilla's glare never diverts from my eyes. "What did you do?"

"Sorry to disappoint but this was all our beloved Everleigh's idea." My lips meet the forehead of said Everleigh now resting against me with her eyes closed, I'd think she was asleep if she could keep her giggles inside. "Let's get you home," I whisper quietly in her ear and she nods gently in reply.

Camilla stands in horror watching us. "Everleigh?" Camilla grabs her hands as I keep my grip tight around her waist, we might not agree on much but we both care about the fierce woman in my arms in the same way. Camilla turns her glare from me into relaxed worry staring into her best friend's eyes. "What happened?"

"I think..." Everleigh closes her eyes, taking a deep breath before her face breaks out into that beautiful smile. "I think I'm happy? I feel so light, like I could just float away into the abyss with Tylan."

Camilla's eyes flick to mine, worry oozing out of her. "I'm worried about you, Leigh. You haven't been yourself lately. You—"

"You're wrong. This is me, Cami. This is who I really am."

"No it's not. You're stuck in a cloud of lust."

"You're jealous."

Camilla startles back as if she's just been hit. "What?"

Everleigh shrugs out of my hold and I let her go, staying close to make sure she doesn't do anything drastic. "Why can't you be happy for me? Happy that I've finally found someone who loves me for all of me, unlike you."

Camilla shakes her head. "Everleigh, I do love you."

"Only when I'm following your narrative. You love me when I need to rely on you. You've been trying to turn me against Tylan from the moment I first mentioned him so that you can have me all to yourself—"

"You're being ridiculous—"

"Don't interrupt me." Everleigh steps closer to Camilla with nothing but hurt written on her features. "You don't get to have me to yourself anymore Camilla. Freddie and Callum may be your little lap dogs, but I won't be, not anymore." With that Everleigh grabs my hand and we walk off together hand-in-hand soaking in the buzzing nightlife around us.

Vengeance

Dear Miss Reaper.

Beware, beware, the ghost of past.

Prepare, prepare, to say goodbye.

Despair, despair, you're too late.

It turns you on, doesn't it, Miss Reaper? Your sins excite you. You had a beaten, dying man, tied up whilst you fucked your toy. But worse, you let him touch you as you watched that man turn to ashes. It's disgusting. It's people like you who don't deserve to be in this world. Don't worry, I will do this world a favour one day. Mark my words.

Count your days, Miss Reaper.

Chapter Forty-Nine

The White Rose

Tylan

When I got the call from Blake asking if I wanted to hang out with my old team at The White Rose, the pub that replaced Harrow Bar, I had to force myself to not overthink why. Maybe they just want a catch up and that's it. There's no way they know about our involvement with Michael Knotts' death. I've been reassuring Everleigh all day and I left her cuddled up with Bailey and Muffin in our bed, with a rom-com movie marathon lined up, promising to message her if anything happens.

I walk through the door surprised at how much the interior has changed. Instead of the split level, it's now just one open floor decorated like a typical, rustic, British pub. I'm still scanning the room when my eyes catch on the young brunette waving her hand in my direction. "Tylan!" I plaster a smile on my face to hide my nerves, weaving through the crowd until I reach the table where my old team sits. Lyla climbs down from the stool, wrapping me up in a hug which I return, the tension leaving my body. "How have you been?"

She pulls away from me climbing back onto her stool as I climb onto the empty one to her left.

"I've been busy, hiding away from the press," I joke.

"They were hounding us nonstop for the first few months once you left." I turn to my left to see Naomi observing me, something about it making me feel uneasy once again.

"What did you expect? They're vultures." I shrug.

"I think that's the truest statement you've ever made." I jump at the unexpected pat on my shoulder from Blake, who passes me a beer before making his way round to the opposite stool. "I was beginning to think I'd never see Tylan Blaese again."

I take a swig of my beer before answering. "My friend was going through a hard time. I was focused on helping them," I half-lie, covering it by taking another sip. "How's the case going?" I know technically they're not allowed to talk about the case to anyone but I was part of their team, and I need to know. What I wasn't expecting was for all of them to look so surprised. "What?" I shift in my seat.

"We closed the case a year ago..." Lyla speaks up. "It was all over the news."

Closed the case? Who do they think killed the men? "You found them?"

"Well, no. It went cold. There were no more deaths, no new leads, we had to close it." I fight hard to stop my smile, using my beer as a cover.

"A lot of cases go cold." I shrug.

"The press was ruthless. We had a lot of questions about your final press conference." Naomi glares at me, something like hatred hidden in her eyes.

I rub the back of my neck. "I had to do it. Their victims deserved for their truths to come out."

No one says anything as we sit in awkward silence, but it all dissipates when the DJ calls Lyla up for karaoke. After I send a quick message to Everleigh to let her know everything's good, the rest of the evening is spent catching up, and the awkwardness disappears nearly entirely. The only thing hanging over me is the fact that they're all acting differently towards me and I can't tell if that's a good thing or a bad thing.

Chapter Fifty

Romeo

Everleigh

Three weeks later

The morning light shines through the small gap in the curtains filling the dark bedroom, placing a spotlight on the man next to me. I'm wrapped up tight in Tylan's strong arms pulled close enough that there's not a slither of space between us. He always looks so peaceful in his sleep, his messy hair disturbed by the silk pillows, his eyelashes fluttering, his chest slowly rising and falling in a steady rhythm.

I'm still staring at him when his voice, heavy with sleep, surprises me. "Some would say it's creepy the way you stare at me."

I rest my head against his chest, relishing in his warmth. "I have to make sure you're real."

My head moves in the same rhythm of his low chuckle, his arms tightening around me. "I'm real, Bubbles."

"Why do you call me Bubbles?" I trace random shapes over his chest, staring into the peaceful abyss.

"The first time we met you refused to tell me your name, the same way you refused to share your champagne—"

"I never share my champagne."

I can feel his smile against the top of my head. "I know, Bubbles," he teases. "I also noticed how much it annoyed you when I first said it and I love seeing that cute fury light up your face."

I give him a playful slap on his chest, giving him my best pout. "You were meant to be a means to an end."

"It's a good thing I wasn't." He brushes a lock of hair behind my ear, holding my chin gently to give me a soft kiss.

I left out a soft sigh. "Can we just stay here forever?"

"I wish we could."

I close my eyes. It all feels so surreal. Two and a half years ago the mere thought of catching the man who ruined my entire life was a fantasy. A dream that would never come true. But now, with the help of Tylan, I found him. Granted I wasn't the one who got rid of him, but I still got my revenge against the other man who ruined my life and now I feel nothing but peace.

"I couldn't have done this without you." I press a soft kiss on his chest.

"You didn't need me to help you find him. You would've eventually. You're too stubborn not to." He chuckles when I playfully hit him again.

"I'm not stubborn." I glare up at him.

"You saying that is exactly what makes you stubborn, Bubbles."

"I just know what I want." I shrug innocently, running my hand down his chest, tracing softly against the top of his jogging bottoms.

"I need to tell you something." He doesn't look at me as he plays with my hair.

"Right now? When my hand is literally right here?" He looks down at me, without a single ounce of playfulness on his face. I roll over onto my front, resting on my arms to look at him more clearly. "What is it?"

He reaches out, playing with my hair around my ears. "I killed my parents."

My mouth drops open, my eyes widening. "W-What? H-How...I thought they were killed in a plane crash."

"They were." He avoids my eyes, still playing with my hair. "I'm the one who crashed it."

I blink, taking in this information. "You know how to fly a plane?!"

He raises an eyebrow finally meeting my eyes, his hand pausing mid-air. "That's the first question you have?"

I shrug. "I would've fallen in love with you a lot sooner if you'd told me that."

"Impossible. You fell in love with me the moment you saw me." He smirks at me.

"Actually that was you. I fell in love with you when you saved me from Michael Knotts' henchman." I blush. I did not mean to admit that.

"Look at you. How could I not?" This man really knows how to sweet talk. My blush deepens even more.

"Moving on..." I push a piece of hair out of his eyes. "How did you crash the plane if there was a flight crew?"

He tenses. "For the record, I didn't want to kill the flight crew or my mother but I was young and thought there was no other way to get rid of my father." I place a soft kiss on his lips in reassurance. I know him. He may have questionable morals sometimes but he still has a heart. "I slipped sleeping pills into their coffees, then when they were asleep I snuck into the cockpit and crashed the plane. I was prepared to die that day but I was strapped into the one seat that was flung away from the rest of the aircraft before it went up in flames."

"It was fate."

He looks at me, his eyebrows furrowed. "You don't believe in fate."

"I believe in soulmates, of course I believe in fate. How else would we be together right now?"

"Does this mean you're finally willing to accept you're not the villain in this story?"

"No. But that's okay, because in this story," I hook my finger under his chin pulling him in for another kiss, "the villain gets the happy ending with her soulmate."

"I'm your soulmate, huh?"

I roll my eyes at his cheeky grin. "I started to believe it after the third letter."

He gasps in fake mortification. "And you still made me put in all that work?"

I giggle. "I had to prove you weren't lying to me."

"I would never lie to you." I raise my eyebrow at him. "Not anymore."

I grin. "Good answer." I giggle as he pushes me onto my back, climbing on top of me. "Can I finish what I started now?"

"If you'll be my good girl." He presses his lips against mine.

"I'm always a good girl." I yelp as he smacks my ass.

"We both know you're a brat." He pecks my lips. "But you're my brat." His kisses trail down my neck, nibbling and sucking along the way.

"I don't think there's any space left for you to mark me." I giggle.

"Is that a challenge?" He smirks at me.

I shake my head. "No. It's definitely not."

He chuckles, continuing his way down my body. "I think everyone can tell you're mine already." I swear in some alternate universe this man would probably be a werewolf given the state of my body. I don't mind though. For once they're not bruises, they're love bites from the one person who will always love me despite all my flaws...even if we still haven't said those words to each other yet.

I relax into the bed revelling in his kisses. His hands grip my waist flipping me over onto my front, a small gasp escaping my lips in surprise. He presses his body on top of mine with just the right amount of pressure for me to feel him without suffocating. "I want to try something a little different, Baby Girl. If you're okay with a little roughness."

"I thought you knew me well enough by now." I grin at him over my shoulder. "You know I like it rough."

"Oh," he smacks my ass, eliciting a small squeal from me, "I know." He kisses me just behind my ear. "I want to tie you up." I squirm a little, the heat rushing to my core, feeling his grin against my skin. "I'll take that as a yes. If you want to stop just say red."

I turn my head to watch him climbing off the bed. "Why not just stop?"

He turns back to me, rope in hand. "Because with what I'm about to do to you, you'll be begging me to stop but really wanting me to continue." He winks at me and walks over to the other side of the bed.

I keep my eyes trained on him, blushing hard when I see what draw he's digging around in. Maybe he won't go too far—

"How did you know that was in there?" I blush hard.

"I heard you one night with it and I just had to do a little digging of my own." He winks at me. "Is it charged?" I hide my head in the sheets offering the tiniest of nods. "You don't have to be embarrassed, Bubbles. I have a feeling me and this vibrator are going to be the best of friends." He lifts my chin, placing a soft kiss on my lips. "Hands." He taps the headboard and I listen, lifting my arms up to a comfortable position. I watch, intrigued, as he ties an intricate knot, connecting my wrists to the headboard. "Try to move." I do but my hands are tied tight enough that it doesn't even budge. "Not too tight?"

I shake my head, grinning at him. "No. It's kinda nice actually."

He chuckles, shaking his head. "You still continue to amaze me." With one last peck to my cheek, he stands up off the bed walking to the other end. "Spread your legs." I spread them until he tells me to stop, quickly tying my ankles to the foot of the bed. I test them noting a little more give in these ones, but they're still enough to keep me in place. "I can see you dripping from here."

And I can feel it. I've always fantasised about being tied up but now that it's actually happening I can confidently say that it lives up to expectations. My little squeal is followed by a soft moan as his tongue swirls over my clit. The feeling is gone a second later only to be replaced with soft vibrations directly on my clit. I let out a tiny whimper, I've always hated this setting, it never offers enough for me to get off properly.

"Please," I beg him.

"What do you need?"

"Turn it up. Please?"

"No." I can hear the smirk in his voice, my whimpers becoming more desperate. "This isn't about your pleasure." I jerk against the rope, his hand connecting with my ass again, which I can feel heating up. I turn my head to the side watching him walk over to my reading chair, which I'm only just realising is no longer tucked away in my reading corner but instead is closer to the bed giving him the perfect view of me spread open for his viewing pleasure. He sits down, smirking at me when I catch his eyes. My eyes travel down his body watching his every move when he takes his hard cock in his hand. I bite my lip whimpering at the small vibrations torturing my swollen clit.

I squirm against my binds, moaning and whimpering in frustration, watching Tylan using his own hand to pleasure himself, his eyes fully focused on me. I try to grind into the sheets below me desperate for any friction, but I fail miserably, Tylan's smirk constantly getting bigger at my struggles. I know what I have to say if I really want it to stop but we both know I won't say it.

I have no idea how long this goes on for but I let out an audible sigh of relief when Tylan makes his way over to me. Finally relaxing when the vibrations ease off my clit, for a few minutes at least. Tylan wastes no time before he's thrusting his cock deep inside me, and I can't hold back my scream as he does – he wasn't kidding when he said he wanted to be rough. He pounds hard into my aching pussy simply using me for his own pleasure.

I muffle my moans into the pillow beneath me, biting hard into it. I shiver at the feel of Tylan's hand running up my back until he's reaching under my hair to grip it at the roots, using it as a lever to pull my head up. "Be a good slut for me. Don't hide your sounds." He leans over to whisper in my ear, pushing impossibly deeper inside of me. "Let them all hear you." I couldn't hide them even if I wanted to, especially when he holds my vibrator against my clit again but this time it's on the highest setting. I tense around him, the pleasure racing to be set free—

"No!" I whimper as the vibrations and thrusts stop together.

"Do you need something?" I can hear his smirk.

"Please," I beg, whining desperately.

"Please what?"

"Please let me come." My pussy squeezes around his cock sitting still inside me, his hand connecting with my ass again.

"Your ass is throbbing baby." I moan at the feeling of his hand massaging my ass, followed quickly by another slap.

"Please. Please let me come," I whimper.

"Hmm." His lips dust my ear. "Only because you've been such a good girl for me." He wastes no time in getting back to his hard, fast thrusts, using his hand to rub against my clit. My orgasm rushes through me like a tidal wave, hitting me almost instantaneously. Tylan fucks me through it, reaching his climax shortly after. He hovers above me, pulling himself out, kissing along the scars on my back as we both come down from our highs. "I love you, Bubbles."

My heart races. He actually said it and I know that he means it. I blink the tears away. "I love you too, Romeo." I lay there with a dazed smile.

"Why Romeo?" He reaches over undoing each of my ankles, massaging small circles along the red marks.

"In a way you were my forbidden love." I twist my head over my shoulder, smiling at him.

"Go on." He kisses my cheek, sitting next to me on the bed and getting to work on the rope holding my wrists in place.

"A detective and a serial killer? What's more forbidden than that?" I giggle.

He helps me to sit up, pulling my legs over his lap whilst massaging my wrists. "You read too many romance books." His smile is so full of love that I have to fight back the tears threatening to spill over.

"There's no such thing. It just helps me to know how I deserve to be treated." I rest my head on his shoulder.

"What would our love story be?" He presses a kiss to my forehead.

"We would definitely be a dark romance."

"You didn't even have to think about that." He chuckles.

"I've been waiting for you to ask that question for days now." I grin at him, revelling in the comfort of his warmth. We sit in comfortable silence, both of us still coming down from our highs. "I need to speak to Camilla."

"I think that's a good idea."

"Do you think I was too harsh on her?" I play with the Tinker Bell charm on my bracelet.

"Did you say anything you didn't think was true?"

"No." I shake my head.

"Don't apologise for being truthful. Just have a talk and clear the air."

"You're right." I nod, pressing a kiss to his lips before climbing off his lap and out of bed. "But first we're saying goodbye to the twins…and Summer."

"I forgot they were moving back today."

"It's going to be weird not living with them after the whirlwind that was the past two years." I stumble over to the ensuite, to the chorus of Tylan's suppressed chuckles. "Don't even think about saying what you're thinking!" I shout over my shoulder.

Chapter Fifty-One

Make The Move

Tylan

I smirk to myself at the sight of Everleigh stumbling towards the ensuite, still as feisty as ever. I walk over to the closet changing into a fresh pair of boxers and grey jogging bottoms. I pull out a white t-shirt when the door to the ensuite opens again. I turn around, my eyes drawn to the bottle of lotion in Everleigh's hands. "My ass hurts." She pouts at me and I can't help the chuckle that escapes.

"I'll put some on for you." I hold my hand out to her as she walks over to me passing me the bottle. "Turn around." I squeeze a little bit of the lotion into my hands, warming it up before gently massaging it into her ass, not stopping even when it's all rubbed in. She looks over her shoulder at me, narrowing her eyes in suspicion. I grin, shrugging my shoulders. "You know I love your ass." She pushes me away, rolling her eyes but her radiant smile is still plastered on her face. I look at the t-shirt I threw on the bed getting an idea. "Arms up." She turns around to face me again, lifting her arms above her head.

I help her into my t-shirt, her eyes narrowing at me again. "This is yours."

I shrug. "You look good in my clothes."

"You're turning into one of those clingy boyfriends." She crosses her arms, looking adorable in nothing but my t-shirt barely touching the top of her thighs.

"I thought we already knew that." I smirk, grabbing a pair of her clean panties and leggings, crouching in front of her. "Use my head for balance if you need to." I hold her panties by her feet struggling to stay still when she presses her hand into my head for balance. I pull them up her smooth legs until they're in their place. "And again." I scrunch her leggings up, placing them by her feet. There's less pressure on my head this time when she steps into them. I stand up, pulling the leggings up with me.

"Thank you." Her smile is the sweetest and I vow to make her smile like that forever. I watch her walk over to her vanity before I turn and grab another t-shirt for me to actually wear this time. I lean against the wall, my arms crossed as I watch her from a distance struggling to get the brush through her hair; I'll never get over her natural beauty, her skin that glows with a slight pink hue to her cheeks that highlights the freckles that dot her skin. She says that she believes her freckles are from everywhere her lover kissed her in her past life – if that really is true then she'll be covered in them in her next life. She huffs, placing the brush back on the vanity, opting to just throw her hair up into a messy bun. She turns to me with a smile. "Ready?"

I raise an eyebrow at her. "I've been waiting for you."

"You're the one who made my hair into this rats' nest."

"I didn't hear you complaining." I grin.

"I-I—" She lets out the most adorable little growl. "Let's go." She leads us down the stairs where everyone else is waiting in the living room.

Summer is sitting on the carpet giving Bailey belly rubs whilst he lays on his back happily offering his stomach to her. "Are you sure we can't keep him?" She has the same wide eyes and pout that Everleigh has when she wants something.

"No. He's Tylan's." Callum shakes his head at her from his spot on the couch next to his twin, it's not hard to miss the adoration in his eyes.

Summer pouts moving her attention to Muffin curled up on her lap. "What about Muffin?"

"Are you kidding?" Freddie asks, raising his eyebrow at her, at the exact same time Everleigh speaks up, their voices blending together.

"Absolutely not." Everleigh storms over to Summer, picking Muffin up off her lap, to a chorus of hisses from the cat. "Excuse me?" She raises her eyebrows at the black fur ball who hisses at her in response. "I'm your mother." I shake my head in amazement as the hisses change to purrs, Muffin nudging his nose against Everleigh's chin. I've heard more arguments between the two of them than I'd like to admit, you really would think they're a mother-son duo.

I join everyone else in the living room, sitting next to Camilla on the other couch. She's staring out the window, seemingly zoning out the other people in the room. "You two will be okay," I speak quietly so that only she can hear.

"I seem to recall telling you the same thing." She turns to me with a sad smile.

"And look how that turned out."

"You're forgetting that I also said she'll forgive you easier than she will me." She shrugs. "She shouldn't forgive me, what she said that night was true." She averts her eyes back to the view outside the window.

"What do you mean?"

"I did use her for my own gain. I'm so sick of the injustice in this world. The number of people who use money to get away with everything is sickening." She turns back to me. "But I'm not strong enough to kill them myself, I knew Everleigh would especially with how broken she was, so I talked her into it." She shrugs sadly. "What sort of friend does that?"

I catch Everleigh's eye over Camilla's shoulder, the longing look in them is evident. I turn my attention back to Camilla. "Just talk to her she might surprise you."

She nods, plastering on a fake smile and joining the other four. "Is the car all packed?"

"Trying to get rid of us already, Camilla?" Callum asks playfully.

"I'm just looking out for you. Don't want you getting stuck in holiday traffic, it is Christmas tomorrow after all." She shrugs.

"Why did you decide to move on Christmas Eve of all days?" I join the rest of the group, wrapping my arms around Everleigh's waist from where she sits on the arm rest, Muffin still secure in her arms.

"We always spend Christmas with my family. It didn't really make sense to go back into the city for one day, back here the next, and then back to the city the next." Summer shrugs. "We thought we might as well just make the move today."

Everleigh tenses in my arms at the mention of Christmas and family, her eyes zoning out like they always do when she gets lost in a memory. I place a soft kiss on her shoulder, bringing her back to the present.

Summer gasps, covering her mouth with her hands. "I'm so sorry, Everleigh. I didn't think."

I squeeze her tighter in my arms, grounding her. She smiles, shaking her head. "It's okay. I think this is the year I want to fall in love with Christmas again, with my new family."

"Really?" We all ask at the same time.

Everleigh rolls her eyes, placing Muffin on the ground as she stands up in front of us. "I realised something three weeks ago. Killing all those despicable men may have brought some justice to the people they hurt but it didn't give me justice. They were holding me back as a person. Ezra Blaese held me back, hell," she huffs out a laugh, "even my own family held me back, and that's not the life I want anymore. Everyone who's ever attacked or abused me..."

She takes a deep breath, all of us watching her in silent awe. "They're the ones who made me into the monster everyone knows the Polaroid Reaper as. But that monster's dead now because I refuse to be defined by my trauma. I want to be defined as me. Everleigh Carlton. A woman who can push through her trauma and come out the other side stronger than ever. And as much as I don't need the help, I am still hoping that I can have the love of my life..." She reaches out to take my hand and I smile at her, squeezing her hand in support. "On one side and my chosen family..." She holds her other hand out to Camilla who tentatively takes it, smiling softly. "On the other to support me through it all. And maybe learning to love Christmas again is the first step I need to take." She shrugs, smiling at all of us.

Callum walks over to the storage cupboard in the corner of the room, leaving behind a confused Everleigh. "It's a good thing we all got you a tree and some decorations then.

"You what?" Everleigh leans against me and I pull her into me, placing a kiss on top of her head. She keeps her eyes on the twins pulling out an artificial fir tree from the closet, dragging it over to the empty corner of the room. Summer and Camilla follow suit with a couple of boxes full of decorations. Everleigh stares open mouthed, her eyes glistening with unshed tears. “H-How? How did you know?”

“We know you, Bubbles,” I mumble against her hair, placing another loving kiss. I try to suppress my laugh as she rushes over to the group, trying to act cool but she just looks like a kid on Christmas morning.

“We would stay to help you decorate but we should really get going, Pixie.” Freddie pulls Everleigh into a brotherly hug.

“What if we face time you when we decorate? It’ll be like you’re with us.” She grins up at him.

“Deal.” He pulls away, ruffling her hair, leaving her to say goodbye to the other two. Freddie walks over to me, pulling his phone out. “She might kill me for this but I can’t not show you.” He turns his phone around to me and on it is a picture of a seventeen year old Everleigh dressed as Tinker bell with a pixie cut. I smile at the memory of her talking about the picture, I never thought I’d ever see it though. One thing is clear from the picture – she definitely does not suit short hair.

“Bubbles?” I call over to her.

“Yeah?” She looks over her shoulder at me with her angelic smile.

“You weren’t wrong about the pixie cut.” I try but I can’t suppress my grin as her eyes turn murderous. She tries to rush past me to the kitchen but I stop her with an arm around her waist.

"I can't believe you showed him." She glares daggers at Freddie, her cheeks reddening.

I lean down to whisper in her ear, "I'll show you the picture of me with a buzz cut." The change in her is instant, her eyes softening, the smile returning to her face.

"You're lucky." She points at Freddie who pulls her into another hug.

"I'll miss you, Sis."

"I'll miss you too." Her voice is mumbled from his chest. They pull apart as Callum and Summer join them. She hugs Callum next, but I can't work out what either of them are saying. The twins leave the girls alone, the tension awkward between the two. At least until Everleigh speaks up. "Look after them for me?"

"Of course I will." I watch Summer hold her arms out to Everleigh for a hug. It takes a couple of awkward seconds before Everleigh accepts the hug.

"And if you really want a pet...puppy dog eyes with a pout at Callum and he'll get you anything you want. Just not when Freddie's around." Everleigh winks at Summer.

"Thanks for the advice." The girls share a giggle, Freddie sneaking up behind Summer.

"Ready to go, Red?" He takes her hand and she nods.

We all walk to the door, Camilla, Everleigh, and I hanging back as we watch Callum climbing into the driver's seat, Freddie helping Summer into the front. "Why is Freddie getting in the back?"

The two girls in front of me share a giggle, Camilla looking back at me to answer. "Because she's their princess." We wave them off until they're out of sight. Everleigh closes the door behind us and the room is full of tension.

"I'll leave you two to talk." I give Everleigh a quick peck. "I'll take Bailey for a walk." I walk over to the back door, calling Bailey over to me. There's no other people within walking distance and he's a very well behaved dog so I don't bother with a leash instead I walk out the house leaving the two behind for a much needed chat. I can't help the smile that doesn't want to leave my face, how could I? I'm living the life I've always wanted with my perfect girl by my side. What more could a guy need?

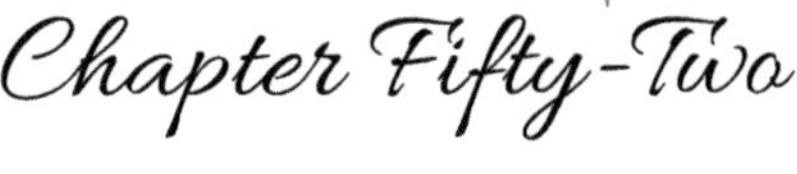

Chapter Fifty-Two

Sisters

I watch Tylan walk out with Bailey, leaving me alone with Camilla, the silence between us hanging heavy in the air. I turn to face her. "I'm sorry."

Her eyes widen. "What for?"

"What I said three weeks ago. It was uncalled for." I hug my arms across my body, seeking the comfort.

"No it wasn't. You only said the truth." I follow her to the couch where we sit on opposite ends. She sighs. "I have this thing about needing to be in control of everything and I don't handle it well when things don't go the way I expect them to."

"I don't need to be your best friend to see that." I smile at her. "It's okay to not be in control all the time Camilla. I thought like that and it broke me, literally."

"What do you mean?"

"It wasn't the betrayal that broke me, it was because I was so set on being in control of everything that when one little thing derailed my control I couldn't handle it up here." I tap my finger against my temple, the same way that Tylan does to me.

"I am happy for you Everleigh. I can tell how much lighter you feel and if you say Tylan's the one for you then I'll support you." She sits closer to me. "I can't promise I'll be his best friend...but I'm willing to tolerate him for you."

I smile, pulling her into a hug. "I guess we really are like sisters."

"What do you mean?"

"Sisters fight and make up all the time." I giggle.

My head turns to the back door as Bailey comes sprinting towards us. I give him a couple of scratches, waiting for Tylan to join us. "Looks like you two have made up." He tilts my head back, leaning down to press a light kiss to my lips from behind the couch.

"Mm-hmm." I nod, leaping off the couch, heading to the corner of the room where the tree and decorations are sitting. "I think it's decoration time." I bounce up and down excitedly, feeling like a little kid again. Tylan joins me as I sit on the floor routing through the decorations. Camilla heads off to her room returning with a tripod for her phone. "Let's start with the tree."

I grin at Tylan who presses a kiss to my nose. "Whatever you want Bubbles, this is for you."

It takes a couple of tries but we eventually manage to face time the other three who are stuck in holiday traffic. Tylan and Camilla get to work setting the tree up whilst I organise the decorations. I settle on the blue and silver decorations, the ones that Tylan picked out – they remind me of my childhood Christmases. It takes a lot of effort the whole afternoon to hold back my tears, all of this is overwhelming. The Christmas music, the decorations, my chosen family...this is the start of the life I've always wanted.

We're nearly done with the tree when Tylan passes me the star to put at the top, I reach up onto my tiptoes but I'm too short. I pout at Tylan who grips my waist, lifting me up to the perfect height. I squeal as he places me back on the ground, tickling my waist. "Stop."

I push him away but he pulls me back to him. "Merry Christmas, Bubbles."

"Merry Christmas, Romeo." Our lips meet in a short and sweet kiss to a chorus of groans from our friends.

"This has been fun but we're about to go into a no signal zone. We'll message you when we arrive," Freddie speaks from the phone. We say our goodbyes before getting to work on decorating the rest of the house.

It's dark by the time we finish decorating the house, which looks nothing like it did this morning. We don't even need to use our main lights with the amount of Christmas lights we put up. I grab the last couple of boxes which were made for outside. "We should put these on the dock." I smile at Tylan.

"How about you two do that whilst I start on some food?" Camilla asks and I don't miss how exhausted she looks.

"Sounds good." Tylan takes the boxes from me, grabbing my hand and leading me out to the dock. I take one box and Tylan takes the other, both working on one side of the dock each. Once they're securely wrapped around the rails we turn them on at the same time and they light up alternating between blue and white. I sit down at the end of the dock watching the lights reflect off the lake. "I should buy a set of lights to tie you up with." His breath tickles my neck from beside me.

I giggle, pushing him away from me. "Is that all you think about?"

"You know it's not, Bubbles."

I rest my head on his shoulder taking in the calmness surrounding us. "I love you, Tylan," I mumble into his shoulder.

"I love you, Everleigh." He presses a kiss to my temple, both of us basking in the comfortable silence. My life hasn't been straight forward but I'm confident that this is where I was meant to end up. A cabin in the woods away from the hustle and bustle of the city, cuddled up with my soulmate overlooking the lake. I still have a lot to overcome, I still need to heal properly. I've always said Tylan would be the one to glue each individual piece of my broken heart back together again and for the first time I'm confident he will. He makes me whole.

Vengeance

Dear Miss Reaper.

Beware, beware, the ghost of past.

Prepare, prepare, to say goodbye.

Despair, despair, you're too late.

My dear Everleigh, you're safe for now. I'll let you live a few years. I'll let you live your "dream" life for now. But don't let your guard down too much. I'll be waiting. The second you're alone your life is mine.

Count your days, Miss Reaper.

Epilogue

1 year later

"Where are you taking me?" I hold my arms out in front of me to make sure I don't walk into anything, Tylan walking behind me, holding his hands over my eyes. I have no idea what he's planning but he seems to have the whole day planned out even down to the red fit and flare dress I'm currently wearing, which he insisted I had to wear. We drove for about twenty minutes, which he had me wear a blindfold for the whole time.

"We're nearly there, Bubbles." We stop just as my hands hit something that feels like an old French-style door. "Are you ready?" I nod against his hands, blinking as my eyes adjust to the change in lighting. My eyes are drawn to the sign on the door *Books and Bubbles. Opening Hours.* I gasp turning to Tylan who holds a single key attached to a book key chain out to me.

"You didn't." My hand shakes as I take the key from him, turning it in the lock of the door. I push it open, my jaw dropping at the aisles of bookcases filled with books, and the elongated desk with a cash register sitting on top of it. My eyes fill with tears.

"I promised I'd make your dreams come true and I never break my promises." I can't stop the tears from falling when I see the loving look in his eyes.

"I-I—" I'm lost for words. What are you meant to say when someone buys you your own bookstore? I hug him tightly, soaking his shirt with my tears. "Thank you."

"I have something else to show you." He takes my hand, leading me in between the bookcases towards the back of the shop. I stop abruptly at the sight of the pin board where photos of all my friends sit, as well as photos of my family.

"This is too much Tylan." I touch the photo of my last Christmas with my family when I was fifteen. We're all wearing matching pyjamas looking like the happy family we were. I hope they're proud of me.

"Your happiness is never too much."

"I never thought I could be happy again," I mumble to myself, my eyes trained on the picture of my family, "and then you waltzed right into my life. What was it? Three years ago?"

"Three and a half. But who's counting?" He shrugs trying to act cool which just makes me giggle hard.

"Is this really all mine?"

"It's ours, Bubbles. But you're allowed to make all the big decisions and I'll just handle all the boring financial stuff."

I grin. “Deal.” I walk back towards the bookcases, soaking in the new store. This is it. This is my dream coming true. Now all I need is a hus—I can’t help the gasp that escapes when I turn back around to Tylan on one knee holding out a white rose with a letter tied to it. I take it from him, holding back the tears threatening to spill and start reading.

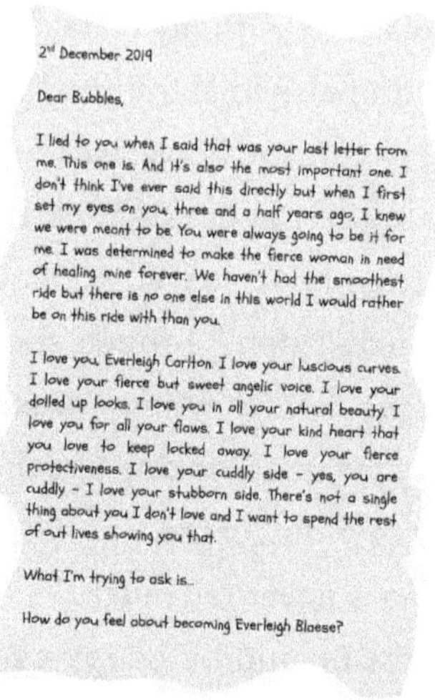

2nd December 2019

Dear Bubbles,

I lied to you when I said that was your last letter from me. This one is. And it's also the most important one. I don't think I've ever said this directly but when I first set my eyes on you, three and a half years ago, I knew we were meant to be. You were always going to be it for me. I was determined to make the fierce woman in need of healing mine forever. We haven't had the smoothest ride but there is no one else in this world I would rather be on this ride with than you.

I love you, Everleigh Carlton. I love your luscious curves. I love your fierce but sweet angelic voice. I love your dolled up looks. I love you in all your natural beauty. I love you for all your flaws. I love your kind heart that you love to keep locked away. I love your fierce protectiveness. I love your cuddly side - yes, you are cuddly - I love your stubborn side. There's not a single thing about you I don't love and I want to spend the rest of out lives showing you that.

What I'm trying to ask is...

How do you feel about becoming Everleigh Blaese?

I look up from the letter, my smile achingly bright, tears ruining my carefully applied makeup. “Everleigh Bea Carlton. Will you marry me?” I stare at the gorgeous sapphire ring held securely between Tylan’s fingers.

I don’t even have to think of my answer. “Of course I will.” Tylan slips the ring onto my ring finger as I lean down, taking his face in my hands and kissing him with all the love I feel for him. There’s not enough words in the English language to describe how much I love him. Three and a half years ago I never would've guessed that this could be my life.

The serial killer and the detective...the most unlikely pairing.

Extended Epilogue

Tylan

Three years later

I feel empty.

This wasn't how the rest of our lives were meant to go. We were meant to live happily ever after. I wasn't meant to be standing here at my wife's grave only two years into our marriage. I thought we left all our demons in the past where they belong. I couldn't be more wrong. The last thing I expected when Camilla called me was for her to tell me Everleigh was in trouble.

I still remember the feeling of my heart dropping. I swear the entire world went silent, the only sound I could hear was my racing heart. I was working the store that day whilst she went to visit the others. It was a little break she deserved. A break from running the store. A break from being mummy to our little girl. It was her chance to relax. How did that end up in her death?

I don't know how I got through her funeral today. I should be thankful there was a bigger turn out than expected. She touched a lot of people in our new community and every single one of them showed up to say their goodbyes and send their apologies. What's the point in apologies? They're not going to bring her back. Nothing will. She was just starting her new life why did she have to go so soon? I've begged every night since the doctor uttered the words "I'm sorry for your loss" for this to all be a horrible nightmare that I can't wake up from. But this is real life, and I have to live the rest of mine without her.

When we were deciding where to bury her none of us had any doubt where we would. I look to the side of her grave where the rest of her family rests. Maybe she's found them again. I hope she's happy even in death. She deserves it more than anyone. I turn my attention back to the fresh one belonging to the other half of me. "I promise I'll avenge you, Bubbles. They won't get away with this." I press a soft kiss to the gravestone. A soft kiss to her. My final goodbye.

I stand up, pushing the pram our daughter sits in, and walk away. I don't stop until I find a quiet spot in the park nearby. I sit on a bench taking our beautiful baby daughter into my arms, rocking her as she cries in my arms, my own tears raining down on her forehead. "Looks like it's just you and me now, Maya."

Acknowledgements

There were times when I doubted I would ever release *Deceitful Devotion* but thank you to everyone who has helped to push me forward and inspired me to finish.

First, I want to give a thank you to you, the reader, for giving me a chance and joining in with Everleigh and Tylan's story.

Stacey – my amazing editor. I don't know what I would have done without you. You helped massively to perfect every single spelling/grammar mistake and make my story readable.

Lauren, Lavanya, Abbie, Sarah-Louise, Alex – my amazing beta readers. Thank you so much to all of you for giving my story a chance when it was still very rough. Your positive feedback helped to motivate me more than you know and made me believe I could actually do this. I appreciate you all more than you could ever know.

Mary, Nick. Kimberley, Rae, SophieAnn, Peyton, Ellie – my beginner street team. It's not easy to market your book as a self-publishing author but thank you for helping me before you had even read the book. You've all helped me push my book out there to find its audience. Thank you!

To all my ARC readers. Thank you to each and every one of you for all your feedback and for giving *Deceitful Devotion* a chance.

Finally, thank you to everyone who has sent me encouraging messages and supported me along the way. I can't wait to bring the rest of the trilogy to all of you.

Also by Lyla Shepherd

The Polaroid Reaper Trilogy

Deceitful Devotion

Broken Devotion

Eternal Devotion – Release TBD

About the author

Lyla Shepherd is a cat and book lover born and bred in the West Midlands, England. She is currently balancing writing with her full time university course, studying International Hospitality and Tourism Management, and still finds to read. Expect to see plenty of books in the future ranging from dark romance to sports romance, to romantasy, there's plenty more to come.

www.ingramcontent.com/pod-product-compliance
Ingram Content Group UK Ltd.
Pitfield, Milton Keynes, MK11 3LW, UK
UKHW020417250726
13967UKWH00007B/2696